LOOK FOR THESE TITLES FROM MAX ROSE

Now Available

The New Detroit Wolves Series

Giving the Alpha an Heir (Book One)
The Lone Wolf's Omega (Book Two)

The Omega's Heir
To Love an Omega
Reclaiming His Omega
Omega Rescue
Chasing His Omega

THE LONE WOLF'S OMEGA

M/M Omega Mpreg Romance

THE NEW DETROIT WOLVES BOOK TWO

MAX ROSE

Etopia Press
1643 Warwick Ave., #124
Warwick, RI 02889
http://www.etopia-press.net

THE LONE WOLF'S OMEGA

First Etopia Press electronic publication: October 2020

First Etopia Press print publication: October 2020

~ DEDICATION ~

For Terrance.

CHAPTER ONE

Henry Wright was being hunted.

He was trapped on the tenth floor of an abandoned apartment building in the ruins of Old Detroit. He'd been scavenging for food and supplies to survive. This top-floor flat had never been looted. So at first, he'd believed his luck was in.

Then he'd spotted his hunters on the street below. An icy chill ran through his body. He had nowhere to go but down, and only by the stairwell because there hadn't been power in Old Detroit in forever. But down was where the danger was.

His hunters hadn't found him yet, but the gut-churning dread of being stalked put him back on the knife's edge of panic. As a wolf shifter, he should be the hunter. But in the burned-out and devastated ruins of Old Detroit, Henry was the prey.

He should be used to it. It was a danger he lived with every day, but even after almost three years of surviving here, he *wasn't* used to it. Every day seemed as dangerous and terrifying as the last. And he was alone, which made it even worse.

The lagodire pack had been hunting him for two days since they'd caught his scent. Usually, Henry was very good at avoiding the packs. He had to be. If they caught him, they would rip him apart and eat him. But he'd been sloppy and desperate. He'd been trying to scavenge food to fill his own belly. Now this lagodire pack knew they had an omega wolf in their territory. They were eager to find him. It wouldn't be pretty if they did.

Henry slowly raised himself up to peek through a shattered window at the street below. The street was a mess of rubble and broken glass. The buildings were long since abandoned. Some of them were only burned-out shells. Four male lagodire made their way up the street. Three of them were shifted into their animal forms. The fourth was still in human form— although he seemed far from human.

An instinctual shudder of disgust always rippled through Henry whenever he spotted lagodire. He figured it was a mammalian reaction, primal and undeniable. Lagodire were neither full mammal nor full reptile. They were a hybridization of a hyena and a crocodile, created in a government lab as a bioweapon.

He didn't hold that against them. No. Henry's kind—wolf shifters—had also been created in secret government experiments. On top of that, Henry was an omega wolf, a kind of genetic mutation of the wolf shifters. So he'd been called abomination plenty of times in his life, just like the lagodire.

But the lagodire...they acted like monsters. He knew better than anyone. They had killed someone he loved. Even after all this time had passed, he didn't forget...and he didn't forgive.

Henry had lived here, trapped in the ruins of Old Detroit with the lagodire hordes, for years. He'd spent those years being hunted, hiding, scavenging, and desperately trying to survive. Hyenas weren't exactly great pets, but whatever crazy scientist had come up with the idea to hybridize them with reptiles—crocodiles, no less—must've been a psychopath. Lagodire were highly aggressive and completely merciless. You couldn't beg or plead with them. They viewed everything as prey. They even fed on each other.

Now these four were closing in on him...

Henry's heart was pounding fast. His breathing was ragged, harsh, and quick. He was almost panting. The fear spun inside him like a tornado as he watched his hunters. He made no sound. He barely even blinked as they stalked along the street filled with abandoned and rusting cars.

The lagodire were the size of Henry's wolf when he was shifted. Henry was an omega wolf and naturally smaller than other wolves, even most females. Their bodies were covered in scaly skin like a crocodile's belly. They had a mane from the top of their head, running all the way down their spine, but no other fur. Their yellow teeth would've felt at home in the mouth of a crocodile, but they had the body shape of a hyena. Their tails were long and thick, more like a croc's. But their yellow or amber eyes…those terrified Henry the worst. He imagined their cold, snake-like scent and shivered. Shifters back in New Detroit had called them "snake-dogs," but Henry only called them monsters.

One of the four-legged lagodire suddenly stopped and cocked its narrow head, listening intently. Its yellow eyes seemed to gleam.

Henry held his breath. He kept absolutely still. Even ducking might draw attention because of his movement.

After a moment that seemed to last forever, the lagodire made a loud grunting and growling noise. The creature lowered its head again. The male in human form looked like some kind of escapee from a post-apocalyptic movie, only naked. He was beyond filthy. So filthy that Henry was glad he was ten stories up and had glass between them. The stench would probably be killer. The lagodire's hair was long and matted, probably filled with lice. His deeply tanned torso was heavily scarred with tooth and claw marks from all the fighting he'd done.

Henry didn't take his eyes off them until they moved farther down the street, beyond the apartment building. They were headed north toward downtown. He could see the dark towers of the abandoned skyscrapers and high rises. Beyond them, he could faintly see the huge walls of concrete and steel that sealed off the city, turning it into a prison.

Old Detroit was nothing but lawless ruins now, cut off from the rest of the world to stop the lagodire hordes. It was anarchy here.

For Henry, it was home.

He waited a few more minutes to be sure his hunters didn't circle back. Lagodire were cunning hunters. They should never be underestimated. They had brutal pack rules, but like wolves, they did have packs.

Or like *most* wolves, anyway.

Henry didn't have a pack anymore. He was alone. That was why he was here. He was alone and trapped in the ruins with monsters who only loved to kill because that was what they'd been designed to do. His old pack had abandoned him here.

Slowly, he left the window. He made his way through the tenth-floor apartment to the kitchen. Hunger gnawed at the inside of his belly. It was an old—and hated—friend.

The apartment was pretty clean except for the epic amount of dust. The rooms smelled musty. That made complete sense. No humans had lived here in a very long time.

He tried not to look at the pictures on the walls or end tables. He tried…but he couldn't help it. He never could. For some reason, Henry was drawn to photos of families long gone. Something about them appealed to him in a way he couldn't define.

These framed photographs showed a human family of four. The kids were of grade-school age. They seemed so happy. There were snapshots of them hiking and together on the beach. There were family portraits, obviously from some studio. Other pics of the kids playing baseball.

He wondered where they were now. Had they escaped Old Detroit during the city's fall? Were they still together? Happy? Safe? Leading their lives while having no idea that Henry was where they'd used to live a long, long time ago, looking at their smiling faces.

He touched one frame, his gaze trailing over the proud father, the loving mother, and two adorable kids, one boy, one girl. He hoped they'd found a home somewhere else in the country, somewhere safe, and had put the nightmare of Old Detroit behind them. He prayed they were safe, even though he had never met them and never would.

Enough. You're wasting time you don't have.

That was true. A few minutes ago, he'd been terrified. Now he felt like he was going to cry. Sometimes he wondered if living alone in this burned-out hell had robbed him of his sanity.

Shaking his head at himself, he began to search through the kitchen cabinets. He needed to focus on keeping himself safe, not worrying about people he didn't know. Things were touch and go enough with him. His big, stupid, and weepy heart was going to get him killed someday.

He'd quickly learned one thing after being dumped behind the walls of Old Detroit. Never, ever, *ever* check the refrigerators for food. The power had gone out in the city decades ago during the fighting and chaos and fires. That had been twenty-four years ago, maybe more. He couldn't remember exactly. Back then, the US military had battled the lagodire hordes. They'd been trying to protect the hundreds of thousands of civilians fleeing Detroit as the city burned around them. People like the family in the pictures around Henry. Normal people whose lives had been upended and destroyed...

But back to his point about the refrigerators. A

quarter century of science projects had been trapped in those fridges. The stench alone might kill him.

Instead, Henry scrounged in pantries and cupboards for canned goods and dry goods that hadn't spoiled or been ravaged by insects and rats. Any food he did find was years and years past the expiration date, but what choice did he have? He was trapped, and no one delivered pizzas here.

At least his digestive system was more robust than a human's. He could eat some chancier things without puking for a week straight. Clean water was the real challenge in some parts of the ruins. He would drink bottled water when he could find it, but he couldn't stay in one place for long. Not long enough to set up something to collect rainwater reliably. He was always on the move through the city ruins. That meant he tried to stay close to the Detroit River as best he could. And yeah, he had to sneak down to the river and fill bottles when he couldn't get anything better. And no, he had no power and couldn't start fires to boil water without bringing the lagodire down on his head.

It was a wonderful life. Still…he was glad to have it. His life, he meant. After all, Max hadn't been so lucky…

He shoved that thought away and opened a cabinet. Inside sat neatly stacked cans of dog food. He grinned at the irony and ignored the canned dog food. He would save it for when he got really desperate.

Luckily, the next cabinet over had stacks of red kidney beans, canned corn, canned green beans, and cans of tuna.

He pulled out his can opener. It was the most important thing he owned nowadays. A can of tuna was his first prey.

Who says omega wolves can't hunt?

He opened the can and used his other most important thing—a metal spork—to dig in. Sporks were abominations—not quite spoons, not quite forks, but a bit of both. In a way, they were like omega wolves. Not quite male, not quite female, but a bit of both equipment, a dick and a womb, go figure that out.

Still, when it came to fine-scavenge dining, Henry tried to avoid eating with his hands whenever possible. He couldn't wash them easily. Sticky hands were the worst. Ms. Manners would hate him.

As he ate, he tried not to think, only to feel. He focused on the rush of pleasure at putting food in his hungry belly. It was simple, primal, but filling these basic needs had become everything to him since he'd been dumped over the wall. The alpha who'd ordered him and Max thrown into this hellhole had expected them to die immediately.

Max had died. But so far, Henry had proved his old pack wrong. He'd kept living, despite everything.

He took a little savage satisfaction from that.

His strength returned as he ate. His thoughts became sharper. The gnawing ache in his belly receded. It would be back, but for now, he had fended off the worst hunger pangs.

.Most of Henry's life was spent scavenging for food, water, and a safe place to sleep. Oh, and hiding from the thousands of lagodire infesting the ruins, even after the battles and all these years. There were no humans and no other shifters in Old Detroit. The lagodire were cannibals. They bred quickly, formed brutal packs, and constantly warred for territory.

They were monsters. His home was a monster's den.

But at least there was tuna fish.

He ate another can of tuna fish and switched to the green beans. He didn't know much about how shifter breeds had been genetically engineered (actually, he knew nothing about it, like the rules of cricket or why it was physically impossible to lick your own elbow). But he did know he couldn't rely exclusively on protein. He needed vegetables too.

Too bad you aren't a goat shifter. You could eat all the grass at Lafayette Park. Problem solved.

He laughed at his own joke, even though it wasn't very funny. The sound of his laughter…was actually a little crazy. That's what happened to you after years alone and on the run. After years of being hunted and saving dog food for when you got *really* hungry. How long had it been exactly? He'd lost track—

A door crashed open ten floors below him, slamming into the wall with a resounding boom. It was very loud, but the stairwell only amplified it to be as loud as a cannon.

Fear and adrenaline shot through his body. He tensed and froze, listening. His heart was in his throat. He stood there listening. Not blinking. Not breathing...

Something was inside this building now, moving up the stairwell. He could feel it. Before, the building had felt abandoned except for him...and now it didn't. Some sixth sense, some prey instinct told him that he was being hunted again. It told him that his hunters were closing in. Henry might be a wolf shifter, but he was only an omega, the weakest kind.

In Old Detroit, he was simply prey.

Slowly, he set the can of green beans down on the counter. He slipped his precious can opener and metal spork into his pack, moving slowly, silently. He shouldered his pack and crept out of the kitchen.

He needed to get the hell out of here. The apartment building had ten floors. He was on the top floor. The elevator didn't work. There was one stairwell and that was it.

Something was coming up the stairs. No. More than one. He heard the *click click* of claws on stairs and a low, rumbling growl echoing up the stairwell.

Lagodire. What else had he expected? Santa Claus?

He fought against rising panic. Why hadn't he left already? The stairs were his only way out...except there had to be a fire escape...

He crossed the apartment, checking the windows for a fire escape. The floor creaked. He froze, his heart slamming as he listened, trying to guess if he'd been heard.

The monsters below him froze too. The growling stopped. The claws clicking on the stairs stopped. They were listening for him. And their hearing was as good as his.

Long, tense moments passed. He stood very still, too terrified to move.

The *click click* began again. They had heard him, after all. They knew where he was—trapped up here with no escape.

He forced himself to move again, no longer creeping. He was running out of time. He was trapped on the top floor like prey chased up a tree. But if he could use the fire escape, he might be able to outmaneuver them and escape.

Except that, when he peeked through the blinds, he could see the human-form lagodire in the street, standing on the top of an abandoned SUV. He was staring at the apartment. Watching the fire escape.

He instantly knew what had happened and why.

The lagodire liked to hunt in their shifted, four-legged forms. But their hunting groups kept a human-form lagodire around to kick in doors and deal with human obstacles. This bastard had kicked down the door for his buddies, and now he was watching Henry's only possible escape route and waiting.

Lagodire were savage, but they weren't stupid.

The fire escape was a death trap. He might be able to outrun them in wolf form, but he didn't have time to shift. As a wolf, he wouldn't be able to lower the ladder on the fire escape's lowest level either.

He was screwed.

In the stairwell, the loud, echoing growls were getting closer.

The roof. It was his last chance. If he could hide there or barricade the door, then maybe...

He had no other choice. If he stayed in the apartment, the lagodire would batter, claw, and bite their way through the door—or shift and kick it in. They were mindlessly feral when prey was near. That was how they were created. They were terrifying. He was about to experience that close-up and personal.

But he wasn't going to cower here and wait for the end. Never. He crossed the apartment to the front door, moving quickly and soundlessly. He opened the door as quietly as he could and slipped out to the hall landing.

The sound of heavy breathing and low growls and

snarls came from the stairwell at the end of the hall, not ten feet away. There was no door to the stairwell. It was open. It sounded as if the lagodire were right there, only a floor or two down.

And that was the way he needed to go to get to the roof. He crept along the landing to the stairs. He looked down but couldn't see anything, only hear the low growling rumble and the *click click* of their claws coming closer. The lagodire reptile stink was powerful, even from way up here.

Henry's mouth was dry with fear. There was definitely no escape that way. The roof was his last chance.

He stepped into the stairwell, taking the final flight of stairs to the rooftop access. He was as quiet as he could be, but not quiet enough. They heard the floor creaks and the pad of his footsteps. It was hard not to. The place was so empty and quiet. Except for the terrifying growling and the sound of those claws that would soon be ripping into him.

Eager, blood-thirsty howls broke out. The howls, yips, and hyena laughing were almost deafening in the echoing stairwell. They were coming.

His blood turned to ice. He broke into a run, taking the stairs two at a time. There was a tiny landing at the very top, right in front of a steel fire door. Hyena laughter and snarls echoed behind him.

The door had a heavy deadbolt, but it was a turn

kind, not a key kind. He turned it with shaking, sweat-slippery hands. He grabbed the door handle. The door locked from the inside and swung outward. He shoved at it, practically ramming it with his body.

It opened with unexpected ease, sending him stumbling onto the rooftop. But he didn't fall, and he didn't go careening over the edge of the roof.

Lucky.

He laughed wildly. Nothing about this was lucky. Nothing about him had ever been lucky.

He spun back to the door to slam it closed.

A lagodire was charging up the stairs right at him. Its yellow eyes flashed. Its sharp teeth gleamed. Ropes of saliva dripped from its open jaws. Its eager snarls sounded desperately hungry.

Henry slammed the door shut with all his strength. It closed right as the lagodire leaped at it. The whole frame shuddered with the impact...but it held. He could hear the frustrated growls and snarls from inside. He could hear them clawing at the metal door.

Henry backed away from the door, his head feeling numb, and his thoughts locked in ice. Now what? They knew exactly where he was.

He ran for the far edge of the ten-story building. He could see the city ruins sprawled all around him, with the taller buildings off toward the downtown areas. He reached the ledge...and stopped cold.

Ten stories was a long way up. Looking down on the street far below made his stomach drop into his feet.

If his hunters got through the door, he would have to jump...but that was insane. He wouldn't survive the fall. But...that was better than being eaten alive, wasn't it?

Or he could try to fight. He wouldn't win against three lagodire, but he could try. He wasn't exactly the biggest wolf in the pack. Not even close. He didn't have time to finish shifting into wolf form to fight with teeth and claws. The change would leave him even more vulnerable if they got through before he was done.

Behind him, the access door shook as the lagodire slammed into it. But the door was steel. They wouldn't be able to knock it down easily.

And then the door simply opened, swinging outward. The lagodire in human form, naked and filthy, stepped out. His yellow eyes locked on Henry. He grinned. It was a hungry grin. A predator grin.

It was over. He was a dead man. He'd been counting on the door to stop them. The fourth lagodire had simply walked up the stairs and opened it. The door locked from the inside, and Henry had no way to barricade it shut.

What a stupid ending. It was almost sad.

He should've felt something more, knowing his

life was coming to an end. He watched as the three other lagodire padded out onto the roof, their scaly, ridged hides a greenish-gray, slaver dripping from their narrow muzzles. Their yellow eyes were locked on him. Their dark manes bristled.

He should've felt fear, but he didn't. Not anymore. Not since the door had opened. The fear had been replaced with tiredness. He only felt weary. He had been on the run for three years or maybe more, he couldn't even remember. He'd lost track long ago.

He had done his best. Most other people, shifters or not, would have died or given up long ago.

Now his luck had run out.

He closed his eyes for a moment, but then decided he wanted to face this with his eyes open. He didn't know why. But he refused to act like terrified prey in his final moments. No one was here to see his defiance, but that didn't matter.

His fists clenched. He didn't have time to shift into a wolf, and he was wearing clothes and had a backpack on anyway. It would've been better to fight them as a wolf, but like everything else in his life, it hadn't worked out that way.

"Come on!" he yelled at them as they slowly closed in on him across the rooftop. "Hurry up, you bastards! I haven't got all day!"

They snarled and laughed. That hyena laugh was the creepiest thing on the planet. It haunted his nightmares. But he guessed he wouldn't be having nightmares for much longer.

The lagodire knew he was trapped, so they took their time closing in on him. They seemed to like the smell of his fear and desperation. One stayed behind to guard the door. The other three sauntered toward him as if they had all the time in the world to enjoy eating him.

Suddenly, something caught Henry's attention. It was motion, something seen out of the corner of his eye. He glanced that way…and couldn't understand what he saw. His breath caught. He stood there frozen, his fists clenched, gaping in disbelief.

A man was in the air. He was in the air with a parachute above him. One of those rectangular parachutes you could control. And he was flying or falling or whatever, right toward Henry.

CHAPTER TWO

Tom Reinhart was on the rooftop of a burned-out high rise when he spotted the man. The guy was on the roof of an apartment building a hundred or so meters away.

What the hell?

Frowning, he moved from his rooftop camp to the edge of the high rise for a better view. He reached for his binoculars as he looked over the building. That was second nature in the ruins. Making sure what you were standing on wasn't going to collapse.

The apartment building was ten or so floors high and looked structurally sound. Plenty of streets in Old Detroit were nothing more than burned or bombed-out ruins. They'd been damaged in the battle for

Detroit by shelling, tanks, bombs, or just the fires that had raged. This building was intact. Hell, it was in far better shape than the one Tom was standing on right now.

He raised the binoculars and focused on the strange man. The guy was thin, despite the bulk of his dirty jacket. Tom was too far away to catch his scent, but Tom was sure the guy wasn't a human-form lagodire. No, this skinny guy was too afraid. He was staring at the door to the rooftop in complete terror. Also, he wasn't naked. Lagodire weren't big on clothing. It got in the way of shifting. Too bad they were the least friendly nudists on the planet.

So the skinny guy was being chased. Now he was trapped on the rooftop like prey that had been chased up a tree. It sucked to be him.

He should've put away the binoculars and looked the other way, putting it out of his mind. It wasn't any of his business. He was here to do a damned job. He wasn't here to rescue any damsels in distress, male or female. Shit. He was a lone wolf in the truest sense. No pack. No ties. No allegiances. He did work for hire, and he was damn good.

Besides, the whole scene playing out in front of him was nothing but trouble. The lagodire pack that controlled this part of the city had been stirred up enough already. They had hunting squads roaming the streets. It had already made it hard for Tom to move around on the street level. He was already a day behind schedule. If those insane shifters were on the hunt for this guy, then maybe they'd calm down after getting their prey.

Or you could help, you selfish son of a bitch.

There were no heroes in Old Detroit. Not anymore. As a wolf shifter, Tom was no pushover. But a pack of hyena-crocodile mutants? That was something that gave even him pause.

He should stop watching, put the binoculars away, and forget this whole thing. It wasn't his business. There was no profit in it. He'd be crazy to get involved.

He *did* give good advice. Advice he never took. He kept watching. It was as if he couldn't look away.

The skinny guy—who wasn't half bad looking…if you ignored all the dirt—ran to the far edge of the building. He stared down over the ledge. Even under the dirt, the guy's face was pale, his body language both desperate and terrified as he peered at the street below.

You can't go that way, bud. Better defend that door—

The man swung around to face behind him, absolute dread in his expression.

Tom swung the binoculars back to the rooftop door. His heart sank at what he saw.

The door was open again. A naked, human-shifted lagodire stepped onto the roof. Three shifted lagodire stalked forward on heavily clawed legs. That human-form dude was covered with grime and old, dried blood. He looked as if he'd parted on bad terms with sanity a long time ago.

He swung the binoculars back to the guy they were hunting. Skinny Guy was still at the far end of the roof. He didn't look like he had any weapons. What kind of death wish did you need to stroll into Old Detroit without weapons?

It was insane.

You have a gun. Are you going to help him or what?

That damned conscience. It was such a pain in the ass.

True, he had a pistol in a shoulder holster. It even had a very illegal sound suppressor on it, making it "silenced." But to hell with risking his neck for some reckless idiot stranger. Tom was in this hellhole, risking his ass for one reason only. Looting. Sure, he could call it "treasure hunting," but it wasn't really. Sure, his kind were technically called "retrievers," but that was a fancy way of saying they were scavengers. But Tom was here for a very specific reason, and for a very specific haul.

An alpha in New Detroit by the name of Eddie Carson had paid for this run. The alpha wanted Tom to find and retrieve a fancy eight-carat diamond necklace. The necklace was called Lumiere Soleil, made by a designer in France. It was valued at well over half a million dollars.

Like so much else, the necklace had been lost in the fires and violence when Detroit fell over twenty years ago. But Tom had a reliable lead on it. That was his deal. If you needed something from the forbidden zone, the dangerous ruins of Detroit where it was illegal for civilians to go, then Tom was the man to bring it out again.

For a price.

He carefully put his binoculars away. He turned away from the distant scene on the far-away rooftop below him.

That was that.

That kid down there needs your help. He's going to die if you don't do something.

Dying was rough. No doubt about it. But it wasn't Tom's ass on the line. He hadn't made the mistake of drawing the lagodire's attention. Nope. Like everything in life, sometimes you rode the tiger...and sometimes the tiger ate you.

Those were the thoughts Tom was thinking as he patted himself on the back for maintaining a professional distance. He kept thinking them right up until the point where he climbed on the ledge and jumped off a forty-story high rise.

The wind rushed at him as he fell. He almost immediately deployed his chute. He had a lot of ground to cover to reach the other building. His BASE jump chute was larger than the skydiving parachute he used to get into Old Detroit. It had a larger pilot chute to help the main parachute fully open and deploy as soon as damn possible. This close to the ground, there was zero margin for error.

He endured the sudden jerk as the chute filled with air and dramatically slowed his descent. This was one of the most dangerous moments in pulling off a BASE jump. When the chute deployed, it could suddenly send him off in an unintended direction—like straight into the side of the building he'd just jumped off. Crosswinds could be murder. Literally.

But the deployment was clean. He used the steering lines to guide himself toward the ten-story apartment building. The wind rushed and roared around him. He was gritting his teeth as he closed in as fast as the ram-air parachute would go.

That was his deal—his special skill set that had kept his ass safe in these ruins. He was essentially a mix of airborne and BASE jumper. He'd done parachute assault training with the 82nd Airborne when he'd been in the military, so jumping out of planes was nothing new to him. Jumping off of things like buildings and radio towers was an interesting and useful twist he'd learned in the years since then. It had always served him well.

Parachuting and skydiving were how he got into Old Detroit for these retrieval runs. It allowed him to avoid the Army checkpoints, blockades, and patrols outside the walls that completely encircled the city. He worked with a pilot—Ian Smith—who owned a DHC-6 Twin Otter. It was a prop plane that skydiving companies loved. Ian didn't fly directly over the ruins—that was restricted airspace unless you had powerful friends or a death wish. But he flew as close as possible without having the US military shoot him down.

After they'd flown as close as they dared to restricted airspace, Tom jumped out the door on the back of the plane and skydived into the city. He pulled his chute at the last possible minute, at the lowest altitude safely possible.

He usually landed on some high rise or skyscraper rooftop somewhere to avoid the lagodire. Even though he usually parachuted in at night, under cover of darkness, he took no chances. Lagodire had no tech to speak of, no radios, so if you kept your head down and didn't stir up the hordes, you could move around as you liked. Pretty much.

But if they ever "treed" him on top of a building like they'd treed the poor bastard he was risking his ass to help, Tom could always BASE jump off the building and land somewhere safer. Those slider down jumps where you didn't reach terminal velocity had saved his ass a few times. Without the slider, the chute opened faster, and you really wanted that when the ground was rushing up to get to know you better.

He was forming a plan on the fly as he descended on the apartment rooftop. The lagodire were closing in on the skinny guy at the edge of the rooftop. In a way, the positioning was as good as it could be for a rooftop with minimal cover.

He was going to land between the lagodire and their prey, and then *he* was going to pray he had the skills to fight four at once.

This was such a stupid and reckless risk. He hated himself for it. What the hell was wrong with him? He was supposed to be a professional. He was being paid to do a job, and this sure as hell wasn't it. Having a conscience must be some kind of genetic defect. There was no other excuse.

On the roof of the big apartment building, the lagodire were slowly closing in on the guy. The man clenched his fists and shouted something that Tom had no chance of hearing with the wind rushing in his ears. Then the guy caught a glimpse of him and turned his way. His eyes widened in shock.

So much for surprise. But it didn't matter now. Tom was coming in fast, right on course.

The lagodire had spotted him now too, but they hesitated. They weren't sure what to make of him. Good. He knew he didn't have much time before they got over their shock and attacked. He needed to make the most of the element of surprise.

He expertly used the chute's steering lines and flaring at the precise moment to slow and position himself. This was the tricky part. There was always wind high up on buildings. The higher the building, the worse the crosswinds were. This building was only ten stories, but he didn't want the parachute to fill again after he touched down and drag him over the edge. He didn't have a lot of time to deal with it either. But if he flared too early, he could stall and cause a hard landing.

Now. He flared the chute, slowing his approach so he could land without killing himself or careening off the other side of the building.

He landed in the open rooftop between the man and the lagodire but with enough room to run off his momentum. He leaned forward and touched down harder than he wanted, but not hard enough to send him to his hands and knees. He had control of the landing and hit almost exactly where he'd intended. As soon as he touched down, he downed the chute, pulling it to the surface of the roof so it wouldn't fill with air from the crosswinds and drag him over the side.

The lagodire watched him with yellow eyes and snarls. They lowered their hyena-shaped heads and bared their yellow teeth.

He made eye contact, knowing they were confused by his appearance and that he didn't stink of fear.

It was hard not to fear them. Creepy-ass laughter. Lots of yellowed teeth. A powerful greenish-gray body covered in scales like the underside of a crocodile. Claws that looked like miniature meat hooks.

The wind blew through the thick brown fur running along their heads and down their backs to their reptile-like tail, making it stand up in spikes. Tom could smell them, even from here, even in this wind. It was a stomach-turning scent—a reptile scent mixed with offensive hyena stink. The lagodire in human form smelled more like sweat and unwashed bodies, but underneath that same lagodire aroma. That stink might be more dangerous than their teeth. And if not, it was a near thing.

His chute was down on the rooftop. He was between the skinny guy and the lagodire. He couldn't smell the man behind him because of the wind, but something about him said "wolf shifter." Tom's intuition was rarely wrong.

Except maybe when he did crazy shit like this.

He pushed away all distracting thoughts and kept his eyes on the danger in front of him. His pistol was strapped into his shoulder holster so it wouldn't fall out when he was in freefall. He reached up and yanked the top strap free. In one smooth motion, he drew the weapon.

"Get the hell out of here!" he yelled at the lagodire, aiming at the closest four-legged super predator. "Go on! *Get!*"

Hell would serve snow cones before these creatures backed off anything they saw as prey. He felt like he had to give them a chance anyway.

His shouted warning did not faze them. In fact, it seemed to provoke them.

With howls and snarls, the four-legged lagodire charged him. They tore across the rooftop, their claws digging in. The two-legged naked guy wasn't far behind.

"Look out!" the maybe-wolf-shifter behind him shouted as if Tom were blind or something.

He ignored the skinny guy. He had enough on his plate already without someone distracting him by shouting the obvious.

Tom's pistol was fitted with an illegal sound suppressor. If you fired weapons in Old Detroit without some kind of suppressor, you were going to bring an entire horde of monsters down on your ass.

The lagodire were not afraid of the pistol. Slaver dripped from their jaws, mouths open to tear into him as they ran at him. Even in his wolf form, he might not be able to take on two at once, much less four—and unlike the man he was risking his neck to save, Tom was a big wolf.

His concentration narrowed down. He took a

breath and let it out. He aimed and fired. Aimed and fired.

There was nothing supernatural about shifters. They were genetic mutations created in a lab. If you shot them in the right place or enough times, they would die like anything else.

The first shot downed one of the lagodire. It crumpled, tumbling end over end across the roof.

His second shot was sloppier but hit home. The next lagodire staggered with the bullet impact. It fell to the roof, lying on its side, wounded but not dead. For some reason, it was doing that hair-raising hyena laugh.

He shifted his aim to the third one closing in fast.

But he ran out of time. Lagodire were fast on four legs. They were almost as fast as any wolf. The third one reached him and leaped at his neck, teeth bared, its yellow eyes gleaming.

Tom was forced to grab the lagodire to stop it from ripping out his throat. The gun was knocked from his hand. It thumped to the rooftop. He cursed, twisting and using all his strength to hurl the lagodire away from him.

It went flying, hit the roof hard, but was scrambling back to its feet almost at once.

He crouched down, reaching for the pistol. Before he could snatch it, the human-form lagodire was on him, snarling as savagely as any beast. Tom ducked the guy's attempt to grab him and hammered him with a few punches that sent the naked guy reeling.

But as he fought, the other lagodire circled and stalked toward him again. Tom's harness and lines were slowing him down. He was forced away from his pistol, driven back toward the skinny guy he was trying to save. The one at the rooftop ledge...

Two lagodire were closing in on him now, utterly fearless even though he'd already shot two of them.

He was going to lose this fight if he didn't get them the hell out of here. Especially since he'd lost his gun and was dragging the parachute along the rooftop. He didn't have the time to cut himself free of the lines or get out of the harness.

There was only one way out of this that he could see. It was crazier than a rat with its tail on fire, but he had no other option.

He turned and ran for the skinny guy standing near the building's ledge. The guy was watching him in shock, frozen in place as if he'd just seen Godzilla fly down out of heaven to rescue him. At least the guy wouldn't be heavy. He looked about one hundred and forty pounds soaking wet.

Tom ran straight for him, dragging the parachute. The chute tripped up the human-form lagodire and sent him onto his bare ass. He loosed a snarling howl.

They hadn't expected him to suddenly break and run. They hesitated a few crucial seconds. Best of all, they didn't think to grab the parachute trailing behind him. That would've been very bad.

He took full advantage of their hesitation. He grabbed the skinny guy he was here to rescue. He simply swept the dude into his arms as he moved in one smooth motion. Then he slammed one boot down on the ledge and jumped off a building for the second time in less than five minutes.

The man in his arms clutched at him desperately, holding on for dear life. It had been a while since the guy had showered, and it didn't help that Tom could scent as good as a wolf. Also, the guy he'd just saved? Yeah. He was definitely a wolf shifter. Now that Tom had him close, the scent was clear as day.

Oh, and the surprises didn't stop there either. The guy was not only a wolf shifter, he was an omega wolf. The rarest shifter breed—one with a genetic mutation allowing a male to carry a child to term. For an instant, the realization was so shocking that Tom lost track of what he was doing.

Which was a bad thing when you'd jumped off a building.

The parachute was still open, of course, so it almost immediately caught air, slowing their descent with a teeth-rattling jerk. He kept a very tight hold on the omega so he wouldn't drop him ten stories. The strain was not pleasant. He was going to need some aspirin after this. Maybe a trip to the chiropractor.

The omega kept a death grip on him. He was holding on so tightly that Tom could feel the other wolf's heart pounding faster than a rabbit's heartbeat.

They had escaped the lagodire on the rooftop, but their problems weren't over. He was carrying the omega which meant he had no hands free to work the steering toggles. That meant he had no control over where they went, and ten stories was not high up. Gravity wasn't forgiving.

"Pull the handle on the left," he yelled into the omega's ear, really hoping the guy wasn't in too much shock to obey. "It's a steering line. We need to head away from the buildings!"

Otherwise, they would smash into the side of one of the other buildings on the street before they could touch down. Not only would they lose all style points, but this would be one of the shortest and craziest failed rescues in history.

The omega could obey orders, at least. He reached out and grabbed the steering toggle. The parachute veered to the left. They barely managed to avoid clipping the side of another tenement building.

Turning increased the rate of descent. The ground rushed up fast. At least it wasn't concrete or asphalt. They were headed for an overgrown lot filled with weeds and thigh-high grass, so he wasn't going to break both legs.

Probably.

"Grab both toggles and pull them downward when I tell you!" he shouted to the wolf in his arms.

"Toggles?"

"Handles!" he yelled impatiently. He continued to look forward, not at the ground, so it was easier to judge distance. When they were just under fifteen feet, he yelled, "*Now*! Pull them down!"

The wolf in his arms did his best. But this was not how a parachute was meant to be steered, and the wolf in Tom's arms made his positioning awkward. You usually flared as stage one, then you tried to glide as long as possible without letting your feet hit the ground as you came in for your landing, slow and controlled.

Tom leaned forward, still holding this wolf in his arms, trying to keep his weight over his feet. They did level out before the ground…mostly. He began to run forward as they touched down. It was a jarring landing, but he didn't fall. He slowed his run until his forward momentum was gone. Then he set the wolf in his arms on the ground.

For a second, he simply stood there in awe. That had been beyond crazy. But here they were. No broken bones. No death. No pistol, either, but he'd still count this as a win. Any landing you walked away from was a win in his book.

But he didn't have time to do a lot of inner pondering on his motives for sticking his dick into the middle of this hornet's nest. The lagodire on the roof could be coming down the stairs after them right now. There could be plenty more lagodire around too, happy to rip them apart and eat them. And now he only had a knife left since he'd lost his favorite gun.

The guy he'd rescued was staring at him with wide eyes, his mouth open. Tom ignored him and pulled out his knife. He sliced through the parachute cords and lines. He didn't have time to deal with them. It meant he wouldn't be able to BASE jump anymore, and he would have to eat the cost of the chute on top of the cost of his pistol.

This run had turned into a nightmare.

So long, jewelry store with your half a million dollar sparkly diamond necklace. It was nice never knowing you.

He was in deep shit for so many reasons, but he couldn't focus on that now. He had to keep focused on the problems right in front of him. Right now, that meant getting the hell out of here.

"Tell me you can run," he said to the omega as he put his knife back in its sheath.

"Yeah..." the omega croaked. It sounded as if the guy hadn't spoken in half a decade. The omega was watching him with those big, light-colored eyes. They were almost amber. Quite memorable.

The guy was handsome, too—under all the dirt. He looked Mediterranean, maybe. Maybe Italian? Or hell, he could be dark Irish and well-tanned for all

Tom knew. The guy had dark hair that was filthy and looked like it had been attacked by a weed-whacker, it was so hacked and clumpy. But he also had delicate features that made him look like he should be a concert violist. Or something like that. Something fancy and dignified.

Tom snorted. Yeah. Dignified. The omega reeked of body odor no matter how he looked, and Tom wondered how long it had been since the guy had taken a bath. Ten years? Or did he sleep in a garbage truck? Detroit might be ruins now, but deodorant didn't have an expiration date.

"Thank you—" the omega started to say.

Tom cut him off. "Not now. Now we run. Follow me."

He set off at a sprint, half wondering if the omega would obey or run in the opposite direction. If he didn't obey, that was going to royally piss Tom off, especially after all he'd sacrificed to save the guy's bacon.

But he heard running footsteps behind him. So the omega wasn't a complete idiot. He was following. Farther off, the city ruins came to life with the haunting howls and vicious laughter of the lagodire. It sounded like they'd stirred up an entire horde.

Wonderful. His life kept getting more exciting with each passing second.

He sprinted along the street and ducked through

an alleyway. The omega stayed with him. That was impressive. Tom was hauling ass.

Lucky for them, lagodire didn't scent very well. Their sense of smell was only a little better than a human's. It was some defect of the genetic mishmash that created them, since hyenas and crocodiles could scent pretty well. He wasn't going to complain. That flaw would save both their asses.

He cut past the burned-out ruins of a big box store, then across another overgrown lot. That was one thing about the ruins of Old Detroit. Weeds and vines, bushes and small trees were growing everywhere. They had swallowed some buildings entirely. They pushed up through asphalt in every crack and crevice. Nothing kept them in check, and plants weren't shy about taking over. The lagodire were more interested in hunting and fighting over territory than landscaping.

He led the way down street after street, sometimes running, sometimes jogging, other times walking fast. He headed toward the Rouge River. The Rouge eventually fed into the Detroit River, but the Detroit River was walled off along the city-side. The river had dammed up against the huge wall. Even though there were outflows, flooding had created a wide lake where there had never been one before.

He already knew they couldn't get out that way. The outflows had heavy steel bars in place, and he had no way to cut through them. Besides, it was one area watched twenty-four-seven by cameras and drones and US military attack boats. Also, the Canadians kept a wary eye on it. Tom didn't want to mess around with the Canadian Army. They were serious chaps when it came to hockey and when it came to defending Windsor.

So no, trying to head out that way would lead to being shot, blown up by a drone-fired missile, or arrested. He didn't like any of those three options.

On the other hand, he *did* want to cross the Rouge River to throw off any lagodire that might be using scent to track them. He might tell himself they were flawed when it came to scent tracking, but he wasn't taking any chances.

Besides, he had to cross the river anyway to get to the only hidden exit he hoped he could use to escape the city. Usually, his exits were simpler. He used the stairs to climb a tall building and BASE jumped off, leaving Old Detroit in his dust. Without a parachute, that wasn't an option.

The howls, yips, and crazy hyena laughter were far in the distance and fading. They might have lost the lagodire already. Still, he hadn't survived this long by taking chances.

Well…except for today when he'd parachuted from building to building to save some omega wolf he didn't know. So much for being a loner, and so much for not taking chances.

He buckled those thoughts down and booted them out of his mind. They had reached the riverbanks. He needed to keep focused on the task at hand.

He glanced at the omega. "Can you swim?"

The omega looked at the water. He nodded.

Good. At least something was finally going their way. His gaze lingered on the omega for a few moments. The guy really was attractive, even as filthy as he was. Tom liked to think he was a pretty good judge of attractiveness—at least when it came to men.

Those eyes were striking. Amber, pale, but not yellow like lagodire eyes. Tom had harsh features, nicks and scars, and a face like a sculpture carved by a chainsaw. But this omega had perfectly symmetrical features, those big eyes, and very full lips. Very kissable lips. Lips that would be soft and yielding when you kissed them—

What happened to staying focused?

Yeah. Right. Focus.

"Come on," he said to the omega more sharply than he intended. "Time to get wet. Ditch the jacket. It will drag you down."

The omega paused before obeying and taking off the heavy coat. Tom threw the coat in the river, watching as the current took it away. They wouldn't need the coat anyway. No one would be freezing to death, even after getting wet.

Together, they waded into the river. The water was cold. He wasn't looking forward to his clothes, supplies, and equipment getting soaked. That was never fun.

The two of them set off swimming. Despite the weight of wet clothes and gear, he made it across the river with no problems. Once he was in the weeds on the opposite bank, he turned to check on the omega.

The guy stumbled the rest of the way out of the water. His wet clothes clung to his body. The omega was very lean, and yeah, you could even say skinny. He was breathing hard and looked exhausted. That was normal. After all the adrenaline of the chase, the fighting, and the escape, even Tom was feeling tired.

Although he sympathized, right now, they needed to push on. They needed to find a place to hunker down and rest. The riverbank was not that place. Distant howls and laughing calls still echoed in the city ruins. Their hunters weren't close, but those calls were a reminder of how much danger they still faced.

"Let's go," he said to the omega. "We need to put more distance between them and us."

"Where are we headed?"

"South. But we need to find somewhere we can rest for a while. Get our wind back."

Once there, he would evaluate their options. It might be best to hunker down for the rest of the day and definitely for the night. Lagodire were quasi-nocturnal.

The omega looked like he wanted to ask more questions, but Tom held up a hand, silencing him. He set off again, expecting the omega to follow. Wet clothes really were a pain in the ass. They restricted movement, made your damn underwear ride up the crack of your ass, and generally felt uncomfortable as hell.

At least bitching about wet clothes kept him from bitching about this entire raid going belly up and costing him big time. How much and how badly had it cost him? He wasn't sure yet. He hadn't been paid by the alpha yet, so he didn't owe money. It was all paid on delivery. Then again, he was already in the hole for the plane ride, the parachute, and his gun. Not to mention the silencer, which cost more than all three of those combined because it was illegal.

You just had to go and play the hero, didn't you?

Yeah. He'd tried to play the hardass who didn't care about anyone or anything. But what could he say? He was a damned pushover. It was disgusting.

He headed south with the omega at his side. Whenever he could, he kept to the back streets and alleys. He avoided overgrown areas. They were easier to hide in, but moving through the underbrush made so much noise. The lagodire might not have the best sense of smell, but they did have sharp hearing. While

Tom might've left the other lagodire pack behind, this was new territory, and it would be held by another pack. Possibly bigger and more savage.

When he noticed that the omega was stumbling and starting to lag behind, he knew he needed to call a halt. It was late afternoon. They would be losing the last of the daylight soon. Usually, moving at night was best, but it was a double-edged sword. Easier to hide in the dark, but more lagodire roaming around, warring with each other. All the same, he couldn't use the secret exit during the night. They would need all the light they could get in order to make it out alive. That meant they needed to hole up somewhere until dawn. Besides, the omega was exhausted, and he was running low on energy himself.

He scanned the surrounding buildings, musing over his dilemma. If he hid them in a basement, that was the place least likely to be discovered. But if they were found, there would be no escape. He usually camped on rooftops if he could, but that was when he had his parachute. Without a chute, a rooftop would be as deadly a trap as a basement.

He glanced at the sky again. Clouds were rolling in fast. If it rained, the rooftop would be miserable. He'd been wet enough already during this lovely excursion, thank you very much.

Then he spotted a four-story building with a water tower on the roof. That caught his attention. Water was even more precious than food in Old Detroit since there was no running water anymore.

The water tower was painted white but had begun to show rust in places. What were the chances the lagodire had climbed up there and used it since the fall of the city? Worth the risk or no?

He had two canteens in his pack and water purification tablets, so they wouldn't die of thirst. But it might be worth checking out the water tower. Carefully. A good supply would mean he could refill his water without returning to the riverside, and maybe the omega could bathe with it. The swim across the river hadn't helped nearly enough.

Water tower it was. He headed toward that building. When they reached it, he found the doors all locked. A good sign. From the faded, in-tatters awning and broken signs, the bottom floor had been a flower shop once. The floors above looked like apartments, maybe. The building was old, maybe from the fifties or sixties. It was clearly abandoned, but there was no fire damage. Another good sign. Large parts of the city had burned during the fighting.

He considered forcing the door, but they had deadbolts. It would be a lot of effort to kick it down. Instead, he broke the back window, cleared the jagged glass from the frame, and vaulted inside.

Once in, he paused to listen. Had the sound of breaking glass drawn attention? He scented the air, but the building only smelled musty and filled with the smell of long-rotted or dried-out flowers.

He moved to the back door and unlocked it for the omega, letting him inside. Then he locked the deadbolts again.

The omega turned to stare at him with those wide, light-colored eyes. Those eyes seemed like they belonged on a deer, not a wolf. When the omega spoke, his voice had a tremor to it. "Who are you?"

Tom held up a hand in warning and kept his voice low. "No talking. Not until we get to the rooftop."

The omega didn't respond, but he didn't talk either. Tom carefully made his way through the building, ready for anything. It was odd. He kept the stranger at his back but didn't feel any worry or unease about the man. He was used to working alone, relying only on himself, but right now, he felt a protective urge inside. It was surprisingly powerful. As if it was his duty to protect this stranger, this omega, even after saving his life once already.

Weird. But everything else about this run had gone tits up. So nothing should surprise him now.

He quickly found the interior stairs. The building had four floors, and like he'd thought, the second, third, and fourth were apartments. He avoided them for now. Later, they would probably hole up in the flower shop. He had enough supplies that they wouldn't need to loot any food. Although, maybe there was a gun inside one of the apartments.

The roof was accessed by hatch and a steel ladder at the top of the stairwell. He used his knife to pry off the cheap clasp and padlock and shoved the hatch open. He led the way again, climbing onto another roof. There was a fire escape on the backside of the roof, but he still felt naked without a parachute around. Or his pistol.

The sun was low on the horizon. Soon it would be dusk.

After helping the omega up onto the roof, he immediately shrugged out of his harness and pack, dumping them on the rooftop. He walked to the edge of the building, crouched, and risked a look at their surroundings. Empty, overgrown streets and alleys in all directions. Rusting shipping containers in a vine-choked lot, and lots of rusting vehicles.

No sign of any lagodire. There were lots of birds, though. Birds were crazy. They hung around like they didn't give a fuck, even though the lagodire would eat them if they could get them.

Pot meet kettle. You're just as crazy. You willingly came into this hellhole. So stop judging a bunch of pigeons.

Too true. Too true.

He headed back to the omega. As he crossed the wide rooftop, he peeled off his wet shirt and draped it on one of the galvanized steel roof vents to dry.

He meant to find out this omega's story and learn

what the hell he'd literally jumped into without thinking.

The omega was staring at him. Well, staring at his bare chest anyway.

At first, Tom thought the omega looked terrified. But that wasn't it. As soon as the omega realized Tom was watching him, he turned a bright red and looked away.

His scent was embarrassed…and aroused. Tom grinned. He couldn't help it.

So. That was interesting. The omega was into dudes. He must've heard that somewhere, right? That the omega mutation made all omegas gay. From how bright this omega blushed, it had been a long time since he'd seen a male half-naked. Or a guy like Tom, anyway, since naked lagodire didn't count. They were filthy and scary, which was not a turn-on.

Also, Tom was in peak shape and covered in well-defined muscle. He had to be. His life depended on strength and endurance. Certainly it wasn't wits, since he'd thrown himself headlong into this mess that wasn't even his problem.

It was clear the effect his body was having on the other man. Tom didn't mean to torture the poor bastard, but he sure as hell intended to get out of these wet clothes. Although maybe he'd wait on dropping his drawers for a little while and let the omega calm down a little.

"I think we're safe for now," he said gruffly, glancing the omega over. No apparent wounds. Lean to the point of skinny, yeah, but not half-starved. Not terrible looking. Aside from being filthy and appearing like a wild man straight from the jungle. "What's your name?"

"Henry. Henry Wright. Who are you?"

"Tom Reinhart." He bowed, just for the hell of it.

The omega gaped at him as if Tom might be the unhinged one. "What are you doing here? I mean, why are you in the city? Did you parachute onto the roof to help me?"

"That's three questions. Which one did you want answered first?"

The omega only shook his head, his amber eyes wide. Henry looked as if he believed this whole thing had to be a wild dream. Thinking back on it, it *did* have a certain dreamlike quality. And by "dreamlike quality," Tom meant "complete nightmare he'd hurled himself into for unknown reasons."

"Where did you come from?" the omega finally choked out.

"I BASE jumped off another high rise."

"BASE jumping?" the omega asked. His voice was rough and raspy, probably from disuse. "Is that parachuting?"

"Sort of. But not from a plane. From structures. It's how I keep from getting trapped on the building roofs.

You should try it if you're going to hide on rooftops."

"I don't have a parachute."

He sighed. "That was a joke." He gave the omega a hard once-over. "What the hell are you doing in Old Detroit? Are you a scavenger or something?"

"No."

He kept staring at the omega, waiting for more. Henry, he'd said his name was. Seemed like an old-fashioned name. Although the name Tom wasn't exactly cutting edge, so maybe he shouldn't talk.

Henry shifted uncomfortably under his steady gaze. "I mean, I do scavenge because I have to. I'm not...one of those people who come in here to take valuable things. I'm looking for food and water."

"Fine. I get it." He paused, considering it. Then he shook his head. "On second thought, I don't get it. You don't have a gun after all that scavenging? What's wrong with you?" He narrowed his eyes. "Are you a pacifist? Because lagodire probably think pacifists taste like chicken."

A flash of irritation crossed the omega's face. A hint of defiance shone in those amber eyes. "Gunshots just bring more of them."

Tom had to give him that one. It was certainly true. Although, when you were already up to your eyebrows in snake-dogs, a gun was really nice to have. Hell, Tom already missed his piece the way he might miss a finger.

Was there a way he could go back to it? Probably not. The lagodire might be insane feeding machines, but they weren't stupid. The human-form lagodire had probably stolen Tom's pistol for himself. Damn it.

Tom focused on the omega wolf again. "Why are you here in the first place?"

The omega looked away sullenly. Tom began to wonder if he would answer. He also wondered if he had the patience for this.

It was far too late for second thoughts. Although, if he had the chance to do it all over again, he probably would've done exactly the same thing. He was a fool that way.

Finally, Henry did answer. Sort of.

"I'm an omega. An omega wolf."

"Yeah. I know." Tom tapped his nose. "This works, by the way."

Henry's cheeks went an even brighter red. "I didn't mean…" He shook his head. "Never mind. It's been a long time since I've…talked with anyone."

Tom took a deep breath and nodded. It wouldn't hurt for him to show a little damn compassion to this omega. "Yeah, I get it. Sorry. I'm a smartass sometimes. Good old Mom tried to beat it out of me with a wooden spoon, but it didn't take."

Henry stared at him. Then the slightest of smiles curved his lips before the omega's wariness and distrust slammed down again.

Great. This guy was never going to be the life of the party. Hell, Tom could deal with that. It wasn't as if he was a party animal himself. He was a loner. That was why he did crazy, reckless shit like parachuting into one of the most dangerous places on Earth.

He tried out a smile of his own. Maybe it reassured the omega, maybe it didn't. He didn't stop there. He went to his pack and pulled out a chocolate bar. Chocolate and nuts. He held it up, raising his eyebrows.

It was a little humbling, actually. He'd believed that the omega had been drooling over his shirtless body earlier. But that did not begin to compare to the absolute lust in the other wolf's eyes as he stared at the chocolate bar.

Guess that was a "yes."

He tossed it to the omega. Henry deftly snagged it out of the air and ripped it open. He took a huge bite, tipped his head back, and let out the most sexual groan in the world.

Tom was surprised to feel himself responding to the raw decadence of that groan. He grinned again. Hell, that was a sound he loved. On top of the deep flare of lust pooling in his groin, he felt a burst of happiness. Simple happiness. Because he'd made this little omega blissfully happy—at least for a little while.

That meant something. He didn't often get that chance with people. So maybe he felt a little happy himself. Not that he was going to admit that crap out loud. It was difficult to play a hardass if you went all melty at the sight—and sounds—of a guy having a chocolate bar orgasm.

Whatever. So the sounds the little omega made got under his skin a little, maybe gave him a bit of a hard-on. Didn't matter. Sex was the least of his worries. He had more than his fair share of problems.

No parachute. No gun. One dangerous way out of the city—a way he wasn't even sure actually existed. Hunted by the lagodire. Don't forget that bit of sunshine.

Worst of all, no diamond necklace, and a client back in New Detroit who wasn't known to be forgiving. Alphas never were. That was one of the reasons Tom loathed them.

Things looked grim. But...he didn't feel desperate. It didn't make sense, but for whatever reason, protecting this stranger, this omega wolf, had come to be important to him. It made zero sense, but it was true all the same.

He intended to get Henry out of Old Detroit alive, no matter what, and he wouldn't rest easy until he did.

You know what? You're a fool. You deserve everything coming to you.

He smirked. He guessed he would find out the truth of that, one way or another.

CHAPTER THREE

Henry was utterly torn. The candy bar was so good that he wanted to shove the whole thing into his mouth at once. On the other hand, he wanted to draw this out for as long as possible, savoring every instant of it.

He tried to find a middle ground. The sugar, the chocolate, the nuts, it all tasted divine. He had a hard time not falling to his knees and worshiping the gods of taste buds. Or chocolate. Or…candy bars. He was willing to worship the whole pantheon.

Maybe his reaction was over the top. Sure, sometimes he found candy bars when he was scavenging. But all of them were long, long past their expiration dates. He risked eating them anyway. And true, he'd built up a tolerance and a steel gut after all this time trapped in the ruins.

But *this* candy bar was fresh and tasty and somehow even better. Maybe it was all in his mind. Maybe it was simply because he hadn't eaten since the cans of tuna and green beans. Maybe it was because he was half-exhausted and loopy from all the running, fighting, and being afraid, and the sugar-spike hit with the power of an illegal drug.

He didn't know. He didn't care. All he knew was that this was the best candy bar he'd had in forever.

When he finished the candy bar, he took a deep breath and let out a sigh. He opened his eyes. The other wolf was staring at him intently. Those gray eyes had an intensity that had Henry's heart beating faster. He felt heat flood his cheeks and the back of his neck. It didn't help that the other wolf was currently shirtless. That only flustered Henry even more.

Tom. The other wolf's name was Tom. He was very distracting. It was even worse because Tom looked like some inner fantasy come to life. He had that rough and roguish handsomeness that had always appealed to Henry...well, back before his life had turned into one long nightmare of survival. He wondered what color wolf Tom would be when he shifted—his fur and eye color. Because in human form, he had thick, shoulder-length brown hair and gray eyes. He had chiseled features, a bit weathered but in all the right ways.

His body was scarred but had no tattoos. That surprised Henry because the other wolf seemed like the type for tats. He was built, too. Perfectly built. In Henry's opinion, nothing was sexier on a guy than ripped, six-pack abs. Except maybe perfect pecs. Oh, and that v-shaped back, heavy with muscle. Those things had him drooling, and not from hunger either.

He had to look away again quickly. Feelings and desires he'd thought lost long ago were surging inside him again. How many years had it been since he'd been with…with another man? Not since Max…

And that was how he'd ended up trapped in this hell.

Sorrow and pain swept through him. He ruthlessly suppressed any desire or need inside him. That was a part of him that had died. He didn't need it stirring back to life. Anger spread inside. He didn't need this stranger making him feel this way. It was almost like an attack.

Tom seemed to sense that something was wrong. He frowned, still watching Henry closely, but there had been a subtle shift to him. At first, he'd seemed amused or pleased at Henry and his maybe way-too-over-the-top reaction to a fresh candy bar. Now his eyes were just as intense but also more penetrating. As if Henry was some kind of prey, and the other wolf was watching, planning a move.

Henry took a step back. His heart was beating faster.

"You don't need to be afraid," Tom said. His voice was deep and rough. It had a natural growl to it. But its very rawness made it seem trustworthy. That made no sense, but it felt right.

Although for Henry, trust was a long way off. Maybe an impossible thing. And why was he thinking of trust, anyway? He could only trust himself. Everything in his life had proven that to him. Over and over again.

"I'm not afraid," he protested.

One of the other man's eyebrows slowly arched. The rest of his face was impassive.

"Fine," Henry said. "Maybe I am. But you're a stranger."

Tom nodded gravely. "You aren't supposed to take candy from strangers."

Heat rushed up his neck and made his cheeks burn. He hated how he couldn't control his body's reactions when he was this close to this wolf. "So, you're a comedian now?"

"Nothing about me is funny." The side of Tom's mouth quirked in a hint of a smile. "But you're welcome."

Now Henry was blushing and added a heap of shame on top of that. Why did he feel so off-balance with this man? Was it because he'd spent the last three years alone? Was it because he'd been cut off from all contact, be it human or shifter, and lost the ability to relate? The lagodire certainly didn't count as company. They would only kill you and eat you.

He took a shaky breath. "You know what? You're right. I should've thanked you for the candy bar. So…thank you."

Tom nodded. He glanced around at the surrounding buildings and street before meeting Henry's gaze again. "I want to get inside again soon. We're going to hunker down for the night. It's safest."

Henry didn't say anything. It was true that roaming at night was the most dangerous. Lagodire were kind of nocturnal, but not completely. Today proved that yet again. But there would be far more of them roaming and fighting and fucking, hunting other packs and eating each other alive after dark. It was mind-numbingly brutal. For him, it was a nightmare that never ended.

"You might be wondering why we're on the roof," Tom continued, his voice low and almost soothing.

Henry shrugged. He hadn't wondered about it…yet. He'd been too afraid during the chase, too numbed by his brush with death, and then too distracted by the candy bar and his disturbing reaction to a shirtless male to wonder about it. All he knew was that they seemed safe. For now.

"I keep to the rooftops when I'm here. I always

had my parachute for a quick escape, but that's not an option anymore. I'm going to get you out of the city. But I need us both to smell better."

That seemed like such a random thing to say that Henry could only blink at him. Sure...he hadn't bathed in...hmm...he couldn't remember. He *did* wash in rainwater when he could. Soap wasn't rare when scavenging houses and apartments, but easy access to water was different. Heading to the river or any lake or pond was a huge risk. The biggest lagodire packs were closest to fresh water.

He shook his head, frowning. "Why does that matter? They don't hunt by smell. Not like us."

"Yeah, they can't scent us all that well. But if we reek, it's still easier for them to find us if we have to hide. I have unscented soap." He jerked his chiseled chin at the water tower and the faucet at the base of a bunch of pipes. "So we clean up and get back down to the first floor. I have food. We need to make it through tonight. After that, I can get you out of the city."

Henry couldn't breathe. Those words... How long had he wanted to leave? But it had been impossible. He'd been trying for years. There was no way to get over the two-hundred-foot-high walls surrounding the ruins. They couldn't be climbed. And if they ever were, you couldn't climb down the other side without being shot. Even now, if he looked hard enough, he would see a military surveillance drone high overhead. No one escaped Old Detroit. Or not people like him, anyway.

But maybe the lie of that was standing here, right in front of him. This man. This wolf shifter. He had been here before and left. He wasn't the only one either…

Henry had seen a handful of outside scavengers from time to time in the years he'd been trapped here. They shot on sight, so he kept hidden. Once, he'd even spotted a small team of them. Other times, he came across the remains of other shifters or even humans who had somehow gotten inside the walls and been found by the lagodire. It wasn't pretty.

But mostly, he was alone. The lagodire owned this place. He was the prey here.

When he opened his mouth to reply, he wasn't sure what would come out. But it was simple. A simple question. "Why?"

Tom cocked his head, a scowl flashing across his expression. "Why the hell would you want to stay?"

"No. I mean…why are you helping me?"

"That's a good question."

Henry waited for the other wolf to go on, to explain himself. But Tom only watched him, waiting, as if it was Henry's turn to talk.

"You risked your life," Henry finally said. "So I owe you…everything. If you don't want to explain…I guess I'll need to accept that."

"You don't owe me anything."

"That's the first untrue thing you've said to me."

Tom chuckled. He scrubbed a hand across his face and sighed. "Listen. The rooftop is not a good place for a conversation. We lost them, but there's nothing wrong with their hearing, and there will be more of those bastards roaming around. I don't have my sidearm anymore, so it's important we stack things in our favor for tomorrow. Let's hurry and wash up. After that, we get inside, look around for anything useful, and set up whatever camp we can. *Then* we can have some more to eat and talk if you want."

Henry glanced at the pipe and spigot at the base of the building's water tower. His clothes were still soggy from the swim. They were definitely uncomfortable. It was absurd, but he did feel a little embarrassed to stink right now. He wasn't the only one, true. Even Tom had a little good old-fashioned body odor to him right now. Although Henry was by far the more pungent one...

Tom seemed to count everything as settled when Henry didn't respond. The other wolf rummaged in his pack and came out with a white bar of soap in a sealed baggie. Without a word or a glance at Henry, he took off his heavy-duty boots and peeled off his socks. As Henry stared wide-eyed, he unbuckled his pants and slid them down. The boxers went next.

Oh, God.

Quickly, Henry glanced away. His skin felt on fire, and the ache in his groin was so intense it was painful. He...he couldn't do this. It was a given that shifters were far more comfortable with nudity than humans, especially since they had to take off their clothes to change forms. But Henry's raging, long-denied libido was going to humiliate him. How sad he would look, standing there with a hard-on, trying not to swoon over this man.

Because...because Tom looked so good that Henry hated him for it. Not really, but almost. He not only had a godly torso, but he had powerfully built legs with dark hair on them and more dark hair around his cock and balls. That...big cock. It was bigger and thicker than Henry's, and that was daunting enough. Even though Tom wasn't erect, it was clear that he would be impressive when the piece of meat that dangled between his thighs woke up.

Henry kept trying not to stare. He kept trying not to admire the other man's ass either as Tom headed for the water tower. His ass looked firm and tight and the perfect muscled package that Henry wanted to squeeze. That ass flexed as he walked to the water tower and turned the spigot. Henry swallowed a desperate groan.

The water spigot squealed, and the pipe shuddered. Finally, a gush of rusty water shot from the nozzle, stopped, then started again. Tom adjusted the flow, and soon it cleared up.

The very naked Tom glanced at him. "Move quick." He pointed at the runoff gutters the water was flowing toward. "I don't want someone to see the runoff and get curious."

Henry nodded, swallowing the orange-sized lump in his throat. But his feet wouldn't move. His body wasn't obeying him. It was taking all his concentration to avoid being turned-on by the very hot, very sexy, very naked man in front of him. He hadn't seen a naked man in years. Not...not one like *this*. And now one that was absolutely stunning was right in front of him. It brought back all the need and desire he believed had died three years ago. When he'd lost—

No. Don't think about that now. I can do this. He doesn't care about me. He's not gay. I'm just another guy. It doesn't matter. I won't show him how attracted I am to him. I'm not going to get a boner. That isn't going to happen.

Easier said than done. Because after almost dying and all the fear and stress, his body seemed hyper-aware and highly aroused. As if his body wanted and needed sex more than anything else.

The universe was messing with him. It had to be.

This whole situation... It was both terrifying and silly. This man, this stranger, had saved his life. Now he was naked. Henry had to forgive him for the torment he was causing too. Or, on second thought, did he? The stranger was a wolf shifter. He would know that Henry was an omega wolf—a genetic mutation on top of genetic engineering. If he knew anything at all about omegas, he would know they could carry offspring to term…and were sexually attracted to other males. So was this guy tormenting him right now? Or was he unaware? Or was he a…a crazy gun-toting exhibitionist adrenaline junkie who jumped off of buildings and out of planes?

Or all of those possibilities combined…?

But it was the memory of Max that was finally enough to put the damper on his arousal. All thoughts of sex, sexy time, anything close to sexual, were stamped out. He kept his gaze off Tom and slowly stripped. He had loved once. He didn't care to have those feelings—even down to desire—ever again.

They washed in silence. The water stank of metal and was oddly warm. The sun on the water tower must've done it. He used Tom's soap, scrubbing harshly, getting off the grime. He soaped up his very short hair. He kept it cut brutally short. Otherwise, he had to worry about tangles, lice, and fleas. But he'd never been good at cutting his own hair…

A wave of self-disgust washed through him, so powerful it was like physical pain. He was such scum. Filthy and disgusting and completely revolting. He scrubbed his body harder as if he could wash all that away. But it didn't wash away. He was ashamed in a way that he didn't think anyone from outside these walls could understand.

Tom had finished. He went to his pack and took out new clothing. Henry was watching him now with quick, desperate glances. Just because he couldn't help it. Like the candy bar, the sight of Tom was something wonderful in his life. He was grateful for it, even though most people would believe him pathetic.

He had scrubbed off as much of the dirt as possible. He blinked out the sting of soap from his eyes as he rinsed his short, bristly hair. After he turned off the water, he felt cold. Goosebumps broke out all along his arms and legs. The sun would be setting soon. In early Spring, the nights could get chilly. All he ever had for heat was his jacket, but he'd lost that today. He was eager to get clothes on again, even though they looked stiff and still damp from getting soaked.

Tom dressed in what looked like dark fatigues and a black, long-sleeved shirt. The shirt clung to his body, outlining his broad chest, wide shoulders, and thick arm muscles. He swept back his long, wet hair with a brush of his hand and bound it with a hair tie into a baby ponytail. The sight of it almost made Henry laugh.

Tom glanced his way, and his eyes locked with Henry's. If the other man had "checked him out" or anything, like...to compare penis sizes, then Henry hadn't noticed it. He'd been too wrapped up in his own dark thoughts. That was actually a relief: that he'd been oblivious...if it had ever happened. He could not physically compare or compete with Tom in any way. But at least Tom wasn't rubbing it in. And best of all, he wasn't gay, so Henry was feeling all shy and self-aware for nothing.

"Here," Tom said, pulling clothes out of his pack. "This is the last of what I have. They'll be baggy on you, but at least they're clean. You won't get a rash from having wet clothes on you all day."

"Thank you." He dressed quickly, and it felt good to be covered again. He knew what had happened to him—the reason he was trapped in these ruins—had broken him in a lot of ways. But he was still glad to have his body covered again. It felt...safer.

Tom busied himself packing his gear. He grabbed Henry's old clothes after slipping his pack on again. He carried everything with them as they headed downstairs again. Henry tagged along with him, feeling like a fifth wheel. But he didn't want to be alone either.

"I want to check these apartments out," Tom said, frowning as he stared down the fourth-floor hallway. "I want a new gun."

"A gun will be loud."

Tom snorted. "I'll take loud over being dead." He glanced at Henry. "Coming?"

Henry nodded. He wouldn't be letting the other wolf out of his sight. In fact, what he really wanted to do was grab on to the guy and cling to him. It could be like one of those movie posters for cheesy fantasy movies where some ripped barbarian man held up a sword while a scantily clad woman clutched his leg. Henry was even happy to play the role of scantily clad clinger if he got to stay around Tom.

He couldn't help it. He burst out laughing.

Tom was surprised. He smiled, but it was a bit bemused. "Either I'm funnier than I thought, or I missed something."

Henry was blushing now. He could feel his cheeks heating. "Oh. Uh. I was just thinking something silly." He cleared his throat. "I don't want to say it out loud. It's really embarrassing."

Tom grinned and slapped him on the back, which almost knocked him into the wall. The wolf was strong.

"Well, whatever," Tom said, smirking. "It's good to hear you laugh. Do it more often. That's an order."

Henry stared at him, not sure what to say. Tom had said that like an alpha giving a command he expected obeyed. He struggled with how to respond.

But Tom was already chuckling and shaking his head. "Sorry. I'm only busting your balls. There's probably a law somewhere about teasing omegas." He rubbed the back of his neck and sighed. "Or maybe

I'm going to Hell for it." The grin flashed again. "And every other naughty thing I've done."

"You were teasing me?" Henry asked, tipping his head to the side.

"Yeah. That's what I said. It's how I show I like you. What? The wolves you knew didn't tease you? What a bunch of assholes." He shook his head. "But look, I only expect you to follow my orders when we're in danger. You already proved yourself."

Henry's eyes widened. "When?"

"When I jumped off the building with you in my arms. I couldn't steer. You saved our asses from smashing into the side of a building. Hell, you landed us."

He didn't know what to say. But a surge of pride swept through him. Because he had done things, hadn't he? He hadn't simply been a spectator, even though he'd needed to be rescued.

The pride made him feel warm inside his chest. At the same time, it pushed back the other, darker thoughts that had been haunting him. He felt...good.

And he had this wolf to thank. A man who had literally appeared from nowhere, descending from the heavens to save his furry butt.

Tom started off to explore the apartments on each floor. Henry stuck by his side, still listening for the howls or laughter from any roaming lagodire on the streets. He remained tense but heard nothing. It seemed as if they'd lost their pursuers. That was unbelievable, especially since he'd thought he was going to die on that roof.

Their luck might've been in earlier, but now it deserted them. Two of the three floors were empty and had been unlived in even before the fall of Detroit. The second floor actually had two apartments. Tom broke down the doors. But once inside, he didn't find any firearms. Neither apartment had anything more dangerous than kitchen knives. He did take some blankets and pillows from a linen closet to sleep on.

Disappointed, they headed back down to the flower shop on the first floor. It was twilight out by the time they'd finished searching the apartments and setting up, including barricading the front door.

"Good work," Tom said, dusting off his hands. The other wolf's voice was gentle. "Are you hungry?"

"I'm always hungry."

"Good. I like a man who likes to eat." He picked up his pack and brought it over. "Now, I hope you're not a gourmet because all I have are MREs."

"What are those?"

"Meals Ready-to-Eat. Field rations. Got used to them in the military. But it's definitely not French cooking, so don't go all celebrity chef on me and start judging left, right, and sideways."

Henry smiled. "It's fine. I've been eating some strange stuff for a long time. Lots of people have cans of lima beans in their cupboards. I never understood why. I detest them."

"I hate them too," Tom said, laughing. "Look at that. We're practically brothers, united by our mutual disgust for canned lima beans."

Brothers. He wouldn't mind having this man as a big brother. But if he were honest, part of him wanted Tom for something else entirely. A fantasy he didn't dare indulge. Something down and dirty and definitely qualifying as lover and nothing else. But that was crazy. This man was still a stranger. A dangerous stranger who had killed two lagodire today and wounded a third as if it was nothing...

Saving your life, he chastised himself bitterly. *He did it to save your worthless life. So you'd better trust him, you little idiot.*

He looked into the man's eyes, trying to decide if he could trust him. This wolf had saved his life. So the obvious answer was yes. But Henry knew he had so much baggage. Sometimes he felt like he'd been grieving for so long.

Was it time to finally stop? Was it time to move on? After all, Max was gone, no matter what Henry did. But Henry was still here. He was alive, and he had hopes and dreams and needs. Meeting Tom today had stirred all of that up. It had his thoughts reeling, his emotions in turmoil...but it didn't feel like a bad thing.

No. It felt like change. Like needed change.

Maybe he would finally be leaving this nightmare city. Maybe he could have his life back.

Maybe he had found a friend.

CHAPTER FOUR

Tom dug in his pack and handed Henry one of his MREs. The Meal Ready-to-Eat was beef ravioli. Tom was going to have maple sausage patty. These two actually didn't taste as much like ass as people might expect. But like he'd said, the French chefs weren't going to agree any time soon.

It was night out now. The building was dark as hell inside, but they wouldn't be risking any kind of cooking fire. And of course, the power had been out for decades.

No, it would be a cold meal. He was fine with that. Once he was home, he'd treat himself to a fancy four-course meal. Really splurge. Or he'd go the trash food route. He'd eat something cheap, plentiful, and completely unhealthy, but oh so damn good.

Or maybe that could wait. Maybe what he *really* needed when he escaped these walls was to get good and laid. Ever since today's cheating death escapades, he'd been completely horny. The low, throbbing ache in his groin never faded much. It was damned distracting. He didn't know if it was being close to an omega or what. Maybe omega pheromones were calling to his cock.

He smirked to himself as he began to eat. Henry had already torn into his food with a vengeance.

There was a half-moon out, low on the horizon. The sky had few clouds now, but the wind was nearly constant. A storm coming in? That wouldn't be good.

The stars glittered. To the south-southeast, the horizon glowed with the lights of Windsor and the searchlights of the Windsor Defensive Line. Farther south, almost straight down the Detroit River and across Lake Erie, would be New Detroit. His hometown these days. He couldn't see it, of course. It felt like it was a thousand miles away.

By his watch, it was almost eight-thirty when they finished eating. They would hunker down on the ground floor flower shop for the night. It really sucked that he hadn't been able to find a pistol or rifle in the apartments. He felt naked without a firearm in a situation like this.

He finished his meal, shoving the last bite of

maple sausage patty in his mouth. After eating, he felt a little better. He felt a bit more energized with some calories to burn.

Meanwhile, Henry had moved on to eating another MRE. The guy had a hole for a stomach. As Henry ate, Tom peeked through the blinds again at the dark street filled with abandoned cars and empty, vine-choked buildings.

No sign of danger. The wind had picked up a couple of hours ago. The building creaked as the wind hooted and moaned. The plants and vegetation that had overgrown much of the street sighed and whispered as the wind shook them. That didn't make him happy. It made it harder to hear things. Wind made it tougher to scent out enemies.

Hopefully, they wouldn't have to move from here. He knew the omega needed some decent rest. The poor bastard looked half dead with exhaustion. He was definitely too skinny, although that made perfect sense, given what he'd endured. Tom still didn't know Henry's story. Curiosity was eating at him. How the hell did an omega end up alone in Old Detroit?

How the hell had he survived?

Whatever the truth was, Henry smelled a thousand times better now. His scent would be less likely to be picked up by the lagodire, so that was good. He actually looked silly in Tom's too-big clothes, but he wasn't going to mention that.

He understood that the small omega was shy. He'd figured that out pretty damn quick, reading Henry's body language. Tom had debated saying something. Maybe teasing the other wolf a little, giving him a compliment on his body, or straight out saying that Tom liked the lean and delicate look. It was almost feminine but not. It was hard to describe, but still attractive. It had gotten his attention, anyway.

But he held his tongue. The omega was probably intimidated by his size. He probably wouldn't believe it if Tom complimented him on his cute little ass. An ass that Tom would love to cup and squeeze and maybe give that bare, pale and silken skin a little love nip.

Damn. What was going on with him right now? He was already half-hard, mulling over these fantasies. See? Ever since nearly dying, he'd been horny as hell. Must be some kind of jacked-up life-affirmation thing.

He needed to slow down and get a grip on himself. He smirked. Not literally.

It was perfectly natural after a brush with death to feel as horny as a triceratops. Sure. That was no big deal. It didn't mean he needed to make excuses for how he was feeling. Because screw that. If the little omega turned him on a bit, then fine and good. He wasn't going to push the issue. Omegas were pretty timid, weren't they? Tom didn't have much experience with them. They were rare, and Tom didn't belong to a pack. He was a lone wolf and damned proud of it.

That was all fine and good. Next problem.

Somewhere outside this building, somewhere out in the surrounding city and nearer than he would like, there were roaming packs of lagodire. After crossing the river, they were almost definitely in a new pack's territory. That could be better because they'd left the pack that knew about them in the dust. Or it could be worse. The next pack might be even bigger and more vicious.

Their escape had been plenty lucky. Sure, skill had been involved, along with pure brazenness and maybe insanity, but also lots of luck.

That luck could give out at any time. If it did, Tom didn't have a lot of options to defend himself or Henry. He'd lost his pistol. He had a knife, but fighting against shifted lagodire would be rough, especially if he needed to stay in human form. Lagodire might not be as fast as wolves, but their thick crocodile skin gave them some natural armor. Sure, Tom could shift into wolf form, but that had its own set of challenges. Some of them were impossible to overcome, like the fact that he would need to swim out of the city, and doggie paddling wouldn't cut it.

His wolf form was bigger and heavier than any lagodire, but they swarmed like hyenas. That made them even more dangerous to fight. Top it off with their heightened aggression, and they were probably the most dangerous creature on the planet. And that was saying a lot.

If he'd been here with a team, it would've been different. But he always worked alone. Like he'd said, he was a lone wolf. He hadn't belonged to a pack since he'd been a punk kid, and he didn't miss it. He'd told the alpha of his old pack in Cleveland to go fuck himself with a pineapple. Sure, he'd been a kid, barely eighteen years old, but that had earned him a savage beating. After that, he'd pulled up stakes and headed off on his own and never looked back. He'd never been much for packs since then. Or even large groups of people, shifters or humans. Hell, more than three and his fur started to bristle.

Now he had an omega to rescue. Nothing had gone according to plan since he'd dropped into the city. Now that he finally had a chance to breathe and take in the situation, it was looking grim. Very grim.

It wasn't only the fact that lagodire were hunting him and he had no gun. It wasn't that having Henry with him would slow him down and put his life at higher risk. It wasn't that he had to sneak out through a drainage tunnel submerged beneath the Detroit River—or that, for a good part of his escape, he wouldn't be able to see a damned thing and would be praying he didn't run out of air before he could surface again.

No. Because even if he managed to escape Old Detroit, things wouldn't be anywhere near good. Not even in the same ballpark.

Because he'd been contracted to retrieve the Lumiere Soleil diamond necklace. He was probably the only person in the country who could pull it off. And the guy who had hired him was not a nice person. Why would he be? He was an alpha. He could make Tom's life hell. He could tank Tom's reputation, make it hard for him to find new, dependable clients. And there was nothing Tom could do about it.

He glanced over at Henry. The omega had finished his meal and was sitting nearby with his back against the wall. He looked content. Hell, he looked sleepy.

When Henry saw him looking, a tired smile crossed his face. It was a sweet smile. The omega's scent was…grateful. He was feeling gratitude, and it must be a powerful emotion to be so easy to scent out.

Hell. Even though this omega had ruined his day—ruined this entire run—it was impossible for Tom to resent him.

"Get enough to eat?" he asked quietly.

"Yeah. Thank you. I'm sorry I ate so much of your food."

He snorted. "Don't worry. When we get out of here, I'll take you to a restaurant, and we'll shovel down all the hot food we can get."

Henry didn't reply for a few moments. He was staring at Tom with those amber eyes that seemed so unforgettable, glittering in the dark.

"Why are you doing this?" Henry finally asked in a quiet voice.

"What? Hanging out in a shop full of dead flowers? It is kind of weird."

"Why are you helping me?"

"Good question. I don't know."

"That's not a good reason for risking your life."

"It's not a reason. It's an answer. I don't lie. You asked. I can't help if you don't like the answer I gave."

"Fine." Henry's gaze dropped to his hands. He held the empty MRE container as if hoping it would miraculously refill. "I just... I mean, I want to say thank you." He looked up again, turning vulnerable eyes back to Tom. "You saved my life."

He shrugged. He didn't want to make a big deal about it, even though it was a big deal. Because that spur-of-the-moment choice might just cost him his furry ass. Tonight. Tomorrow. Maybe even back in New Detroit, if they made it out.

He wouldn't tell Henry that. He didn't need the omega feeling guilty. It wouldn't solve anything.

But Henry seemed to expect something more than a shrug. So Tom gave him a half-smile. "You're welcome."

"I guess I might be the luckiest wolf alive to have you drop from the sky to rescue me."

"You *could* say that. But I wouldn't."

"Why not?"

"Because you're here in this hellhole. You were being hunted by snake-dogs. I don't call that lucky."

"Snake-dogs." Henry shook his head. He pulled his knees up against his chest, wrapping his arms around them and resting his chin on his knees. "I'm an omega wolf."

"I know." He frowned, wondering at the wild change in conversation topics. Did Henry think he hadn't noticed or scented him out right away? It was a strange thing to say.

"You must know the slurs they use about my kind."

Tom shrugged. "Sure."

There were dozens of them. From ugly things like "dick bitch" to more obscure stuff like "fur traps" because you could screw a male and end up with a baby or something. Like all slurs, they were nasty and mostly stupid.

"Is it weird to feel sympathy for something called a 'snake dog?'" Henry asked.

"Yeah." The question irritated him. "Especially since they almost ate you today."

"That simple, huh? I guess things are black and white for you."

"Don't put words in my mouth. But I'm no bleeding heart for lagodire." He gave Henry a hard stare. "If you are, then you're crazy. This isn't my first rodeo in Old Detroit. And you've been trapped here for I don't know how long. And today, they almost killed us both. So don't lecture me about ugly names."

"Maybe you're right." Henry was staring at his empty food container again. "I hate them. I'm terrified of them. But I also feel sorry for them."

"Well, don't. There are plenty of people to feel sorry for on the planet, but lagodire aren't on the list." He nodded toward the grimy windows. "They destroyed this city. Killed tens of thousands. Now they eat each other. I don't shed any tears for them."

He didn't understand people like Henry. Maybe they were big, tenderhearted softies. He guessed it was good to have compassionate people running around in the world. They made up for bastards like...well, like himself. He killed lagodire when he had to, although it was always best to avoid them if possible. But it didn't keep him up at night. Maybe because of all the gnawed human bones around Old Detroit. That was hard to forgive or forget. They had destroyed an entire city.

Besides, the lagodire had put a bad name on all shifters with the humans. Even though humans had created them. Even though both Tom and Henry had a big share of human genetics.

Whatever. It was a mess. It would give you a headache thinking about it. Besides, he wasn't the brooding type. He dealt with the problems in front of him and moved on.

Problems like this omega. But was he second-guessing himself? No. Well, not much, anyway. He had made a choice. He would deal with the fallout. There was no use spending a lot of time and energy worrying about it now. He needed to finish what he'd started and get this omega to safety. And safety meant out of Old Detroit.

That was the problem right in front of him.

The silence between them had drawn out enough to start getting uncomfortable. Tom reached for his pack and dug around in it. He pulled out his last candy bar and held it out to Henry.

"Here. Eat. It's a peace offering."

Henry's eyes went wide. He took the candy bar, unwrapped it, and began chomping away. His enthusiasm amused Tom to no end. The little omega had a sweet tooth.

"So what's your story?" he asked after the omega vacuumed down the candy bar. For someone so skinny, he ate like a horse. "What the hell is an omega doing alone in Old Detroit?"

Henry didn't answer. He went back to hugging his knees, staring at the floor.

Tom moved to his side. He squatted down,

reached out, and put a hand on the omega's shoulder. He gave a reassuring squeeze.

Henry sucked in a sharp breath and stiffened. Then Tom felt him relax. He cast a quick glance into Tom's eyes. The omega did have thick lashes on those pretty eyes.

Yeah. He could feel the tension of arousal low and persistent inside him. He was definitely attracted to the other man. But at the same time, Tom knew he was a stranger. He was a stranger, even if he felt strangely protective of Henry. It was a wolf thing, but still a powerful urge. Definitely not one he was used to. It had crept up on him too. He hadn't felt protective when he'd been watching Henry through his binoculars. Hell, he'd almost turned his back on the omega.

But…he was glad he hadn't.

"Tell me," he urged Henry. "I want to know."

"It's a hard story for me to tell."

"If you can't, you can't." He shrugged and drew back his hand. "I can talk if you want. It's not like we have television to watch. Or we can get some sleep. I'll take first watch."

"Will you talk instead?"

The omega watched him wide-eyed, as if talking was some big thing or as if Tom might suddenly refuse. Tom felt a burst of sympathy for him. If Henry had been trapped in the ruins for long, he was probably desperate for some interaction. After all, you couldn't exactly get chatty with the lagodire.

"All right. I'll talk. So what do you want to know? My life story?"

"What's it like out there? Over the wall."

He frowned. "How long have you been trapped here?"

"Years. I think three. But I don't really know now. A few winters. Those are the hardest."

"Damn." Three fucking *years*? He was starting to appreciate the hell this omega had suffered. He was starting to appreciate it on a raw, gut level. "You're tougher than I am."

Henry sucked in a quick breath. His scent was embarrassed but pleased. "No, I'm not. I've been trapped here, trying not to get eaten."

"I guess trying not to get eaten is high on the list of important things." He took a deep breath and started talking about random big things that had happened over the last few years. Some of it was local stuff from the New Detroit packs. Some fat cat St. Clair alpha was pouring money into rebuilding the city and breaking ground on a new hospital. He figured Henry might want to know about that kind of stuff—what little Tom knew, anyway. He generally kept his distance from shifter politics and especially wolf packs.

Henry latched on to the mention of the St. Clair

Pack. "I remember him. Kross. Everyone said he wanted to take back Old Detroit."

"Did he? Well, he's doing a shit job of it." He snorted. "Look, I'm no power player in New Detroit pack politics. I can barely stand the bullshit. I'm no fan of alphas."

The omega turned those big eyes to him. "What about you, Tom? What's your story?"

It was the eyes. Those damn pretty amber eyes. Were omega eyes bigger than everyone else's? They certainly seemed that way. Yeah, maybe omegas weren't tough and physically strong or any of that shifter bullshit, but those big puppy dog eyes had to be some kind of protective adaptation.

"All right. Hold on to your boxers. You ready for this epic tale?"

Henry burst out laughing, his expression surprised. His eyes warmed. "Yeah. I'm ready. I think..."

It made Tom feel good to make the omega laugh. For a few moments, all the harsh lines of care in his face had vanished. Everything weighing on him seemed to fall away. His laughter had a nice, light tone to it.

"I'm ex-military," he began. "82nd Airborne. I joined up after getting my ass kicked out of my pack. After I turned eighteen."

"*What*? How? And what pack?"

"Archwood."

Henry shook his head, frowning.

Tom smirked. "A big Cleveland wolf pack. As for how I got tossed, it's just an ugly story. The alpha's this bastard named John Dyer. He's connected to a lot of shady shit. I was eighteen or so, full of piss and vinegar. I wanted to move up in the pack ranks. Dyer had me doing a few things for him. Small-time stuff. But...it never sat right for me. The alpha kept talking about how this was good for the pack, but it was only good for his pocketbook."

"Was it illegal stuff?"

"It was borderline. Bullshit that rich and powerful men get away with. Shifters are the same as humans. Maybe worse, with all this pack loyalty bullshit."

Henry was leaning forward, watching intently. "What happened then?"

"I told him I didn't like it. He laughed and called me some kind of starry-eyed idealist or something like that. Actually, what he said was more like—'a wet-behind-the-ears punk like you needs to shut his fucking muzzle and do as he's told.' I essentially told him to ram it up his ass with a snow shovel."

"You *said* that to an alpha?"

"Why not? They're mostly all bark and no bite."

Most of them were anyway. Sure, there were a few hardasses. But then again, he had long ago soured on packs. They were worse than the military at dominating your life.

"Did he hurt you?"

"That's not his style. He has bodyguards. Some tough guys acting as muscle in the pack, protecting him. He exiled me from the pack. As a going-away present, he ordered them to give me a beating to remember."

"Did you fight them?"

"I landed a few punches, but I was just a kid. Outnumbered. You're always outnumbered when it really counts."

"I know."

Tom glanced at him. He was looking down at his hands again. But it made sense that the omega had seen some shit. He was here in the ruins of Old Detroit, after all.

He decided to continue the story. "After that, I joined up and didn't look back. I got out of the service after a couple of re-ups. Since then, I've been on my own. Doing my own thing."

"No pack? No family? No...girl?"

"I'll never belong to a pack again." He flashed Henry a cocky grin. "They're not worthy of me. My dad was one of the first generations of wolves. But he died defending Detroit. My mother was human. After my father was killed, she found God and decided shifters were an abomination. Haven't talked to her in years."

Henry was watching him closely. "I know... I know about that."

"Yeah. Figured you would. As for girls..." He grinned again, looking right into the omega's eyes. "I go for men."

Henry's cheeks flushed. He looked away quickly. It was pretty damned adorable. It had been a long time since he'd been around someone who blushed so easily. Of course, maybe that was a side effect of surviving alone in this hellhole for three damn *years*.

He liked this guy. Henry was definitely endearing. The word "cute" seemed to fit him. Those puppy dog eyes were going to be a problem, though. He smirked. If Henry ever learned the power of them, it was going to be a dark day for the rest of the world.

Then again, he couldn't tell how much of his reaction to the omega was just his cock talking. You had a few run-ins with death, and suddenly, all your primal instincts kicked in. A big, powerful example of those instincts was fucking. So right now, yeah, he felt the sexual tension coiled inside him.

Tom let the quiet settle before finally breaking it again. "Yeah, I like dudes. But I haven't had a lasting relationship in years, if that's what you want to know."

"Why?"

Why. That was a good question. He didn't have an equally good answer.

"That's a mystery I haven't solved. It could be me."

"You jump off buildings with a parachute."

"Yeah. It could be that."

Henry smiled. "And you're in Old Detroit. Who comes here?"

He had to grin back. "Crazy people."

"See? Now you have a good reason. You're crazy."

"Can't argue with that one." He rubbed his jawline. His stubble made a rasping sound against his fingers. He decided to go for it again. "What about you, Henry? Why are you here?"

Henry took a deep breath and closed his eyes. Then his expression grew determined. It was almost comical, how he steeled himself, chin raised, shoulders back. He looked Tom in the eyes, and he told the story.

CHAPTER FIVE

"It's a stupid story," Henry said. "Don't expect much."

He cleared his throat and took a sip of water from one of Tom's canteens. All this talking was hurting his throat, and he hadn't done all that much yet. But after going so many years without speaking to anyone, he realized how much he missed it. Being alone for so long was hard. It wore you down on the inside.

He took a deep breath, knowing he was stalling. He knew he should tell this, clean out an old wound, but he still hesitated. Would telling a near-stranger what had happened to him help or hurt? Would sharing the things that had been done to him make

Tom feel contempt for him, or pity, or... Or what?

Tom waited, watching him. It was strange to be the focus of the other man. The lone wolf was fascinating and a little frightening. He was big and strong, but that wasn't all. Henry had been around bigger and stronger men all his life. But Tom had a self-contained intensity to him. Maybe it was his time in the military. But you also felt like you could trust him. As if he'd keep you safe if he gave you his word, no matter what came after you.

And he had put his mind to keeping Henry safe, hadn't he? Tom parachuted onto a building to save his life. A guy he didn't know, didn't care about, didn't even know was there. A man so brave he might be a little crazy had come to save the life of someone stupid enough to get trapped on a rooftop with no escape.

That was part of the theme, though. Henry was stupid. His story would only prove it.

He took another deep breath. It helped steady him. Now that the moment had come, he realized that he didn't really want to tell his story. It was painful. It brought back a lot of painful memories. Yet, he felt like he owed Tom something. He owed him his life, that was clear. But something more. An explanation. Maybe something to let Tom know he hadn't put his life in danger for nothing.

"I lived in New Detroit. I'm gay. I had a boyfriend. He was human."

After that rapid burst of sentences, he fell quiet again. Thinking back on it, it felt like a hundred years ago. Another lifetime.

"Did you have a pack?" Tom prompted gently.

That was the usual question with wolf shifters. What's your name? What pack are you with?

If you didn't have a pack…it changed things. Life was harder alone.

"I did have a pack once. The Metro Pack. In New Detroit. I…I lost them."

Sympathy flashed in Tom's eyes. Sympathy and anger. But Tom would understand what that meant better than anyone. He'd left his own pack at eighteen, and now he was alone too. Alone, and he seemed like he was doing just fine…

Doing fine, except for having to babysit Henry inside walled-off ruins teeming with predators…

Henry pushed on. "I was betrothed to Alpha Carson's second in command. A wolf named Jason Weis."

"That's right. I've heard things like that. Omegas are usually claimed. Used as bargaining chips. That kind of shit."

Tom sounded disgusted, but he was essentially right. That was just the way things were for Henry. Or the way they had been, once.

"They told me that was my role in the pack," Henry said. "My alpha was Eddie Carson. He was already married and had an heir for pack succession. He had a family and didn't need something like me. So I was betrothed to Jason Weis when I was sixteen."

"That's too damn young," Tom growled.

He could only shrug. "They couldn't have me legally marry him until I was eighteen. Then Weis got another girl in the pack pregnant and decided to make her his mate. I thought I was off the hook."

"But you weren't, of course."

"No. Alpha Carson betrothed me to another man in the pack. Daryl Underwood. By then, I was twenty, and they could force the marriage. I wanted to run...but I didn't have anywhere to go. I was afraid."

He glanced at Tom, expecting to see disapproval or contempt in his eyes. After all, Tom had told his alpha something really obscene, shrugged off a beating, and left his pack forever.

But Tom's eyes, faintly visible in the darkness of the store, were only filled with sympathy. He looked as if he was hanging on every word.

"I was going to be married to him," Henry continued. "But...then I met Max."

"Max, huh?" A knowing smile showed on Tom's face.

"Yeah...Max Taylor." Remembering him was like squeezing razorblades. Even all these years later, it hurt with a bright red pain. "It was love. Or at least I thought it was. I was stupid and young." Even now, it hurt him. The wound was deep. It hurt more than any of the kicks and punches from wolves in his pack after the truth came out. "He was human. He...he didn't care that I was a shifter. Or an omega. We fell in love and told each other we'd leave New Detroit. Head to New York. Or Los Angeles. Anywhere but where we were."

He stopped, feeling the intense pressure of tears behind his eyes. He hugged his knees and closed his eyes. He didn't have a picture of Max. His wonderful face had faded in his memories.

"You didn't make it," Tom said quietly, the statement urging Henry on.

"Not even close. Someone found out. Maybe they followed me. I don't know. Daryl...he was furious."

"He hurt you."

A humorless, jagged chuckle left Henry's lips. "It's like you already know this story."

"I know werewolves. Or maybe it's just that all people suck."

"You're a glass half empty kind of guy, Tom."

He smirked. "It's that obvious?"

"It doesn't matter. Being trapped here doesn't exactly inspire much hope." He shook his head. "Where was I?"

"They found you out. They hurt you."

"They found me out." His voice was getting raspy. Tom handed him his canteen. Henry took a deep drink and handed it back. "Thank you." He took a second to center himself again and continued. "My alpha didn't approve. He thought like should stay with like. He didn't protect me from Daryl. I never loved Daryl. I didn't want to marry him. So I don't believe I was cheating on him. No one else in my pack saw it that way. Especially not my alpha."

Tom grunted. "Alphas. Such assholes."

Henry slowly shook his head. "I would never have the guts to say something like that. I'd just get my ass kicked."

"My mouth has been getting me in trouble my whole life. Even the military could barely rein me in. I behaved, sort of. Mostly because the whole squad got in trouble if I ran my mouth, so it wasn't just me paying the price." He leaned back, rubbing a hand across that strong jawline. "Sorry. Didn't mean to make this about me. Go on with your story."

"There's not much more to it. I tried to run away with Max. My alpha got to him first. They terrified him. They...hurt him. They were waiting for me when I showed up at Max's house." He stopped, his words catching in his throat. The memories were still painful, like swallowing glass. But he pushed on because he was almost done. "My alpha told me I was exiled—dead to him. He walked out. That was the last I ever saw of him. After that, Daryl... He took his time beating me and making me watch as he hurt Max.

Then they put us both in a car. Four wolves from my pack were there, including both men I'd been betrothed to, guys I'd known forever, and no one would speak to us. No one would say anything. Max was so terrified. I could smell his fear. I was certain they were going to take us somewhere and kill us. Dump us in the lake."

"What did they do?" Although, from his knowing eyes, Tom had already guessed.

"I guess my alpha paid off some people in the military to look the other way. They... My alpha owns yachts, helicopters. They flew Max and me to Old Detroit in a helicopter. They threw us off from almost twenty feet up, not even bothering to land. Max broke his leg in the fall. They left us in the ruins and flew away."

Tom's voice was so very gentle. "And Max?"

"The lagodire killed him. That first night. That's...that's the only reason I escaped. I tried to save him, but I couldn't... I'm not strong. Not strong enough to save anyone."

A sound of anguish and raw pain escaped him. His breath came out in a shuddering gasp. So much emotion was boiling inside him. Things he'd kept inside for so long. His eyes were burning as the pressure of tears built up even more.

He closed his eyes again, desperate to keep his sorrow under control. But he felt the burning trail of tears wind down his cheeks. He looked away, hoping the darkness would hide them.

A rough hand reached out and wiped those tears away. "I'm so sorry, Henry."

The kind words and the touch were too much. Henry couldn't help himself. He leaned into the gentle touch desperately. It was sad how he was so vulnerable and needy in front of this stranger. But he couldn't seem to control himself. Tom felt like a good person inside. It had been too long since Henry had been touched. And he'd been so alone...

Tom moved close to him. Strong arms wrapped around Henry and pulled him close. He let go of his reservations and simply sank into the hug. He sobbed a little, ashamed to be so emotional but unable to help it.

But Tom didn't judge him. He didn't say things like, "It will be all right." But he didn't let go, either. He comforted without words. He comforted with his actions, holding Henry tightly, letting him sob against his chest. It was strange. He felt so safe in the other man's arms. He didn't understand it, but he didn't try to fight it either.

Gradually, Henry managed to pull himself together. He was mortified, but he also knew he shouldn't feel shame at losing control. Tom wasn't making him feel that way. The other man had only been kind and good to him.

He had cried for Max a lot in those first few desperate months when he'd been alone and terrified, trapped in the ruins and scavenging to survive. He'd grieved, but he'd grieved alone. But that grief felt...empty somehow. Almost as if it didn't heal him. But this...right now, it felt... It felt right.

But everything comes to an end. As much as he wanted to stay like that, being held and comforted, he knew it couldn't last. He drew back, and Tom let him go.

The lone wolf's eyes were kind. That surprised him. He'd expected the shifter to be all grizzly badass, tough and kickass and...well, alpha. But his gray eyes were so kind that it almost hurt.

Henry couldn't hold that gaze for too long. If he did, he would either lose himself in it or begin bawling again. His eyes already felt like they were full of sand and grit. The ache behind his eyes still throbbed. He knew he was a wreck, but he also felt better. As if a wound might be healing.

He took a shuddering breath, trying to pull himself together again. "I'm sorry. I don't usually fall apart like that. It's pretty humiliating. Crying my eyes out like that..."

Tom shrugged. "What crying? I didn't see anything."

Henry gaped at him, unsure if the man was joking because his delivery had been so serious. Tom stared back with a kind of mock innocence that had Henry shaking his head slowly and smiling. This guy was something else.

"It's nice of you to pretend you didn't see me breaking down and blubbering," he said softly. "But I lost my pride a long time ago. So there's nothing to protect."

"That's fair. It's also fair to say you have nothing to be ashamed of. You've been through hell."

He stared down at his hands. Right now, it was too difficult to look anywhere else. "I went through hell because I was stupid. Reckless. If I hadn't fallen for Max…"

"When did the heart ever listen to the head?" Tom asked gravely. "You can't control falling in love. You don't have anything to feel ashamed of. You didn't kill Max."

Henry burst into tears again. He was shaking with the emotions tearing through him. "I did! My pack hurt him because of me. They threw us in here to die."

Just like that, Tom was holding him again. And just like that, Henry was helpless to stop it. It wasn't a strength thing. He was helpless because he wanted it, he *needed* it so much.

"What they did to you was horrible. You loved Max. You didn't want that to happen to him. But your alpha killed him, not you. Max will always be a part of you. Ask yourself—would Max blame you for what happened?"

Henry buried his face against Tom's chest and sobbed. He was shaking.

"No," he said, his voice barely a whisper. "No, he...he wouldn't."

"Good. So let all that pain and blame go. It's eating you alive."

Tom didn't let go of him. Henry simply cried for a while, feeling so emotionally wrung-out that he no longer felt ashamed to be sobbing in a stranger's arms. But it was weird, too. Because Tom didn't *feel* like a stranger. He had known Tom for less than a day, but the lone wolf felt like...like an old friend.

Maybe Henry could finally let Max go. He would put aside the pain of his loss, the fear that he'd cost his lover his life, and he would go on. Because Max had been a kind, happy-go-lucky guy with a great sense of humor. He always made Henry laugh. Max wouldn't want Henry to suffer. He had been suffering. For years. Even though Henry told himself enough time had passed for the wounds to heal, they clearly hadn't.

So why did he feel like they could heal now? Why did he feel like he finally had a chance at life again? Was it simply because Tom was here, promising a way out of this hell?

He moved back enough to look up into Tom's rugged face. His jaw was covered with dark stubble.

His hair was cut short but was spiky from air drying after the rooftop bathing. His gray eyes were watching Henry back, the understanding and strength there so very tempting. So very tempting.

He drew away again, but…not too far away. They were still touching, pressed close against each other.

"Thank you," Henry said in a shaky voice.

"You don't need to thank me."

"I do. And I'm sorry. For all of this. I know you didn't come looking for this kind of headache." He sighed out a long breath, rubbing his temple. "I wear my heart on my sleeve. I can't help it. I'm weak."

"That's not weak. It's just who you are. Don't be ashamed of caring about people or feeling things. It's like apologizing for the color of your eyes or your skin. You are who you are."

Henry had to force himself to draw back and raise his emotional drawbridge again. "Why are you so nice? What's wrong with you?"

That earned a surprised laugh from Tom. "Don't know. Couldn't say. Don't care to find out either."

"I'm serious. You're kind to strangers. You saved my life. You're a hero."

He shook his head. "I'm no hero."

Henry wasn't going to let this go. It was too important to him. He stared up into Tom's eyes. He would be honest. It was far too late for anything else. "You *are* a hero. To me."

But the smile on Tom's rugged face was a little sad. "To me, my dad was a hero. He gave everything to his country. He let them change him. He believed in what he was doing, right up until he died."

Henry's heart went out to Tom. He had the feeling that Tom didn't open up easily or often, so he was incredibly touched that Tom was letting him get close. Besides, he owed Tom. He would listen to anything the man wanted to share.

"You said your father was part of the first generation of shifters… That he died defending Detroit. Will you talk about him? If you don't mind me asking…"

"I don't mind. I'm proud of my daddy. Like I said, he died defending Detroit. He died the night the lagodire swarmed the city."

"I'm so sorry. You must've been so young."

"I was just a kid. They told me he died trying to defend everyone. Shifters, humans. It didn't matter. He did his duty."

"So he was a soldier? Like you?"

"Damn right. He was part of an elite shifter unit that worked for the government. They were sent in to stop the lagodire. But that was impossible at the time."

There was a lot that Henry didn't understand. If he had been in Tom's shoes, he would've stayed far away from the lagodire. Especially if they had killed his father. He didn't understand it, but he admired it in a way. Then again, Tom's bravery had never been in question. He'd saved Henry's life by parachuting onto a rooftop. Henry could let that go. It was the kind of wild thing an action hero would do. But Tom didn't even brag about it.

He was amazing. Henry owed him so much. He knew he had to do something. He felt so incredibly close to Tom right now. What they had shared had brought them together, both the things that had happened and the truths they had told each other tonight.

His heart was pounding. His thoughts were shooting through his mind like fireworks. He could feel his body's desire stir to life as his attentions shifted. Or maybe that desire grabbed hold of his brain and shifted his attention for him.

It didn't matter. His desire smoldered inside him, growing hotter. The touches, the hugs, the intimacy had stirred him. All the fear and brushes with death... All the chaos and emotions. His brain wanted to find something simple that it needed, wanted, and have that one thing drive away all the fear and loneliness that had haunted him for so long.

Henry threw everything aside, all caution, all reservations, and leaned up to kiss Tom. Right then, it felt like the kiss had to happen. It sounded sappy. But he *wanted* sappy...and he was desperate. He hadn't touched anyone in so many years.

His mouth crushed against Tom's firm lips. The lone wolf's body felt warm and tight with muscle. Tom was surprised by the kiss at first. Henry felt the other man's body tense. But that tension was gone in an instant. Because then Tom was kissing him back.

His arms came up to hold Henry, pulling him tighter against his body. Tom deepened the kiss Henry had started. He took control of it, then teased Henry's lips open, claiming his mouth for his own.

A needy groan escaped Henry's throat. His eyes were closed. He was lost in the sensations, the feelings, the touches. The kiss became his world. It had his heart soaring.

Tom's hand slid up Henry's side, across his chest, and settled on the nape of his neck. His palm was so warm.

But Tom slowly stopped the kiss, moving back a little. His hand moved from Henry's neck to cup his cheek. His other hand did the same. Henry opened his eyes to find Tom looking at him.

Tom's expression was so tender as he held Henry's face and looked deep into his eyes. "Are you sure?"

Tom's ragged voice held restraint but also hope. Henry hid a smile at that hope, delighted that Tom seemed to want this too. Henry wasn't bad looking, although he wasn't ever going to win any awards for being the manliest male around. But the interest, the desire in Tom's eyes, made him feel amazing.

"I want this," Henry whispered.

It might be the moment, it might be nearly dying, or simply finding a friend who was sympathetic to him, but he wanted this. He wanted to lose himself in something beautiful, something wonderful. He wanted to feel alive, his body singing with pleasure. And he wanted to thank Tom. He had nothing to give him. No money. Nothing. But he could give him this. If Tom was interested, Henry could give him *this*.

But those were thoughts. They were emotions. They were things inside his head. The blunt truth of it was far simpler. He had been attracted to Tom from the beginning. His body ached for Tom's touch. On a core physical level, he wanted this with all his heart.

He didn't need to say another word. Tom's eyes flashed with their own heat. He captured Henry's lips again in a ravenous kiss that had Henry's heart in his throat and his stomach full of butterflies.

After that kiss, Henry gave up trying to think. It was too much to ask of him to deny this passion. It had been too many years. He'd been too alone, too afraid. Part of him knew he was throwing himself at the first person to show him any kindness. He realized that...and at the same time, it didn't matter. He didn't care. Because he might be giving himself as a thank you to Tom in one way, but in another, he was doing this for himself. To fill a hole inside him. Even if only for a while, it would make him feel warm and loved instead of cold and alone.

Their kisses grew even more intense. Tom made a growling noise deep in his throat when Henry pressed his groin against the man's big thigh, grinding his hard cock against his body. Henry wasn't in the mood to play games. He intended to show Tom exactly how much he needed this.

Tom's hands roamed his body, caressing him, stroking him. It felt so good that it nearly took his breath away. He couldn't help the eager, encouraging sounds that escaped his mouth. Words weren't an option because Tom was kissing him so well. But he could sense that the wordless encouragement only drove Tom's desire higher and hotter.

He opened his eyes again when Tom began to undress him. He was normally shy, but right now, he felt zero shyness or hesitancy. He let Tom pull his shirt over his head, baring his chest. Then Tom pulled off his own shirt and tossed it aside. Henry bit his lip, a desperate groan escaping him. His cock throbbed. He already knew the man's body was magnificent. Yet, seeing it now, knowing what was coming, knowing he could touch it? It drove him out of his mind.

Henry leaned forward, putting his hands on Tom's chest. The man's skin was so warm and soft. He leaned in, meaning to take one of those tight pink nipples in his mouth and play his tongue over it.

But Tom never gave him the chance. He caught Henry easily and drew his head up for another plunging kiss. While he ravished Henry's lips, Tom's deft hands undid the button of Henry's trousers, the too-big pants he's borrowed from Tom. Tom opened the fly, all while slipping his tongue into Henry's mouth and keeping his head trapped in that deep kiss.

Tom carefully pulled Henry's hard and aching cock out. He began to slowly stroke it, gripping just under the head and sliding down the shaft to the base. Long, slow strokes...

Henry endured the pleasure for as long as he dared. Already, he could feel his balls pulling tight, that increasing pressure, the building climax, that told him he was about to lose control.

He drew back from the kiss, breathing so hard he was almost gasping. "Wait. That feels too good. I'm going to lose it."

Tom said nothing, only trailed his hand up Henry's abdomen to circle his belly button, then higher, to gently rub one of Henry's nipples with the pad of his thumb. It was still pleasure—every touch this man gave him was pleasure—but it wasn't so much that it had him ready to lose control.

But a boldness came over him. Henry slid one of his own hands down Tom's bare chest. He fumbled with the belt buckle until he got it undone. His hand was shaking as he undid the button by touch alone. He was too busy kissing Tom to look. But he finally succeeded and drew the zipper down.

He was rewarded with exactly what he wanted. Tom's thick cock was straining at the cotton of his boxer-briefs. Henry traced his fingers over the cloth-covered shaft and felt Tom's shuddering in-draw of breath. Grinning into the kiss, he slipped his hand into the waistband of Tom's boxer-briefs and settled his fingers around that cock. Carefully, he drew it out, pushing aside the fabric of the underwear.

The warm silk of Tom's skin was too much. All he knew was that he wanted that cock in his mouth to see if he could drive Tom wild. Henry might be an omega, but he wasn't any blushing virgin either. He knew what a man liked, and he liked to give it.

He broke from the scorching kisses, a hand on Tom's chest to keep him from gaining the upper hand again. Tom played along, watching him with heated, half-lidded eyes.

Henry drew Tom's trousers and boxer-briefs down and went to his knees. He used his shirt to pad his knees against the hard tile floor. He probably wouldn't have cared anyway. He was so eager to see Tom's cock when it was hard for him.

He gripped the base of Tom's thick cock and licked the tip, teasing the slit. Then he slowly settled his mouth on the shaft and took him as deep as he could go. At the same time, he worked Tom's cock with his hand, stroking him. Because he was too long to take very deep. With his other hand, he gently stroked Tom's balls, just skirting his fingers over the sac.

Tom gave out a groan of pure pleasure. His hand was on Henry's head, lightly fisted in his hair. The sounds of Tom's pleasure only made Henry want to give him more. He wondered if he could make the lone wolf come in his mouth. He would swallow every bit of that hot seed. Giving him that kind of pleasure made him feel powerful.

But his plans were thwarted when Tom gently but firmly held his head and moved his hips back, pulling his cock free of Henry's mouth. Henry gave the tip one last flick of his tongue as that beautiful cock drew away.

"God," Tom said in a desire-roughened voice. "You've got one hell of a mouth. You know that?"

Henry only grinned and reached for Tom's cock again. Tom hadn't seen anything yet.

Tom caught his hand, grinning now, his eyes hot with desire...and promise. "Not so fast. I want this to be about you."

He drew Henry back to his feet. Henry's legs were a bit wobbly, his heart pounding fast. His cock was so hard it ached and throbbed. Tom quickly stripped him of all clothing so that they were both naked now.

After that, Tom pulled him into another blazing-hot kiss. The man's thick, hard cock was pressing into his stomach, the silken hardness feeling hot and wonderful. Henry began to grind his own cock against Tom's body, but again, Tom showed he was in control and completely happy about that. He turned Henry around so that his back and bare ass were pressing against Tom's body and cock. Tom's cock, wet with Henry's saliva, was between Henry's ass cheeks, thrusting upward along the crevice.

Tom moved back enough to reach Henry's ass. They had no lube, but Tom used saliva to prepare him. The rawness of it might've turned him off another time, but he was so desperate to be filled right now that he only felt the pulse of desire in his head, driving out any thoughts, any second thoughts, everything.

As Tom's fingers entered his hole, teasing him, preparing him, Tom kissed Henry's neck, nibbled at his ears, and sent shivers of pleasure and anticipation through him.

He assumed they would fuck like this, standing up, but again, Tom surprised him. Henry exhaled a surprised breath as the wolf lifted him clear off the ground. Tom's strong arms were under his thighs, spreading him and lifting him in the air from behind. Henry leaned forward enough that he could brace himself against the wall with his arms, arching his hips, silently begging for Tom to take him.

That anticipation was soon rewarded. Henry felt the large head of the man's cock brush across his hole, lining up, then slowly, carefully sinking inside him even as Tom drew him down and closer.

It did hurt at first. Burning. He gritted his teeth and ignored it, breathing through the discomfort. But then Tom was sheathed inside him, the discomfort faded, and his pleasure was building again.

He was effortlessly held in the air. He had braced his arms against the wall. It gave him a way to push back as Tom began to slowly thrust into him. The thrusts were powerful. They moved his whole body, pushing him against the wall. He gave a whimper as his pleasure built.

Tom fucked him slow and deep, drawing it out, driving Henry's bliss even higher. He felt so connected, so close to the other man, this intimacy satisfying something he'd long missed.

He was doing pretty well, edging along his orgasm, when Tom suddenly shifted his angle of penetration. Then the other wolf's hand slid from where he held him under his thigh down to Henry's erection. The man's big hand enveloped him. The grip was the perfect pressure, the strokes sending Henry's pleasure peaking so fast—

He came hard. The orgasm gripped his body, pulsing out from his groin, exploding in his mind like fireworks. Waves of pleasure took him front and back, the sensations so powerful that he had to bite down on his tongue to keep from crying out. But keeping silent only seemed to increase the pressure, the sensation inside him, and he jerked in Tom's arms, shuddering. His cock spurted his seed all across the wall.

The orgasm left him so overwhelmed he was almost dizzy. But Tom shifted his grip again, grabbing him and relentlessly pounding into his ass, each powerful thrust driving him up and forward. His arms were trembling, pushing back against the cock taking him. He closed his eyes, letting his head loll as Tom owned him completely.

It seemed impossible, but Tom only increased the speed of his thrusts, driving hard and deep, still holding him aloft as if he weighed nothing. His dazed mind wondered at this. The wolf was so strong. So much stronger than he was. But it wasn't a frightening realization. No, it was wonderful and comforting.

When Tom reached his peak, he let out a primal growl that nearly had Henry coming again. He gave another hard thrust, and his body tensed. His muscles were rigid. He held Henry tight against him, sinking into him balls deep. His cock pulsed, pouring hot seed into Henry.

They remained there for a few moments. Both of them were lost in the afterglow of such intense pleasure. They were coming down slowly. He didn't want it to end. He wanted Tom inside him, connected to him like this for...for an even longer time. He knew he was being greedy, but he had missed this so much.

He had missed love. Years of grief had shadowed him. He'd never believed he would have this again. Today he had almost died...and he'd found this. This incredible man. A hero. A lover, if only for this once. It was more than he had ever hoped for after all that had happened to him.

Tom tenderly kissed him on the back of the neck as he lifted Henry and pulled out of him. Henry felt a sense of loss as their connection ended. He always felt that way when the lovemaking was over. But then there was cuddling, and he liked that too.

Gently, Tom set him down again on his feet, holding him tightly while Henry found his balance. His knees were definitely wobbly. His thoughts had a pleasant, happy fuzziness to them. He might still be trapped inside these ruins, but right now, he felt at peace with that. He felt at peace with all kinds of things.

More than that, for the first time in years, he felt a spark of hope.

That was enough for him to turn back to Tom and hug him tightly, pressing his face against the man's chest almost desperately.

Tom held him. Those strong arms wrapped around him, and he placed a gentle kiss on Henry's head.

The night was not quiet around them. The wind gusted and moaned. Somewhere far away, but not far away enough, a lagodire was doing that hyena-like laugh. The sound echoed from the buildings and down the empty streets. That sound had terrified him for years.

Now he closed his eyes, hoping against hope that soon, thanks to Tom, he would never hear it again.

CHAPTER SIX

The next morning, Tom gave the last of his energy bars to Henry. He wanted the omega rested and fed for this last part of their escape attempt. It would be the most difficult.

Henry chewed on his energy bar, peeking out one of the flower shop windows at the surrounding buildings and deserted street. The sun was still low over the city, not even over the tops of the building yet. The light was that bright dawn yellow, full of promise. No clouds were in the vibrant blue sky. Tom hoped that was a good sign.

The omega seemed different today—and that was a good thing. His scent was just as tempting, but much of the tension and worry had left his face. He was quiet, but he didn't smell upset. He seemed content. Maybe even happy.

Tom held back a smile. Best not to be caught grinning. Seemed a bit arrogant. But taking the little omega last night had been one of the hottest things he'd ever experienced. Making love in such a dangerous place, hunted, in ruins full of enemies. The passion overcoming the danger. Giving everything he had to the man whose life he'd saved... Maybe he was a reckless idiot. Maybe he was a romantic idiot, believing something sappy like *love would find a way*. He snorted. Sex certainly found a way.

Henry glanced at him and gave a shy smile. Tom went to him and brushed a kiss across his lips. The omega tasted like the energy bar.

"You ready?" Tom asked softly.

"I've never been so ready to leave." His eyes were solemn. "Tom... No matter what happens, I owe you everything."

"You can thank me when I get you out. It's not going to be fun."

"Somehow, I didn't think it would be. Do we have to climb down the wall?"

"No. That's over two hundred feet of sheer drop. If I still had my parachute, I would BASE jump with you again. That's how I always get out. Getting to the top of a high rise building closest to the wall and simply gliding over the wall. I touch down, and I'm gone before the authorities get their knickers in a twist."

"Is there a way out under the wall, maybe? I've searched before… But there are parts of the city I don't dare go."

"There were a few. Army engineers blew one scavenger tunnel and collapsed it. There used to be one hidden way out on the north side of the city, but the last I heard, the area was swarming with lagodire, and the air inside the tunnel was bad. You needed some kind of breathing apparatus to make it out alive."

"But you know another way?" Henry was watching him with a sharp gaze, those amber eyes intent on his own.

"Yeah. That's where we're headed. There's a drainage tunnel that feeds into the Detroit River. It's partially collapsed. And most of it is underwater. There isn't a lot of light either."

"Have you used it before?" Henry looked uneasy but still determined. That was a good sign.

"Never. I know someone who has."

Miles Deacon was his name. That had been the last time Miles had risked scavenging in Old Detroit. But before he'd retired from the game, Miles told him about the secret way he'd used to escape. Miles was human, but retrievers, salvagers, and scavengers shared a lot of the same small circles. Bars they hung out in. Gossip. That kind of thing. Tom had shared more than a few beers with Miles and teased the story out of him.

"And he lived?"

"He lived. Afterward, he retired from the salvage game. Can't really blame him for quitting while he was ahead. Last I heard, he was living in Oklahoma somewhere with six or seven dogs."

"He retired after getting out through this drainage tunnel. So I guess it was pretty harrowing."

"I'd say he crawled out the other side of the wall a very different man."

Henry seemed to consider this. "But at least he survived. He got out. That's what we need."

"That's what we need." He moved to the window and took one last look at the street. The street and the surrounding buildings were empty, as they had been since they'd holed up here. It was time to leave. "Let's go."

"Yeah. Let's go."

They left the building the same way they'd gotten in. All his senses were on full alert now. He had already carefully considered what form to use for this escape. Wolves ran faster. He could outrun any lagodire, which were slower than hyenas, a downside of their crocodile genetic profile. But lagodire weren't exactly slow either...and Henry's wolf form might not be able to keep up with Tom's. At this point, that was simply an unknown but a potentially dangerous one.

If it came to fighting, Tom would be more effective in wolf form. Especially since he'd lost his firearm. But it wasn't that simple. They were going to have to swim out, and humans were faster, more agile swimmers, and better divers than wolves. The human form was a better all-around shape to stay with, allowing them to climb and talk and haul their last food and water. The downsides? His ability to scent and his hearing would be diminished, even if they remained sharper than most humans.

So that settled that.

Tom used his compass and got his bearings, then headed southeast. Henry walked along beside him, tense and quiet but not as terrified as yesterday. He was putting a lot of trust in Tom.

That wasn't exactly a burden Tom was eager to take on, but it was what it was. If he hadn't expected complications, he never should've saved Henry's ass in the first place. Things in life had a way of snowballing. But not always in a bad way. He had no regrets about his choices anymore. Sure, there might be hell to pay in the future, but right now he was focused on getting Henry to safety.

Everything else could wait.

It was almost noon by the time they reached the huge wall sealing off Old Detroit. Twice they'd needed to hide from roaming groups of lagodire. But their luck held. They weren't discovered, and soon the unsettling laughing cries of the lagodire moved off deeper into the ruins. It was going to be hard not to hear that laugh inside his nightmares.

The wall was over two hundred feet high. Originally, the barrier had been nothing more than huge piles of scrap metal and rubble, pushed into place by Army bulldozers to stop the lagodire hordes. Or to slow them enough that they could be shelled and shot climbing over it.

But after the lagodire destroyed the city, the Army rebuilt another wall out of reinforced concrete. It took over a year of nonstop work and nearly constant fighting by tens of thousands of soldiers and engineers. The end result was something like a huge dam that surrounded the ruins, winding along the Detroit River, Lake St. Clair, the burned-out ruins as far as Troy to the north, past Rouge Park in the west, and dipping down to Southgate in the south. The fighting had been constant, but the military and construction crews had pulled it off. The lagodire had been sealed off from the rest of the nation and basically contained in their own zoo cage. To this day, debate raged on whether it was inhumane to have trapped them and whether the lagodire could be negotiated with.

Tom had no illusions on that front. The lagodire had been created by the government to be monsters.

In all his experiences with them, they had never shown him any different. Hell, the bastards had killed his father, hadn't they? And they'd killed Henry's lover and so many others.

Yeah, they were merciless predators. He only needed to glance around him at the ruins of a once-proud city. Now it was only street after street of abandoned buildings, burned down homes, rusting cars, and the destroyed shell of what had been the home to so many.

It was grim. It was depressing. It was hard enough to scavenge this place on his occasional retriever run. He couldn't imagine being trapped here, forced to live under a constant cloud of death and fear and hunger. He glanced at Henry. The omega was small and skinny, not the most intimidating person Tom had ever met. Not by a long shot. But he couldn't deny that Henry had amazing inner strength and determination. Hell, Tom admired him. That wasn't something he said about many people.

Henry sensed him looking and glanced at him. He gave a shy smile. He guessed wrong about what Tom was thinking, though.

"It sure is high," Henry said, glancing up at the wall again. They were in the wall's shadow now. The last hundred or so feet to the wall was a fifty-foot-high tangle of rusted metal, broken wood, concrete, and junk—the remains of the first barrier. "Guess I should apologize again for being such a pain in the ass."

"You don't have anything to apologize for."

"I do, though. You're putting your life at risk for me. Over and over again."

The omega's gratitude made him feel a little self-conscious. He didn't want to strut around believing he was some big hero or anything like his father. After all, Tom had only been in Old Detroit for one reason—to find the Lumiere Soleil diamond. His reasons had been completely mercenary.

"You can buy me a beer after we're safely on the other side. How does that sound?"

Henry's smile was brilliant. "Deal."

It took over another hour of searching to find the drainage culvert. They had to climb over the tangled wall of rusting metal and debris and make their way along the bottom of the wall itself. He was going to need a damned tetanus shot booster for sure after this. The going was slow and dangerous, and they were both drenched in sweat by the time they found what they'd been searching for.

Some of the storm runoff from this part of the city was directed into the Rouge River. A river which was now a lake all along where the wall stopped the Rouge from emptying into the far larger Detroit River. The rest of the storm runoff in this area was sent directly into the Detroit River.

This particular drainage culvert was in a low

section of land, something like a wash nestled in all the metal and rubble. His old friend Miles hadn't been lying. The culvert, hidden in so much debris, did seem to go under the wall. It had stained concrete sides. There was standing water in it and spreading out into a small pond. The top of the water was coated with bright green algae. Clouds of insects swarmed across the surface.

Wonderful. He was so very thrilled to be getting wet and filthy again.

The drainage pipe was set into a concrete retaining wall a dozen meters from the huge barrier wall. It was almost impossible to see in all the wreckage and twisted metal. If he hadn't been searching for it, he almost certainly would've missed it.

"I should've brought my swim trunks," Henry said quietly.

Tom grinned. At least the omega wasn't flat-out refusing to go. Again, it showed how brave he was. Or how desperate. But you couldn't be brave unless you were first afraid, right?

"You and me both. You ready to get the hell out of here?"

"So ready."

"Good."

Henry's hand closed on his wrist. His voice turned tense as he glanced up at the blue sky. "Wait, there's a drone overhead."

Tom had heard the rotors of the drone high overhead too, but there wasn't much he could do about it. The military constantly had armed drones patrolling, making sure the lagodire didn't build a ramp or somehow escape the walls. Those drones had powerful cameras and missiles on them to deal with problems.

"If they saw us, they saw us. Either way, we'll lose them when we go under the wall."

That was his hope, anyway. But he had to face one problem at a time. Right now, getting the hell out of the city before the lagodire found them again was priority number one.

Tom climbed down the slanted concrete sides of the drainage aqueduct. He walked at an angle to give himself better traction and control of his descent. Henry followed behind him with one hand on his shoulder, gripping hard.

The water was warmer than he expected. It also stank of stagnation. The algae clung to his pants, coating him with green slime. He moved carefully, testing out where he placed each foot. He was wearing heavy boots, but that didn't mean he wanted to gash himself with rusting metal or rubble hidden beneath the water. Right now, the water was knee-high, but it was getting deeper as they moved toward the huge drainage pipe. The wall towered over them.

He helped Henry over a mound of rubble. The water was waist-high now as they sloshed forward. Henry made a soft sound of revulsion but kept pressing forward.

They finally reached the concrete and galvanized steel drainage pipe. It was half-submerged in the stagnant water, overgrown with weeds and vines and moss, surrounded by rubble. The rusted metal mesh to keep out animals had been bent back and out of the way. The tunnel beyond was black.

He glanced at his waterproof Casio G-Shock watch. Plenty of time before they started losing daylight. They could go slow and safe. Or as safe as this could possibly be—which wasn't safe at all.

Damn it. Time to get this over with. The wall was forty or so feet thick if he remembered right. The drainage tunnel started about a dozen meters from the base of the wall. He didn't know exactly how far the tunnel extended into the river. All he knew was that it was now underwater. Or at least partially submerged.

He pulled out his tactical flashlight from his pack. It had cost almost as much as the pistol he'd lost. It was waterproof, impact-resistant, used batteries for the high power beam but also had a hand crank in case the batteries ran out. Right now, this thing was going to be their savior, so he made sure he tightened the strap around his wrist. He was *not* going to drop it.

The flashlight beam pierced through the darkness in the drainage pipe. He swept the beam around the interior, looking for dangers. There was nothing but stagnant water.

Carefully, he slipped past the bent metal mesh. Once inside, he turned back to help Henry, shining the light so the omega could better see. Henry was smaller and had an easier time slipping past the mesh. Tom clasped his hand, helping him through. He reluctantly let go after giving Henry a reassuring squeeze.

He didn't know what he was feeling toward the omega, but now definitely wasn't the time to go thinking about it. His protective urge surprised him, though. Although maybe that wasn't really a surprising thing at all. They'd been intimate. It connected people, even relative strangers. But what was strange was that he felt little regret now. Before, he'd been worried about not getting the necklace and the fallout and all the money he'd lost. But those worries had faded. Or they'd been drowned by bigger, closer worries.

They pushed forward, Tom leading the way. The drainage tunnel was free of debris, although the water was still disgusting. The stagnant stink was overpowering. Times like these made him regret his heightened sense of smell.

The tunnel had a downward slope. Ten feet in, the water was up to his chest and nearly at Henry's neck.

He kept the flashlight raised. The top of the pipe descended steadily down into the water. Soon enough, they came to the place where the only way forward would be underwater.

Henry was breathing fast. The sound of their breathing and splashing echoed loudly all along the tunnel. Tom turned and looked at Henry's face. The omega's skin appeared very pale in the bright white flashlight beam.

"We need to swim the rest of the way," he said. He kept his voice calm and matter of fact, even though he was uneasy himself. He wanted to focus on reassuring the omega. That was most important right now. "I'll lead the way, shining the light forward. Keep right behind me. We'll have to swim single-file."

He had a lot of worries right now. First, he was worried about running out of air—that was obvious. Second, he was worried that Henry would get in trouble and need him, and he wouldn't know about it because the omega would be behind him. But he needed to go first, in case there was something they needed to deal with. Danger or debris that needed to be moved. The tunnel was about six feet in circumference, but it would still be difficult if they were forced to turn and swim back out again.

"I'll be right behind you," Henry promised.

"Are you a strong swimmer?"

"Average. I took lessons as a kid."

"All right. We're going to take a deep breath and then try to expel all the air in our lungs. Then we'll take another deep breath—as deep as you can—and we'll go for it. Ready?"

Henry nodded. They locked gazes. Tom took a deep breath and blew it all out, trying to empty his lungs completely. Henry did the same. Then Tom took another deep breath, turned, and slipped under the water. The water was murky. Even the bright flashlight beam could only pierce six or seven feet in front of them.

He swam forward, kicking hard. The underwater drainage tunnel seemed to go on forever. Eventually, he could see a faint glow ahead of him that wasn't from the flashlight.

His blood was rushing in his ears. His lungs were burning. He fought against the urge to suck in air. It would only fill his lungs with water.

The end of the drainage tunnel seemed to appear out of nowhere. The light was filtering down from the surface of the river. He pulled himself out from the concrete edge, then turned to shine the light back to look for Henry.

His heart was pounding. For a second, he was sure the tunnel was empty behind him.

But no, there was Henry. His eyes were wild, but he was swimming as hard as he could. Tom grabbed hold of him, pulled him from the mouth of the old drainage tunnel. They were so close. So close to freedom and escape. The surface of the river was only a dozen or so feet above them.

He swam toward it, kicking furiously, pulling Henry along with him. His lungs felt like they were on fire. He wasn't going to let the omega go until they reached the surface. They hadn't come all this way for Tom to lose him now.

They burst from the surface in the river beyond the wall. He gasped in a huge lungful of air. Next to him, Henry was clinging to him and gasping too.

He wiped the water out of his eyes, taking deep, shaky breaths. They clung to each other clumsily, treading water. It took a moment for Tom to realize that Henry was laughing. He was gripping him hard, shaking and laughing.

Tom pressed a kiss on Henry's lips, grinning himself. Then he began to swim for shore, dragging Henry along like a lifeguard saving someone from the water. Maybe he didn't need to do that, but some part of him wanted to keep Henry in his arms, to be sure he was safe until they reached land again.

The water from the river had washed away the slime that had coated them. They staggered from the river onto the riverbank below the immense wall. They were drenched. Breathing hard. Adrenaline still popped in his veins. His mouth tasted like he'd been chewing on pennies.

He felt ecstatic, though. Relief and victory all entwined. A natural high that couldn't be beaten—

A male voice blasted over a loudspeaker, startling them both. "You are under arrest! Don't move! Keep your hands where we can see them!"

Now he could hear the rumble of a boat engine. Or he'd always been hearing it, hadn't he? But getting to safety with Henry had been his priority.

It was a military patrol boat with huge machine guns. A half dozen soldiers were pointing assault rifles at them. None of them looked in a particularly friendly mood.

Shit.

He slowly raised his hands and glanced at Henry. The omega's eyes were wide, and he looked confused and afraid.

Tom gave him a wry smile. "Well, we're out. Guess we'll have to celebrate later. Beer is on me."

That was if he didn't end up in jail for criminal trespass, illegal scavenging, and a slew of other charges they could throw at him.

It was classic. Lucky one minute, unlucky the next. He wasn't surprised. Out of the frying pan and into the fire might be cliché, but it certainly applied.

But at least Henry was safe. There was that. He had kept his promise. Hell, maybe he had even done his dad proud.

CHAPTER SEVEN

Three days later...

Henry hated everything about the New Detroit downtown lockup. It was loud. It stank of concrete and metal, but that wasn't the worst odor. It also stank of sweat, fear, and desperation from the people all around him. It was worse for him. He'd been alone for so long that he'd lost the ability to block it all out. The emotions around him sliced at him like knives. It took all his self-control to keep from fleeing.

He was sitting in a hard plastic chair with a huge Plexiglas barrier in front of him. There was a phone mounted there. He was staring through the glass at an empty yellow chair. Beyond the chair, a jail guard stood near a metal door. He was glowering at everyone in the room.

They would bring Tom out soon. Henry had been sitting here for ten minutes, trying not to listen to the anguished conversations of the people around him. It wasn't easy to keep focused.

Henry was staying in a shelter. He'd been staying there since being released from military custody two nights ago. The military had handed Tom over to police custody, though. Apparently, the military really didn't like "retrievers." Apparently, Tom had a reputation.

The prosecutor had let Henry go without pressing charges because of his story. No, that wasn't right. He'd let Henry go because Henry was the Metro Pack's problem, and the district attorney wasn't eager to get involved in "shifter affairs." Henry thought the jerk was a complete coward. So much for justice for the weak.

But they'd jailed Tom and charged him with almost a dozen counts—trespassing and illegal scavenging, entering forbidden "no-go" zones, undermining national security, things like that. They were throwing the book at Tom, eager to make an example of him. It didn't help that Tom had a few run-ins with the military and law enforcement. At least Tom wasn't locked in some military brig where Henry had no chance to ever see him.

Henry had been having trouble sleeping ever since their arrest. Worry kept him awake and restless. Worry for Tom. He wasn't worried about himself. His life had already been as low as it could get. Tom could easily have let him die on that rooftop. But he hadn't. He'd come to the rescue like some kind of superhero. He'd saved Henry's life. The time they'd shared had been so brief but so powerful, so memorable. It had been amazing. One of the best things he'd ever experienced.

He wanted more. That was the worst part about this. He'd been given the taste of something wonderful...and he desperately wanted more.

The door on the other side of the security barrier opened. Tom walked through, wearing an orange jail jumpsuit. A guard walked behind him. Tom had heavy-duty cuffs on, the kind used to restrain shifters.

Tom's gaze immediately locked onto him. A broad smile appeared on his face. He crossed the room to take the seat in front of Henry.

Henry looked him over closely, worried he'd had a hard time in lockup. But Tom didn't have a visible scratch or bruise on him. Or not any new ones, anyway. He seemed to be one of those people with a lucky aura and nothing could touch him.

Of course, they were sitting in a downtown lockup, so that luck only went so far.

He picked up the phone receiver, eager to talk. Tom's hands were cuffed in front of him so he could use the phone receiver on his side of the barrier.

"Hey, there," Tom said, his deep, rough voice sounding pleased. His eyes were warm. Henry felt a thrill inside him because it was clear how happy this man was to see him.

"Tom," he managed to say, his voice sticking in his throat a little. "It's good to see you."

His heart was beating fast. It was tough to talk, like it always was at first. So many emotions were swirling inside him that he got choked up on all the things he wanted to say. Most of all, he wanted to keep thanking Tom, even though he had thanked him so many times already. But it felt like he couldn't thank Tom enough for all he'd done, for all he'd risked getting Henry out of Old Detroit.

"Good to see you too. It's always the highlight of my day." Tom's devil-may-care grin only widened. "Way better than seeing my high-priced and yet worthless lawyer."

"Thanks." He grinned back. "I think."

Tom leaned forward. "How are you doing?"

"Great, considering I'm not locked up. They aren't going to charge me with violating the Old Detroit quarantine or anything else."

"Good. I was worried about you."

Those words made Henry feel like he had just

taken a big sip of the perfect-temperature coffee on a chilly day. He took a deep breath, trying to keep himself under control.

The only way he could do that was to keep the focus on Tom. "Are you okay in there? Has anyone messed with you?"

Jails were almost as bad as prisons. But the judge had denied Tom bail because of the "national security" elements of the case and because Tom had been inside a prohibited military zone. He'd also labeled Tom a "flight risk" because Tom was a shifter without a pack.

None of it seemed fair. All of it made Henry feel a sharp sting of guilt.

Tom's smile didn't fade at Henry's question, but it did get a dangerous edge. "Yep. I had fun."

"Fun?"

He shrugged. "I'll spare you the punching details. It gave me a chance to stretch my legs and work off some steam. Don't worry. Nobody got really hurt. As in dead hurt." He raised his eyebrows. "But they have me in my own cell now. I'm a VIP."

"Are they going to charge you with anything else? Fighting or something?"

"Don't know. It doesn't matter."

"What? Of course it matters!"

"Look. I'm staring down a lot of problems right now, but they aren't your problems." Tom's gaze sharpened. "I want you to leave New Detroit. Now. Today. Get away from here. The farther, the better."

He knew right away why Tom wanted that. He was afraid Henry's old pack, his old alpha, would come to finish what they'd started. And even though the shelter where he'd stayed the past few days locked its doors at night, it was far from the safest or securest place in the city.

So he understood. But he wasn't going to obey either.

"I won't run," he told Tom grimly. "Not when you're here. Locked up because of me."

"I love your loyalty, I really do. But I might not be out there to watch your back any time soon. You know your alpha. I don't need to dredge all of that up again. I don't want them to finish the job they botched. You already lost someone close to you. I don't want to lose you the same way."

Tears burned behind Henry's eyes. Despite his bold words, he'd been worried about that too. The city was huge, but the packs were powerful. The media had been sniffing around after the story, alerted by Tom's arrest, possibly even tipped off by a cop. So far, Henry's name had been kept out of public attention, but he didn't believe that would last. Sooner or later, his old pack would find out he'd survived.

"But—"

"Promise me you'll get the hell out of here," Tom

said, cutting him off. His expression was deadly serious. "I know you're grateful, but you don't owe me anything. If this goes sideways for me, I want you to move on. I don't want you visiting me in prison or any of that nonsense."

Panic gripped him hard. The thought that Tom might end up in prison over this—because of him—made him feel a crushing sense of guilt.

"Why did you do this?" he asked, his voice an unsteady whisper. He'd asked the question before, but he couldn't help but ask Tom again. "You ruined your life for me."

"Don't. Nobody gets the blame. I do what I do. Just so happens I got caught this time. Shit happens. I don't want you to throw it all away, risking your life, coming to see me like this."

Henry took a deep breath. What Tom was saying made sense logically. But Henry's heart wanted something else entirely. It was strange how much this man meant to him. There was a connection between them far deeper than the small amount of time they'd shared. As if he'd found his mate...

"I don't have anywhere to go," he protested, still not willing to give in or give up on seeing Tom again.

"I know. If I was a free man, you could stay with me and keep your head down. But I can't even get you my house keys right now."

He blinked. This man would trust him like that?

Let him stay alone in his house? It seemed so strange, yet like such an honor. The only other person he could imagine doing that was Max.

But maybe it was too risky to feel anything this powerful for another man again. Max had been gone for so many years. Henry still loved and mourned him—he always would. But he was afraid. Not to love again, but that he would love too strongly, too soon. That he would give his heart to this man who was so handsome and brave, and it would end up hurting him. He would end up losing him. And that was what was happening, right? Tom was facing a prison sentence.

Tom watched him closely. "You seem surprised. Because I'd let you crash at my place?"

"I...I have a hard time believing you would trust anyone like that. A stranger..."

"You're not just 'anyone.' You're sure as hell not a stranger to me, Henry."

He closed his eyes, loving the words but still doubting them. Not because he thought Tom was lying. Tom had nothing to gain and everything to lose by keeping him around. But the man kept surprising him.

Maybe he simply didn't believe he could get lucky enough to have this man care.

He looked at Tom again. It broke his heart to see Tom behind bars and know he was the reason. He struggled to find the right words, hating the growing tension between them. God, he couldn't do anything right, could he?

Tom's eyes were still intent on him. His voice was soothing. "I love seeing you, Henry, but this is the last time I want to see you coming here. When I get out, I'll find you again. That's a promise."

"No." His desperation was raw in his voice and twisted inside him like rope. "There has to be something I can do. Something. Some way—"

"You can't fight an entire pack." Tom's voice was pitiless, even though his eyes were full of regret. "They went to great lengths to get rid of you. They took your lover from you—"

"You don't need to remind me of that. I'll never forget." He looked away.

"You're right. I'm sorry. I pushed it too far." He took a deep breath and ran a hand through his hair. "Damn, I wish I could touch you right now."

Henry's chuckle was almost a sob. "I wish that too."

"But I can't. And I can't watch your back from in here, either."

"You don't need to," he said fiercely. "I've been watching my own back for years. Losing your pack will do that to you."

Tom nodded slowly. "You and me, we share that. Most humans wouldn't understand. Hell, most wolves wouldn't understand. Not really."

That was true. Packs were as tight as family. But what happened when your family turned on you?

The guard walked over. His voice was muffled by the barrier. "Time's up."

Tom didn't even look at the guard. His eyes were locked on Henry's. "Promise me, Henry. Don't risk coming back here. Get out of town any way you can. Even if you have to hitchhike."

"I promise." He didn't know how he would pull it off, but he owed Tom. The man was right. It wasn't safe for him to stay here alone. With Tom facing charges and a trial and maybe prison time, he couldn't protect Henry. So he needed to leave. He didn't believe Eddie Carson would risk throwing him back into Old Detroit off a helicopter again. This time, the man would simply have him killed outright. And no one was going to care about some dead omega shifter.

Tom gave Henry one last grin and hung up the phone receiver. Then the guard escorted him out of the room. Henry sat there and watched him go, never taking his eyes off the other man until the heavy metal door swung closed again.

A few minutes later, Henry left the jail behind, walking out into a too-warm Spring day. It gave him a headache, going from the over-air-conditioned inside of the lockup into the hot and humid parking lot.

He started across the parking lot, headed for the

bus stop. He would take the bus back to the shelter. He had so much to think about. He had no idea how he was going to get out of the city. He only had a tiny bit of money given to him by the shelter. Not even enough to buy a bus ride out of town. He was stuck here. He had nothing. No job, no place to stay aside from the shelter. No family. The people he knew in New Detroit were all part of his old pack.

A man was crossing the parking lot, heading in his direction. It was a human. He was wearing a gray suit jacket, a blue dress shirt with no tie, and gray trousers. He was looking right at Henry.

Henry started to angle away from him, suddenly unsure. But the man started to jog toward him and cut him off.

"Henry Wright?"

Henry froze. He wanted to run, but his legs wouldn't obey. His throat was dry. Instead of answering, he began to walk faster in the other direction.

The man chased him, cutting him off again. He had his smartphone out now and pointed at Henry as if recording.

"Henry Wright? I'm Tom Collins with the Associated Press. Is it true you were picked up by the military after escaping from Old Detroit?"

He fought against rising panic. He raised a hand to block his face from the camera on the phone.

"Please, go away. I don't want to talk to you. Don't take my picture."

"How do you know Tom Reinhart?" the reporter asked, following alongside him. "Are you both involved in criminal activity in Old Detroit? Did you escape the ruins? Are you facing charges from the government? How many others are living illegally inside Old Detroit?"

The questions were absurd but came so fast that he could barely register one before another rushed at him. The man kept thrusting the phone at him and shooting off those rapid-fire questions.

He was so rattled that he was considering running away. Would anyone blame him if he shucked off his clothes, shifted into a wolf, and fled on four feet instead of two? Even worse, he was terrified that Eddie Carson or Weis or Dylan or anyone from his old pack would recognize him or his wolf.

A limo suddenly appeared from nowhere, rolling to a stop and blocking their way. Henry froze; his stomach felt filled with dry ice, so cold it burned.

Was this his old alpha? Had they found him already? Had they been waiting in ambush?

He was all set to flee, but the driver got out of the limo…and he was a human. His ex-alpha would never hire a human to drive him around. So this couldn't be Carson. That was a little relief, even though his heart was still hammering.

The driver hurried to the rear door and opened it as Henry and the reporter both stared at the limo. The reporter looked eager, and his scent was excited. He thought there was a story here...and that wasn't good news for Henry.

A man climbed out of the back of the limousine. The man was wearing a spiffy suit and a blue tie that matched a pair of intense blue eyes. He was very tall, very regal-looking, and Henry instantly knew he was an alpha wolf. Henry could feel the power coming off him in waves. It was different from the strength that Tom gave off. He didn't like it as much. It reminded Henry of his old alpha too much.

But then Henry recognized the man in the suit. It hit him all at once. Of course. A rich alpha. The familiar face. It was Kross. He'd been the alpha of St. Clair wolves for a little while before everything in Henry's life had gone up in flames. He remembered seeing things in the news, and shifters loved to gossip, especially about other packs.

Alpha Kross looked at him. His voice was deep, commanding, expecting an answer. "Henry Wright?"

Henry didn't say anything. Panic drove all coherent thought from his brain. He still felt like running away. What did this alpha want with him? This was an ambush, first by the reporter and then by this rich alpha in his limo. Had they staked out the jail for him? But why? None of this made any sense.

He still didn't answer. Fear had stolen his tongue. He could only stand there staring, with his heart pounding and his eyes wide.

The alpha didn't seem angered by his failure to answer. His look was grave. "I'm Jacob Kross, alpha of the St. Clair Pack. I'd like to speak with you."

Henry took a step backward. He didn't know anyone from the St. Clair Pack, so there shouldn't be any reason why they'd be interested in him. He knew they were powerful. And he'd already had enough dealings with alpha wolves to last his entire life.

He took another step away from the limo. The reporter was recording all of this avidly, watching with eager eyes. Henry didn't want to make a scene, but he didn't trust any wolves now, no matter what pack they were from.

Only Tom. He was the only person that Henry trusted.

Jacob Kross lifted a big hand and made some kind of calming gesture, as if he were trying to soothe a spooked horse. Maybe that was more accurate than Henry wanted to admit. He certainly felt like bolting.

"Henry, don't be afraid. I want to help you."

"Only one person has ever helped me." He jerked a thumb at the huge concrete jail building behind him. "And he's in there. So you can leave me alone."

He surprised himself with those words. He had no idea where he'd found the spine to talk like an alpha—an *alpha!*—like that, but he just had. It was both thrilling and terrifying. Maybe he would end up running away after all. Alphas didn't like to be disrespected.

Good thing he'd had lots of practice running. Years of being hunted would do that to you.

Someone else was in the back of the limo. He scooted across the seat and climbed out. Kross immediately turned to this other wolf with a look of relief on his face.

Henry froze, staggered once again. The newcomer was short, even shorter than Henry. He had big brown eyes. You could easily call those doe eyes. He had short, dirty-blond hair and delicate, pretty features. He wore faded jeans and a simple T-shirt with a rock band name on it—so at odds with the alpha's expensive business attire, it was almost absurd. The newcomer was not only a wolf, but Henry knew at first scent that the other wolf was an omega.

Just like him.

"Henry," the omega said quietly, looking at him with warm, kind eyes. "I'm Gavin Harris. I know you're afraid and alone." A reassuring smile appeared on his face. "Believe me, I know better than anyone. But I promise you, we won't hurt you. Would you come with us? Please?"

"Why?" Henry demanded. The kindness in Gavin's eyes immediately pulled at him, and he felt like he could trust the other omega. But that was why he didn't want to. Henry had believed he could trust his pack once. But they had turned on him. He knew he was too naïve and ignorant to trust his instincts about anyone but Tom. Because Tom had put everything, including his own life, on the line for Henry. Actions spoke a thousand times louder than words.

Gavin's expression remained kind, but his eyes were wise and knowing. It really felt as if the other omega understood…and had compassion for him. "Because we want to help. We really do. I know it's hard to trust. Especially for us omegas, but I'd like you to give us a chance."

"So you're playing that card? The omega card?" His confusion was making him obstinate, maybe even rude. But he didn't want to be deceived again.

Kross still seemed very grave, watching him with intense, intelligent eyes. He didn't respond, giving his omega the lead. Which was surprising.

Meanwhile, Gavin's smile turned knowing and a little sad. "I want to play the friend card. But I know we have to earn your trust." He moved beside Kross, and their hands intertwined. Once again, he asked, "Will you give us a chance?"

Seeing an alpha and an omega wolf holding hands out in public left him speechless. He knew alphas and other high-ranking pack wolves used omegas for their needs. Since omegas were always homosexual and always produced male offspring, they could be a valuable asset. But the love and affection these two showed each other by their looks and body language... Well, he'd never imagined it could be possible between an alpha and an omega wolf. Their feelings for each other seemed to radiate from them like heat. When Kross looked at Gavin, the tenderness and love in his eyes were impossible to miss.

It was the love and that alone which finally changed his mind. Unless he was wrong and making another horrible mistake, these two wolves were different. Different than he expected. Maybe he could trust them. Henry couldn't deny that he needed help, but maybe these two could help Tom somehow. Alphas had lots of connections. They had money and could pull strings.

The possibility made his heart leap. He would do anything to repay Tom for everything he'd done. He didn't care about himself. Tom might want him to flee town, but what if he didn't have to? What if he could find a way to get Tom off these charges and make him a free wolf again?

Henry had to take that chance. "Okay. I'll hear you out."

Kross nodded almost curtly while Gavin beamed at him. The other omega left Kross's side and walked to him. Henry held out his hand to shake, but Gavin brushed it aside and hugged him tightly.

Henry was shocked at first, then touched. He didn't even feel distrustful. With anyone else suddenly hugging him like this, he definitely would have.

Timidly, he brought his arms up and hugged Gavin back. It felt good to be hugged. More than that, it felt good to have another friend.

Maybe. Don't get ahead of yourself. Be careful. Don't trust anyone too easily. Don't make a fool of yourself.

He needed to be careful, that was true. But he couldn't be so hard-hearted that he refused simple friendships. He knew they still existed. He'd had friends once. He just needed true friends that he could trust.

The reporter swooped in like an eagle. "Mr. Kross, what does helping Henry Wright mean for the St. Clair Pack? Are you going to take back Old Detroit like you always claimed? What do you think of the charges against Tom Reinhart?"

Gavin drew back but took Henry's hand in his and guided him toward the limo.

"Come on. Let's get out of here. Reporters are too stressful." Gavin smiled. "Besides, there's tons of great food in the limo. Fancy food. Junk food. Whatever you like, we have you covered."

Henry smiled back. He couldn't help it. Gavin's smile was infectious.

He threw one last glance over his shoulder at Jacob Kross. The alpha was discussing something with the reporter, and his expression was fierce. But the reporter didn't look frightened. He actually looked more eager than ever.

The chauffeur smiled at Henry, holding the door as Henry climbed inside.

The limo was amazing inside. He'd never taken a ride in something so extravagant. There was a fancy TV, a fancy bar with lots of crystal and fancy drinks. A fridge was elegantly hidden near the leather seats. It was like sitting in a moving penthouse. Or at least, that was what he imagined.

Gavin climbed in beside him. "Thank you for coming. Believe me, I know it can be difficult to know who to trust."

"I'm willing to hear you out," he said warily. He was already second-guessing his decision, but he tried to make a joke. "And I hope you'll give me a ride. I'm tired of walking and taking the bus everywhere."

"That's the least we can do," Gavin said, laughing lightly.

Jacob Kross got back into the limo. He adjusted his tie as the driver shut the door. Then he glanced at Henry.

"It's good to meet you, Mr. Wright. There's a lot we have to talk about."

CHAPTER EIGHT

"Don't be so ominous," Gavin chided Jacob Kross. "We don't need the drama."

Kross looked amused at the rebuke. He glanced at Henry and rolled his eyes. "Fine, fine."

Henry had to hold back a smile. He didn't want to be suckered into thinking these two were adorable. He needed to stay wary.

Gavin turned in his seat. He looked out the back window at the reporter as the limo pulled away. "Is that reporter going to be a problem? What did you tell him?"

"That I wanted him to sit on this story. That I'd give him a bunch of exclusives on St. Clair business if he did. I promised he could have the scoop when we were ready. That kind of thing."

Henry watched the alpha with wide eyes. "Mr. Kross...I don't want to make problems for you—"

"Call me Jake," the alpha said with a casual wave of his hand. "And it's not a problem. I have interests in this, but I definitely don't want the press involved."

Gavin snorted. "That's going to be impossible."

"Nothing's impossible," Jake said with a confident smirk. It reminded Henry a little of Tom. He turned his ice-blue eyes to Henry. "Now. You don't trust us. That's smart. Let me be blunt. I want to make a deal."

It was Gavin's turn to roll his eyes. "Alphas. They love to talk like kings, don't they?"

Henry risked a chuckle. He was reassured when Jacob Kross looked amused at the teasing. The alpha was so different from Eddie Carson. They both seemed to radiate waves of power, but with Kross, it felt like...like he was a better person.

Of course, intuition couldn't be trusted very far. It had landed Henry in trouble before. He didn't know what kind of "deal" he could make that was worth anything to people like this.

"I'm not part of the Metro Pack anymore," Henry admitted quietly. "If that's what you mean by deal. I'm only an omega—"

Gavin reached out and stopped him with a touch on his hand. "You *are* an omega. Not 'only' an omega.

You're special. As special as an alpha in your own way."

He blinked. He'd never thought of it like that. So much was made of strength and wealth and position that it surprised him that wolves could value anything else.

"Gavin's right, as usual," Jake said. "I'm the head of the shifter council. I can help you, and you can help us."

"Before we talk about help, I want to know how you found out about me."

"Easy," the alpha replied. "I have friends at court, in the police department, and I know a lot of lawyers." He flashed a wry smile. "But don't judge me too harshly about that last part."

Gavin nudged Jake, giving him a fond look. "Get to the point, will you?"

It still boggled Henry's mind seeing an omega interacting that way with an alpha. The teasing, the affection, the love so easy to see. It tipped his world on end. It made him question everything he'd known, everything he believed.

So much had changed for him in the past few days that half the time he feared it was all a dream. He was terrified he'd wake up and still be locked in the nightmare of his life before Tom.

"The *point* is, I want to help you, and I want to help Tom."

He wants to help Tom.

Henry struggled to control his excitement. There was always a catch. "Why?"

"Because what happened to you wasn't right," Jacob Kross said grimly. "If what I hear is true, anyway. Will you tell us what happened to you? I'd like to hear it from your own lips."

"What will you do to help Tom?"

Gavin answered this time, his expression kind. "We'll do everything in our power. You can trust us on that."

He knows I have feelings for Tom. He knows...and he understands. But he's not using that against me...

"If you want specifics," Jake Kross said, "I'll get him a great legal team to start."

"He's a hero. He shouldn't be in jail at all."

"We're going to do everything we can to get him out, Henry."

"But first, you want me to tell you my story?"

"That's right," the alpha said. "I need to hear it from you."

So Henry told them his story. All of it. It was easier the second time. Easier than it had been to share with Tom.

He told them about the betrothals. About falling in love with Max, a human. His alpha finding out the truth, stopping him before he could run away with Max. The beatings. Being locked up. Max's kidnapping. Both of them taken by helicopter into Old Detroit and thrown to the monsters.

"Max died. His leg was broken. He couldn't run. The lagodire...killed him." He tried not to break down and cry. He didn't want to seem weak and distraught in front of these two. But he couldn't help it. The memory was still a wound that hadn't fully healed. Some tears escaped anyway. He'd never been good at bottling up his emotions.

Gavin was there, pulling him into a hug. "I'm so very sorry."

He allowed himself to be held as he wept. It didn't feel the same as having Tom hold him, but it still felt comforting. Maybe he was a fool, but he truly believed that Gavin understood. Maybe it was because of who they were. Omegas. But he also felt a spark of hope. If Gavin had found happiness, then maybe Henry could too...

Kross stayed silent, letting the two of them have some space and letting Henry pull himself together. This was difficult to talk about...and in less than a week, he'd poured out his heart to three different strangers. It was surreal.

"Tom wants me to leave New Detroit," Henry said helplessly. "But I don't want to leave him sitting in jail... That doesn't feel right. It feels like running away. And I've spent years running away."

Kross was frowning. His lips were pressed into a

grim line. "This is some dark news about Eddie Carson."

Gavin snorted. "Especially since he wanted you to marry his daughter. He sounds like a wonderful father-in-law." He glanced at Henry and leaned in conspiratorially. "Eddie Carson's not my biggest fan. I threw a wrench in his plans. But the feeling's definitely mutual."

"He's not a good man," Kross said, his scowl fierce. "But I haven't heard anything like this before. He went to such great lengths to do that to you and your lover. The costs. The risks. The damned vengeful spite of it."

"Why, though?" Gavin shook his head. "That's what I don't get. Didn't he think it might come back to haunt him? Karma's a bitch."

"He must have been sending a message to the rest of his pack," Kross mused. "Making an example. Or a personal vendetta against omegas. With an alpha like Carson, it could be anything." His glance fell on Henry again. It was a powerful gaze, commanding and fearless. Again, it made Henry think of Tom. Tom was fearless too—and had proved it over and over again. "I'll bring this up at the next council meeting. The other packs deserve—"

"No, please!" Henry said, feeling as if he'd just been punched in the gut. Panic stole his breath away. "He'll know I'm back. He'll come after me to finish what he started."

"He most likely already knows you're alive," Kross said. "If I know, he must know."

Henry felt the blood drain from his face. Sounds in his ears seemed tinny and faint. He struggled to draw another breath.

This was what he'd feared. His old pack coming after him again. Tom had been right to tell him to leave.

"We can protect you," Kross said. "The St. Clair Pack will keep you safe. You have my word."

He openly gaped at the alpha in shock. "Why would you do that for me?"

Henry had been exiled from his old pack, but that didn't mean Alpha Carson would allow him to find a new one. That could be seen as a provocation—an act of war. It made no sense why these two were so eager to help him.

Of course, it made no sense why Tom had risked his life to help him either.

"It's the right thing to do," Gavin replied simply. "That's why we want to do it."

"You don't need to join our pack," Jacob Kross said softly. "I'm sure you don't trust anyone, and no one can blame you for that. But we can keep you hidden. We can keep you protected. That means security and bodyguards."

"That means I won't be able to see Tom. Not if

you tracked me here so easily. Carson could too."

"That's true. You should stop visiting Mr. Reinhart. At least until his trial is over. We'll keep you in hiding. You can send him all the letters you want. Then, when Tom's a free man again, we can go from there."

"*If* he's found not guilty." Henry couldn't shake the dread that Tom might be sent to prison for saving his life. It was so damned unfair.

Kross looked skeptical. "With the high-powered lawyers that I'm throwing at this? He's going to get off."

The alpha's frank confidence sent a wave of relief through Henry. He had to bite his lip not to break down into grateful sobs again. The dark and suspicious part of him still didn't trust why they were being so kind. They must want something, but he couldn't imagine what that might be. Henry had nothing of value.

Still, the offer was so tempting. So extremely tempting.

"Tom wants you to leave town," Gavin said softly, "but we can keep you safe here. We can give you a nice place to stay. Food. A safe place to recover, to heal." He smiled. "Friends."

He wanted that. Who wouldn't? Yet, to him, it seemed like such an impossible dream. "But...what do you want? What do you want for all this help? I don't want to join your pack. And I don't want to be betrothed or married off again. I won't do it."

Again, Gavin placed a comforting hand on Henry's arm. "We have a lot to talk about. But I promise you we won't do anything like that to you. From one omega to another."

"Gavin is right," Kross said. His smiles were far rarer than his mate's, but Henry couldn't shake the feeling that he could trust this man. It was intuition, and intuition was dangerous, but he still couldn't deny the feeling. "But I'll be completely honest with you about my motives. I made a promise to my father that I'd reclaim Detroit for the pack and drive the lagodire out. I had to give up that dream for something better." He reached out and pulled Gavin to him. The omega snuggled against his side, closing his eyes, utterly at home in the arms of the alpha. "Instead, I've dedicated my life, my pack, and the fortune I've made to improving the lives of everyone in New Detroit. This is our home. It's home to all sorts of shifters and humans of all races and colors. But I feel an obligation to you because your pack failed you. You were abandoned and alone, trapped in Old Detroit, left for dead, and you lost someone important to you. There must be justice. I needed to hear the whole story from you. Now that I have, it only makes me certain I was correct to extend the hand of friendship to you. I want to make things right. That's what I like to do."

Gavin opened his eyes, and his expression was serene as he looked at Henry. "It's true. It's what we like to do. Will you let us help, Henry? You don't need to join our pack, but you can still be our friend. Friends help each other."

He wanted to let them help. He ached to have something similar to what the two of them, alpha and omega, shared together. He wanted it with Tom. He didn't want to flee the city. That would break his heart. Worse, it would make him feel like he was abandoning Tom, and Tom had never left his side. He owed the lone wolf so much.

Now he would owe Jacob Kross and Gavin Harris too. It was frustrating to owe so much to so many other people without having anything valuable to repay them with. But at the same time, how could he turn down their offer? They were going to protect him, and his old alpha had tried to kill him once already.

"What about the Metro Pack?" he finally forced himself to say. "You could be putting yourselves in danger."

Kross nodded. "This is no small thing. But evil prospers when good men stay silent. For a long time, I've been having serious doubts about Eddie Carson. I lead the council, so I have a lot of power at my disposal, including the support of the other packs. So my offer stands. We'll keep you safe until after Tom's trial. After that, the two of you can decide what you want to do." The alpha's gaze grew even more piercing. "Tell me if I'm mistaken, but you have feelings for him, don't you?"

Henry found himself nodding. His heart was beating fast, his tongue felt thick in his mouth, yet it was the truth. He'd only spent one incredible, unforgettable night with the lone wolf, but that night meant everything to him. He knew he'd lost his heart to Tom that night, even if he was still reluctant to acknowledge the depth of his feelings out loud. He doubted those feelings because they'd only known each other for such a short time. Yet the power of those feelings, those emotions, was like nothing he'd felt since...since Max. And that was saying enough, wasn't it?

"I do. And I...accept."

"Good." Gavin's smile was so bright and happy that Henry couldn't help but smile back. "You won't regret this, Henry. Get ready. I speak from experience when I say things are going to change for you. For the better."

Henry took a deep breath and nodded. So much had changed already that he felt as if his life was in freefall. But good things were happening to him after such a long, dark night. Now, if he could only get Tom out of jail, things would be perfect. With friends like these—if he could trust them—he was sure that would happen. He chose to believe it would happen.

Things really were changing. It was terrifying, but it also filled him with hope for the first time in so very long.

CHAPTER NINE

Being stuck in jail had Tom nearly climbing the walls. They'd kept him in solitary after he'd busted a few heads in the main lockup. It was pecking order shit. But he'd warned them he wasn't in the mood. They'd pushed it, so he'd patiently explained himself with his fists.

But that hadn't endeared him to the guards or to the judge. So now he had his own little jail cell. It was certainly quieter. And he didn't have to share a toilet. So there was that.

He was lying on his bunk, hands behind his head, staring at the ceiling. It had been three days since he'd told Henry to leave town and never come see him here again. He was surprised at how hard that had been.

Or how empty he felt right now.

He hated the feeling. He desperately wanted to see Henry again. To talk to him and find out how he was doing. He was worried. That's what it came down to. He was worried sick that Henry was in danger and Tom could do nothing to save him.

The feelings were powerful. Sometimes it was hard to separate the wolf and the wolf's needs from his human emotions. But he cared for Henry deeply. He wasn't afraid of feeling that way, either. And he sure as hell didn't waste time pondering if his feelings were valid.

A guard appeared at his cell door. "Reinhart. You have a visitor. Come over here so I can do your hands."

His stomach suddenly felt frozen solid. Who the hell would be visiting him if Henry had left town? His good-for-nothing lawyer wasn't scheduled to see him today. Maybe one of his friends from Cleveland? He didn't know.

He let the guard put him in cuffs and headed for the visitation area with the guard on his heels. Tom's heart was firmly lodged in his throat. He hadn't felt this on edge since Old Detroit.

They headed down a gray corridor with fluorescent lights and ugly linoleum tile. They passed through another heavy steel door, walked down another depressing hallway, and finally went through another door.

There were six chairs on the jail side of the visitation area. Five of them were full. His gaze went to the empty one and then to the person on the other side of the security glass.

It wasn't Henry. The relief he felt was almost immediately replaced with wariness. Because he recognized the guy in the fancy suit.

Keen, ice-blue eyes. Too damn handsome for his own good. Short, dark hair without a strand out of place. Looked like it should be in a damned shampoo commercial. Tall, powerfully built. The guy would be a tough fight if it came down to it. Jacob Kross. Tom recognized that big-shot alpha mug from the papers and the TV news.

The tall alpha was sitting in one of those ugly, uncomfortable plastic chairs, wearing what had to be a ten thousand dollar suit. The guy was the head of the wolf shifter council for New Detroit. He was powerful, and he knew it.

So what the hell did a New Detroit alpha want with him? Tom might live in New Detroit, but he didn't mess around in wolf politics. That fact kept him on edge. Alphas were all the same deep down. They expected to be obeyed. You were on *their* side. They weren't on yours. And if you defied them...

Well, if you defied them, then God bless your little heart.

The alpha picked up the phone receiver. Tom picked up his. They stared at each other.

"You don't know me," the alpha had said. "I'm Jacob Kross. I have Henry somewhere safe."

So Kross immediately shot straight to the point. Tom appreciated that. He hated a lot of schmoozing and politicking and talking in circles. But the man's words sent a lightning bolt of fear right through him all the same. Because Henry wasn't here, and this alpha had him.

Tom leaned forward, his voice all growl. He didn't give a fuck about alphas or their protections and certainly not their "help." He could kick enough ass on his own. He routinely parachuted into one of the most dangerous places on the planet and got out alive. So if this was a threat, it was going to backfire for the alpha big time.

"If you hurt Henry, you're gonna answer to me. I won't be in here forever. Your entire pack won't stop me from kicking your ass."

They locked stares. Slowly, Kross's lips turned up in a tight smile. "You're protective of him."

"Damn right."

"Good. That will make this easy."

He didn't like the sound of that. Then again, he didn't like the sound of any of this. He wished Henry had gotten the hell out of New Detroit like Tom had wanted. But he said nothing, giving the alpha a hard stare. If the bastard thought he could stroll in here wearing fancy suits, throw his weight around, and have Tom knuckle under, he was badly mistaken.

Kross continued to talk, keeping his voice neutral. "I like you. And I adore Henry. So you have no worries there. He's in no danger from me or my pack."

Tom leaned back slowly, but his grip on the phone receiver was still tight. "I'll be the one to decide that."

"Fair enough. You have questions. Ask."

"Mighty kind of you." Although, in a way, it was mighty kind. Alphas didn't usually submit to being interrogated. Bastards. No wonder he loathed them.

Kross waited patiently for him to begin.

"I told Henry to leave the city," Tom snarled. "Why are you suddenly involved?"

"That's a tough question to answer."

"Try your hardest."

Kross shrugged. "Because Henry is an omega. I happen to have an omega in my life too. A wolf I love more than anything in the world. You could say my omega made sure I got involved with yours."

"Henry doesn't belong to me."

"Do you care about him?" Kross asked, eyebrows raised.

"That's my business, not yours."

"Fair enough. But like it or not, I'm involved now. I believe I can help."

"Of course you do. I've never met an alpha who didn't think the same."

Kross chuckled. "I can't argue with that."

Tom didn't like Kross agreeing with him so easily. "So. You're protecting Henry. Is that what you came to tell me?"

"I have Henry living at my mansion right now. I have tight security in place. He'll be safe from the Metro Pack. You have my word."

"He doesn't need your protection, damn it."

"Oh? And you can protect him? From in here? Impressive."

"He sure as hell isn't a pawn to me. You're using him in some game."

"He's no pawn to me either. But he was witness to a murder, ordered by an alpha of a large and powerful pack. I'm head of the council. I have a duty to protect the innocent and victims in my city. The same way I have a duty to justice."

"You'll have to forgive me if I don't fall down on my knees believing you. It's not *your* city anyway. And I don't give a damn how much time you spend with your personal trainer in your posh gym, but unless you're ex-military, you can't protect Henry like I can protect Henry."

"So are we comparing dick sizes now? Who is tougher? Who can protect him the best while beating his chest?"

"If we were, I'd win. All categories."

Jacob Kross chuckled, shaking his head. "Listen to us. Is this helping?"

Tom smirked. Maybe he had derailed things. A little. "I want Henry safe."

"I understand. You want to be the one to protect him. But you can't. Not right now. You don't like being dependent on anyone. Certainly not a stranger."

"Certainly not an alpha."

"Fine. Believe it or not, I understand. But Henry will be safe until you can look out for him again. If that's what you want." The handsome alpha tilted his head, his expression almost sly. "You do want that? To claim him. To protect him. To make him yours forever? Or am I misreading things completely?"

Was that what he wanted? Having to watch out for someone? He hadn't had a serious relationship in, what? Four, five years? Just flings. Now he was ready to throw his whole life away for some omega he'd just met?

Pretty much. Yeah. It certainly looked that way. He wasn't going to blab on about his feelings, but there had certainly been a powerful connection between them. Not just the incredible sex. A real connection.

"Yeah," he finally answered. "That's what I want."

"I'm not going to tell you to trust me, but trust

me."

Tom snorted. He didn't want to feel reassured, but he did. Alphas were controlling bastards, and they would definitely lie if it suited their needs, but for some reason, he believed that Kross would keep Henry safe. Maybe it was the other man's eyes that convinced him. Maybe Tom was simply desperate.

It didn't matter. He still needed to make certain Kross understood the stakes. "You know his alpha tried to murder him."

Kross's expression went dark. "He told me everything. He lost someone already. A young man named Max."

So Henry really had shared the truth with this alpha. Fine. He only hoped Henry wasn't making a mistake and trusting too easily.

"So you know the story. Are you going to do anything about it?" Tom didn't bother keeping the anger and challenge from his voice. "Aren't you head of the council? Or will this be swept under the rug like this kind of shit always is?"

"Carson won't get away with what he's done."

"Big promises."

Kross shook his head. "You can believe me or not. I want to stay focused on the problems right in front of us. Right now, Henry needs somewhere safe to stay. You're behind bars. Until that can be fixed, you'll have to rely on some outside help."

He still didn't want to be in this alpha's debt. "Henry could leave town like I told him to."

"The news media was already sniffing around. Like it or not, you two aren't a secret. Getting caught might mean his death. Besides, he had no money, no friends to help him, nowhere safe to stay. So I intervened."

"You make it sound as if it was my fault that we aren't a secret. I didn't have much of a choice. It was either risk getting picked up by the military or having the two of us eaten alive. I took a risk. My luck ran out."

"I understand. Options were limited. Luck runs out. But Carson most likely knows that Henry's still alive. If Henry flees town on his own, Carson or some Metro Pack wolf might be able to track him down. Your heart was in the right place, but now *I'm* involved. You'll find out that brings some advantages to your corner of the ring."

"Fine." Alpha arrogance. Holy hell, it irritated him. He hated that he was trapped in a damn jail cell and couldn't protect Henry himself. It was one of the worst feelings ever. He hated feeling helpless. It pissed him right off. "What do you want for your 'help?' Nobody does anything for free. Is this some move against Metro? Or do you want me in your debt? Are you looking for me to retrieve you something out of Old Detroit? Jewelry? Bonds?

Weapons?"

"I don't need anything from you. I merely wanted to tell you that Henry is safe. He really wants to see you, but I don't think that's a good idea. It would be the perfect place for the Metro Pack to find him. Even with security, it could get ugly."

"I agree. Don't let him come here. It's too risky."

Kross nodded. "He made me promise to tell you that he'd write you. Every day."

That brought a smile to his face. He was already looking forward to his first letter from Henry. "Well, I'm no poet, but you tell him that I'll write him back. I have plenty of time on my hands."

"I will. That's settled, then. Now, do you have a lawyer?"

"I called one. Morgenson." Lawyers. He was paying retainers out the ass, but he had the hardest time getting the man to call him back or come in to see him. It was like the guy barely gave a damn. Oh, and he hadn't been able to get Tom bail. So there was that.

"Let me hire you a legal team."

He bristled. "And put me in your debt? No, thanks."

"No debt. No nothing."

Tom shook his head. "I don't get your game. Why would you help us? And don't give me the 'I like omegas' line. Or say anything about *justice*."

"If you won't believe that, I don't have much more

to say." Kross's voice held some irritation as he slowly rubbed a hand along his jawline. Maybe Tom had finally gotten under his skin. Still, he didn't seem very angry, even when Tom pushed him hard. That level of self-control in an alpha was impressive. Usually, there was far more chest-pounding and "respect my authority" and threats, real and implied. So far, the only one making threats had been Tom.

"I don't believe you," Tom said. "But right now, I don't have any good cards in my hand." He let out a long breath. What it came down to was simple. If he wanted to have any hope of seeing Henry again, he needed to get out of here. Using Kross seemed like his only hope of that. "Can your lawyers get me bail?"

If he could get his ass out of a cell, he could see Henry again. Protect him. That was part of it, but he also missed the omega. It was as simple as that. It wasn't something he would admit aloud, but the ache never faded.

"They'll try. But the judge seems to buy into this 'flight risk' problem the government's trying to push."

The judge had definitely been a hardliner. He gave off the impression that he believed Tom was some kind of traitor to the country because he'd broken the government's "martial law" zone quarantining Old Detroit. It was infuriating. But at least he was getting a jury trial.

"Fine. I'll take your lawyer team."

But he was still sure Kross would want something in return. Maybe not right away, but eventually. Maybe he would even have the right to ask for it. Hell, if he kept Henry safe, Tom would owe him.

Thinking of Henry only sharpened the need to see him again. "Give Henry a message for me."

"What do you want to say?"

"Tell him to..." *Wait for me.* "Tell him to be careful."

"I will. This will be our only meeting until after your trial. It was enough of a risk coming here today to talk to you. Henry will write. I'll have the lawyers pass messages from me if I have information for you. Do you agree?"

It was odd hearing an alpha ask a question like that. Then again, maybe he was too hard on this guy. Maybe he was judging the hell out of him without giving him a chance. Tom was suspicious like that. He had reason to be.

"I agree."

"That's all I have then. I'll send the lawyers. And I'll give Henry your message."

"Thank you," he growled. That was a pretty aggressive thank you. He followed it up with, "I mean it."

Kross smirked. "Noted."

There wasn't anything else to say. Tom had big problems, but he couldn't stop worrying about

Henry's problems first. Hell, he'd been watching his own ass, dodging bullets and bites all his life. But Henry...

Henry deserved a break.

They both hung up the phone receivers. Jacob Kross stood, nodded once to Tom, and headed for the door out. Tom signaled the guard to take him back to his jail cell.

He hated to feel helpless. That was the worst part about being in jail. Knowing Henry was still in danger and not being able to be there to help. He hated having to rely on Kross—or anyone for that matter. But he was smart enough to realize he had no options.

He was going to have to trust. He would have to trust that Henry would keep himself safe.

He clenched his fists and had to fight the raw, powerful urge to rip apart these cuffs and smash his way out of here to get to Henry again.

This wasn't going to be easy. Trapped here, he could only hope that Kross would keep his word and keep Henry safe. And that, when this trial was over, Tom would finally get to see the omega again.

That was going to be a good day. Still, there would be a lot of bad days between that good day and now. He only had to get through them. Oh, and win his trial. But at least now there would be no more surprises.

At least now they had a fighting chance.

CHAPTER TEN

A month and a half later...

Henry stared at the results of his pregnancy test. He held the piece of paper in shaking hands. The torn-open envelope had already fallen to the floor near his feet.

Positive. The test results were positive.

It wasn't one of those pee-on-a-stick things that could be wrong either. No, these results were from a lab. Dr. Arlington, personal physician to the St. Clair Pack, had sent the blood work to a lab for analysis. The results showed he had hCG in his blood. That meant Henry was pregnant.

He should've guessed it. In fact, he'd known,

hadn't he? Way in the back of his mind…

A week ago, he'd woken up in the middle of the night, certain he was pregnant. Just like that—wide awake and in a cold sweat. He'd been feeling off for the past week or so. Fatigue. Puffy bloatiness. Some fleeting nausea. Putting on weight—although it had been hard to tell because he hadn't exactly been sexily plump after scavenging in Old Detroit and eating out of cans for years.

He'd mentioned the dream to Gavin the next afternoon. After hearing how he'd been feeling, Gavin had suggested that Henry might be pregnant. The other omega had been playing in the pool with little Ryan at the time. Gavin had been holding Ryan's body on the surface, carefully supporting his weight as Ryan squealed and splashed and waved his arms enveloped in arm floaties that were bigger than his head. Both Gavin and Ryan seemed to love the water as much as fish.

"Maybe you're pregnant," Gavin had merrily suggested, raising his voice to be heard over the splashing.

Henry had nearly fallen off the floating pool chair in panic. He spilled half his iced tea in the pool. "What? No way! Not even. Don't joke about that."

Gavin raised his eyebrows, eyes twinkling. "I know a little something about it." He made his voice melodramatic, like a bad actor during a soliloquy. "I got knocked up at such a young and tender age. I became one dangerous man's baby factory to support my addiction to chocolate desserts. Alas! It is a warning tale for our generation."

Henry shook his head at the silliness. He didn't feel like laughing right now. He felt more like running around as if his hair was on fire and then maybe hiding under the bed. "I'm glad you think this is funny. You're going to give me a heart attack."

"I know. I'm a terrible person. But Ryan still loves me. Don't you, sweetie?" He lifted Ryan up and kissed one of those cherub cheeks. Ryan frowned and flailed, unhappy to be taken out of the water for something annoying like a smooch. But once Gavin put him back in the water again, he shrieked and splashed and sent wide sprays of water onto the pool deck with his kicks. Gavin glanced at Henry again. "Don't worry. You'll make a great dad. And I'll be there to help you."

He opened his mouth to say—*again*—that he wasn't pregnant. But he only ended up shaking his head.

"I wish I was more like you," he said. "You're so..." What? Vivacious? Caring? Effervescent? "Crazy," he finally managed to say. "I mean crazy fun. Like...as a compliment."

Gavin laughed lightly. "I wasn't always, you know. I've changed a lot. I was very shy and quiet and unsure of myself. I think Jake was ready to kick me out on my ass because I was always hesitating when I said anything."

"You were shy and quiet? I don't believe it." The omega practically shone in any room he was in. He was radiant. The pack wolves all adored him. And he had quickly become Henry's good friend.

"Believe it. Every word is true."

"Fine. But I don't believe Jake almost kicked you out."

"Okay, that was an exaggeration. Jake makes me feel like the most important person in the world. Me and Ryan. I love him with all my heart."

Henry felt his chest tighten inside. An ache, a desire to have the same with Tom. "That's why you're his baby factory?"

"Exactly. Although I only have one baby so far. If you're having one, I'll need to have another to maintain my dominant lead."

"I'm not pregnant!" He shook his head and looked down at his belly. It hadn't changed...had it? No. He pushed the thought out of his mind. "So, how did you change?"

"Change? Well, first there was fatigue. Occasional morning sickness. My belly started to get big like I was smuggling basketballs under my shirt. And then—"

"I *meant*, how did you change how you act?" he

said, giving an exasperated roll of the eyes. "You're really enjoying this, aren't you?" He didn't bother letting Gavin give the obvious answer. "I didn't think people could change..."

"They definitely can. For me, part of it was having a baby to love and care for. Part of it was falling in love with Jake and being loved back even more. Jake gave me the confidence I needed to escape my fear. Now I know he loves me, and that makes me feel secure. I can be myself. I can grow."

He knew what Gavin meant. He had that with Tom. Every day, he poured out his thoughts, feelings, fears, and dreams onto stationary and mailed the letter to Tom. Every day, he waited for the mail to arrive so he could see if a letter had come from Tom. Then he spent the next hour reading and rereading the letter. It was the highlight of his days—and these days, his life was wonderful.

Except that he didn't have Tom to touch, to kiss.

Gavin picked up Ryan, balancing him on a hip as he climbed up the steps and out of the pool. Henry watched as Gavin dried the little one off and put him in the playpen in the shade of a patio umbrella. Gavin had shaded his eyes, looking at Henry as he floated on the pool chair.

"Hey, you want me to call Dr. Arlington today? He can do a test—"

"I'm not pregnant!" he'd yelled, splashing at his

friend in outrage.

But he *was* pregnant. He was standing here now, almost a week later, being pregnant. Pregnant was a state, and it was now *his* state of being. He had the test results on a sheet of paper in front of him. Dr. Arlington had even included a note in terrible doctor handwriting. He wanted to see Henry as soon as possible. He wanted to get Henry on a vitamin regimen. He wanted to math out the due date. He wanted to run some other tests.

I'm going to have Tom's baby.

The thought left him staggered as it truly sank in. Slowly, he made his way through the big mansion on legs he didn't feel. His head seemed stuffed full of cotton. He was wandering in a daze.

The mansion felt strangely empty. His footsteps echoed in the foyer and on the grand stairs. Jacob Kross was at his downtown office. Gavin was putting Ryan down for his nap. Carl and Duncan, the bodyguards on duty today, were outside on the grounds. He could hear Linda in the kitchen, prepping dinner, but he didn't want to bother her when she was cooking. Even Terry, the butler, didn't seem to be around. He liked Terry...but he didn't know what the butler would say if Henry suddenly announced that he was with child.

On second thought, Terry would probably say, "Very good, sir. May I get you a refreshment?"

Henry finally ended up back at the guestroom where he was staying. He hadn't meant to come here, but this was where his legs had taken him.

The room was by far the most beautiful room he'd ever stayed in. And the bed...it was like sleeping on clouds. Also, the pillows were goose down and very fancy. He even had a little cup coffee maker *and* a mini-fridge in here. That seemed so decadent.

He sat down on the edge of the bed. He only sat there, his hands in his lap, staring at the sunlight coming through the blinds.

He was pregnant. Soon his belly would grow. He would experience other things that were probably a true pain in the ass. He didn't know what those physical changes were yet. He'd have to go online and look up everything to expect on being pregnant. But after finding out the truth, he probably wouldn't be able to sleep for a week.

What would Tom say? He was going to be a father. Would he be happy? Would he be angry with Henry? They'd only made love once...but once was enough to get pregnant.

He clutched his hands tightly. That was what he dreaded. Telling Tom that he'd gotten Henry pregnant.

Tom was still in jail, in isolation. Things were moving so slowly. The prosecution kept asking for more time, and the trial date kept getting pushed back. It was frustrating beyond belief. If Tom knew Henry was pregnant, but they couldn't see each other, wouldn't that make his time in jail even worse? Would knowing the truth now hurt or help?

He didn't know.

No matter how much Henry loved the intimate letters they sent one another, he didn't think this was something that should be announced through a letter. He needed to tell Tom in person...but he couldn't go to the jail to see him either. It was too dangerous. Henry hadn't left the secure mansion grounds since moving into the guest room. He felt safe here...if a little stir crazy sometimes.

As he sat there and tried to come to grips with all the huge changes coming fast, Henry realized he didn't know how he felt about this. He didn't know whether to be happy or terrified or both. Was he ready to be a father? Would he make a good one? He'd have a tiny, helpless life in his hands, depending on him for everything. It was a huge responsibility.

Someone knocked on his door, startling him out of his thoughts.

"Henry?" Gavin called through the door. "Ryan's down for his nap. May I come in?"

"Come in. It's open." He felt a surge of relief. If anyone would know how he was feeling, it was Gavin.

His friend entered and walked to the bedroom. He

saw Henry sitting on the edge of the bed. The ripped-open envelope was in Gavin's hand. His other hand held a cordless baby monitor. The little lights on the front pulsed. Henry could hear Ryan's soft baby snores through the speaker.

Gavin held the envelope up. "I found this downstairs on the floor. Do you want to talk about the results?"

Henry showed him the letter. His hands were trembling. "I'm pregnant."

Gavin put a hand on his arm. "You and Tom, I assume?"

He nodded. "Our first time. We didn't use protection. We...didn't have any."

"I know you might be afraid right now. I know it's a huge change, and it looms over you. But you will make a great father, Henry. From all the stories you've told me about Tom, so will he. This baby's going to have some of the best parents in the world."

He shook his head. He didn't feel right accepting encouragement about something so far in the future—something so unproven.

"I need to tell Tom about this," he said in a choked, raspy voice. "I should do it in person. I don't want to tell him in a letter." He lowered his head, blowing out a long breath. "Or maybe I should wait. I don't want to stress him out in jail." *Or drive him away.* "And...I want it to be a special moment. Not something in that depressing visiting room. But I don't know what to do."

"That's your call, Henry. I think you should tell him right away. Maybe over the phone?"

"But what if he goes to prison? Because of me? And he never gets to see his son. Won't it make things even worse, knowing that?"

Gavin smiled and nudged him gently with a shoulder. "All right. All right. Let's not get crazy here. Let's not borrow more trouble than we need right now. One thing at a time."

"But I don't know what I'm going to do. This baby will be coming. The clock is ticking. I don't have health care or a job or a car—"

"Listen, don't worry about that stuff. We'll take care of hospital bills and get you and your baby on a health care plan. Danny can drive you wherever you need. And you have a place here, with us, for as long as you need."

Henry stared at him. Gavin was his friend. He trusted Gavin. But it was still hard to believe the offer he'd just heard. "Why would you do that for someone like me? It's too generous."

"Henry, it's only money," Gavin chided. Then he laughed. "That's something you say when you have too much money, isn't it? So I just made my point. Jake will be happy to help you. And so will I."

"But I'm not part of your pack. Why would an

alpha want to take care of an outsider? He has his own problems. His own people to look after."

"He doesn't think that way. Listen, I'm serious. Don't worry about that stuff. Stay here. It's safe. Help me with Ryan. It will be great practice for being a parent. You'll be a pro at diaper changes."

He was right. Staying here was definitely the best choice. It was the only choice. How could he turn down health care? "Do you think Dr. Arlington will be my physician too? Even if I'm not part of St. Clair?"

Gavin grinned. "Of course! But if you're worried about it, why don't you join our pack?"

"What? I...I couldn't!"

"Why not? You told me what your last pack did to you. We're *very* different. My Jake is a good man and a good alpha. He treats the pack like family. I'd love to have you as part of our family."

Henry sat there, his thoughts bouncing around erratically in his brain. He had been frightened of Jake at first, but the alpha was a good person. He loved Gavin with all his heart...and he absolutely cherished his son.

The rest of the pack was friendly and warm as well. He'd liked the ones he'd had a chance to meet so far. He could imagine having them as friends. He'd been a little...wistful? Needy? Envious? He wasn't sure. But he wished he'd been in this pack instead of the one he'd been trapped in before.

"I'd love to have you as part of our family…"

He wanted to be part of a family. He'd never felt like family before with anyone. He'd always felt like…property. Soon, he would have a son. Tom might be tough and competent enough to go it alone, but Henry wasn't so confident. Without a place to stay, without a job, he could definitely use a pack behind him, supporting him. He could use a family to count on. He could use friends…

"I want that," he said. "I want to be part of your pack. I want to have a family."

Gavin beamed. "That's wonderful news! I'll go call Jake. He's going to be pleased as punch."

"What then? How do I…join?"

"Oh, it's nothing huge. I did it, so you don't have to worry…you know, if you're worried that you'll have to donate a kidney or something."

"I wasn't worried about that. Until now…"

"Don't worry. No kidneys. There's a ceremony, and then you're golden."

"What's the ceremony?"

"It's a huge cookout. Everybody comes. You meet the pack." He frowned. "That *is* a little intense, come to think of it. I was pretty nervous at the time." He shrugged. "But I'll be with you. Until I have to change a diaper, anyway. But then I'll be back, I promise. As for official stuff, you swear to be part of the pack and accept Kross as your alpha. We all clap and cheer and celebrate and tell funny stories. Social drinking—but that's off-limits for you now. I've been to three of those ceremonies now, including my own."

"All right. I can handle that. I think."

"And what are you going to do about Tom? Are you going to tell him you're pregnant?"

"Yes, of course. Of course. But...I need to do it face to face."

He felt that very strongly. He needed to look into Tom's eyes when he told him. He wanted to judge if the news made Tom happy and excited...or if Tom didn't want a child, and Henry had become a burden. He feared that last part...so he would wait. He didn't want to wait, but he didn't have much choice.

Henry would wait until he knew for certain whether Tom would end up a free man...or if the father of his child would be going to prison because he'd saved Henry's life.

CHAPTER ELEVEN

Six months later...

Life was always a surprise. That never changed. One thing that surprised Henry about being pregnant was that his shoes didn't fit anymore. He had to get new shoes. Not that he'd had a huge shoe collection to begin with, but it was weird. Almost as strange as the child growing inside him. He put his hand on his stretched and huge belly. It was strange and wonderful.

You're rambling. Pay attention.

The jury would be giving their verdict today. Henry had barely slept at all last night. He'd had to force down food today. Gavin had alternately cajoled, nagged, and babied him all morning to get Henry here in one piece. But the omega had been a good friend from the beginning...and a shoulder to lean on with Tom gone.

Henry was sitting in the back of Jacob Kross's limo. Gavin was with him. Jacob was inside the courthouse, witnessing the proceedings.

The hand on his belly visibly moved as his baby seemed to do a complete somersault while kicking wildly. He really, *really* hoped their child didn't turn out to be an adrenaline junkie like his father. One person giving Henry potential heart attacks was more than enough, thank you very much.

He still wasn't paying attention. It was a defense mechanism. Underneath all his thoughts about the baby, he was terrified.

Tom still didn't know he was a father.

Henry had kept it secret. He hadn't seen Tom since the lone wolf had told him to leave Detroit. There had been hundreds of letters back and forth between them, but Henry never talked about the child growing inside him. He clung to his reasons, even though both Gavin and Jake disagreed.

He wanted to tell Tom in person. That was the biggest reason. He needed to look into Tom's eyes, take in his scent, read his emotions. Then he would know if Tom truly loved him and would love this child...or if the words in the letters meant nothing. If it had only been a one-night stand in Old Detroit. If Tom was with him for the long haul, no matter what, or…if he wasn't.

But there were other reasons too. Henry didn't want to heap on the stress when Tom was on trial and in isolation at the jail. And…because Henry was afraid. He was afraid to lose what happiness he finally had…

He had no idea how Tom would react when he learned the truth. They'd shared one night together. It was an incredible night that Henry would never forget. But now the two of them had created a new person. He didn't want to sound silly, saying it was a miracle, but…it *was* a miracle.

Henry's life had changed so much. Who was responsible for that? Tom.

He owed the man so much. All the changes in his life still left him feeling like he was in a dream, even after all this time. One of the biggest surprises was that he didn't feel afraid anymore. Not for himself, anyway. He was still terrified that Tom would be sent to prison. That kept him awake at night. That, and worrying about protecting and caring for his child. Or maybe caring wasn't the right word. He already loved the little guy with all his heart. Maybe being worthy of his child was closer to the mark.

But he did worry and stress over Tom. It was even worse because he couldn't see him, only send him letters. So he wrote him a letter almost every day. He wrote about everything. About Gavin and Jake and how much they loved each other. He wrote about silly, inconsequential things, like what he saw on television. He wrote about heavy, intimate things, like how he felt about Tom or his dreams for the future. Sometimes he even wrote about his past. But he kept the most important thing secret.

He was pregnant. Tom was the father. And very soon, their child would be here.

He stared out the limo's tinted window at the huge courthouse. In his opinion, they built those buildings to look like fortresses to scare you to death. Tom was inside. Right now, some jury of strangers was determining his fate.

Tom had to be worried about being sent to prison, no matter how cavalier or dismissive he always sounded in his letters. That was one of Henry's justifications for not telling Tom about his son yet. He worried it would be like pouring gasoline on the fire by telling him he had a son coming. It would only raise the stakes for Tom. That wouldn't help.

Or maybe it would. Maybe it would give him something to fight for alongside his freedom. Henry didn't know.

But it was far too late now. He'd made his choice, and everyone around him had respected it, even if they didn't completely agree. Still, he couldn't shake the feeling that he had done the wrong thing. It made him feel a constant, low-grade panic. It was almost as bad as the tension and worry he felt right now, waiting for the jury to come back into the courtroom and give their verdict.

He was so afraid to lose Tom. The letters from Tom had been the highlight of his day since the very beginning. He kept every one of them, reading them over and over again. Tom joked around a lot and talked about things with a wry and sometimes sarcastic sense of humor. Henry could hear Tom's voice in his head when he read the letters. It was strange. Not something he'd noticed from emails before, but definitely something from old-timey, handwritten letters. Or maybe it was just him. God knew he was strange enough as it was.

He even had his favorite letter in his back pocket right now. He usually carried it with him. That was sappy. It was cheesy. He knew it. He embraced it. Carrying the letter made him feel close to Tom when he couldn't be with him.

"I'm on the edge of my seat," Gavin murmured. "I can't imagine what you're going through right now."

Henry shook his head. "I just want it over with. I want him back."

"You had such a short time with him. It breaks my heart."

He couldn't deny that it had been torture. It was

torture to find someone like Tom and then be separated from him for so long. But the letters helped. In a way, he felt like he was getting to know the real Tom. The things he'd done. Little observations and jokes of his. The way he thought. How he viewed the world. The Tom inside the rough, tough ex-soldier badass exterior.

And one of Henry's favorite parts was when the lone wolf got dirty. The man didn't have an ounce of shame—and Henry loved it. He didn't care that people at the prison probably read every word of the letters going out and coming in. When Tom talked dirty, those hot words always had Henry melting in his seat. It was wonderful torture. But now he was aching for the real thing again. Real touch. Real warmth. True kisses.

Gavin reached out and put a comforting hand on Henry's arm. "Are you worried about how he'll react to the baby?"

Henry closed his eyes and nodded. He struggled to find words and couldn't. The worry was so massive. It threatened to drown him. But the choice had been his. He needed to own it.

Still, that didn't make him feel any calmer about the moment when Tom would finally learn the truth.

"*Don't* worry," Gavin chided. "My Jake likes your Tom. He says Tom will make a good father. That he'll protect his 'cub' with everything he has. So things will work out. I know it. You know it."

That lifted Henry's heart, but he was leery of getting blindsided or taking anything for granted. "But Jake only met Tom once. What if he's wrong? This is...so much to take."

"Jacob is definitely wrong sometimes." He grinned. "You can tell him I said that, too. But he does have good instincts. After all, he chose me, didn't he?"

Henry laughed lightly, his spirits lifting a little. It was hard to be around Gavin for long and not end up with a smile. The other omega was so deeply caring. He was a great father to his son. They were both great fathers. Henry got to see and admire it every day. And it was great practice for him too. He helped Gavin care for Ryan as the ten-month-old baby crawled everywhere and was even pulling himself up on things, sometimes even walking for a few steps before falling on his diaper-padded baby butt. Right now, Ryan was being watched by the pack so Gavin and Jake could come here and be with Henry today.

The pack. He still couldn't believe he was a part of it. He was part of the St. Clair wolf pack. They had taken him in like a lost puppy. It hadn't even cost him a kidney, just a pledge of loyalty to the pack and to the alpha and he was in. Now he had a family. He didn't regret that decision for an instant. He was still deeply grateful to Gavin, who had been the driving force behind it.

He never thought he would say it about a wolf pack, but this one felt like a big family. He could sleep at night, knowing he had people who cared about him and who would do everything to protect him. He felt the same about them. And Gavin's story with Jake and how he came into the pack? Henry found it uplifting beyond words. Almost like a fairy tale.

Gavin's smartphone suddenly chirped. A message had just come in. Henry's heart began to thud in his chest. His mouth suddenly felt as dry as desert sand.

Gavin swiped at the screen and read the text. He glanced at Henry. "It's Jake. The jury just filed in. The foreman's going to read the verdict."

Henry sagged in the leather seat, covering his face with one hand, his other hand resting protectively on his big belly. His boy responded with a kick. Henry felt a faint smile on his lips even though right now, he felt like throwing up.

Gavin was still staring at his phone screen when Henry peeked through his fingers. His heart was still thudding in his chest like a drum. He could feel his pulse throbbing in his temples.

This was it. Finally. He'd find out if Tom was headed to prison. The very thought nearly panicked him, smothered him because it was so close. This was the moment. He couldn't lose Tom. It would be his fault. How could he live with that?

Gavin suddenly reached out and seized Henry's

arm. "It's a hung jury! The judge ruled it a mistrial!"

Gavin was grinning from ear to ear, but Henry's head was spinning.

"Wait, is that good? I wanted not guilty."

"That would've been best, but they did catch you pretty much red-handed leaving Old Detroit."

"But what does this mean? Can they keep him in jail?"

"Let me ask." Gavin's thumbs tapped the smartphone screen in rapid-fire. Henry was vaguely jealous. He still used the hunt-and-peck method of texting.

A moment later, Gavin's phone chimed as another text came in. Gavin read it and explained it to Henry. "The lawyers say he isn't convicted, but he's not acquitted. The case can be retried if the government wants to keep coming after him."

Henry let out a long breath. That wasn't great, but it wasn't a guilty verdict. "So he can leave jail?"

"He's out of jail! He walks out right now, a free man. I guess all those lawyers are worth something after all!"

The omega's enthusiasm was contagious. Henry felt his smile stretching wide across his face. Relief nearly drowned him. But then he realized that the other shoe was about to drop. He was going to see Tom again.

And he had some explaining to do.

He tried to fight through another wave of worry. He needed to keep a positive attitude. After all, so much had changed for him. He wasn't trapped in ruins anymore, always hungry, hiding from hyena-crocodile monsters that were hungry for him.

Now he was a father. He had friends. A family. A pack.

But he also wanted Tom more than anything…and that suddenly felt at risk. Because of a secret. A gamble. A choice that might have been a horrible mistake…

It took a while, but people began to file out of the courthouse doors. He craned his neck, nearly pressing his face against the limo's tinted windows, trying to see Tom.

And there he was. Tom Reinhart, dressed in a suit and striding through the crowds.

Henry wanted to get out of the limo and run to meet him. He wanted to throw himself into the man's arms. But he was pregnant and always felt as if he moved with the grace of an elephant with swollen ankles. And even if he wasn't unwieldy, he needed to stay out of sight. That was the only reason Kross agreed to let him come. He needed to stay in the safety of the limousine. Danny and Duncan were in the front of the limo. Duncan was armed. Just in case there was a problem with the Metro Pack.

So getting out was forbidden, but Henry never

took his eyes off Tom as he crossed the courtyard. Jacob Kross walked at his side. Both men looked amazing in their suits, but Henry only had eyes for Tom.

The lone wolf ignored the few reporters who were hanging around. He headed directly for the limo parked on the street as if he could sense Henry inside. His long strides rapidly ate up ground. If Jacob Kross hadn't been just as tall, he would've been left in the dust.

Henry's heart was pounding so hard he wondered if it would burst. It was too late to stop this from happening. He couldn't drive away. He couldn't run. Literally. This was going to happen. Right now.

You've faced worse than this. Be brave.

That was true. He had managed to survive alone in Old Detroit. So why did this feel completely different, yet just as terrifying?

Danny got out of the limo and opened the door for Jake and Tom. Duncan got out too and stood there glowering and looking dangerous and exactly like a bodyguard. Jake held back and let Tom enter the limo first. Henry's breath caught in his throat as the lone wolf bent down and climbed inside.

He knew it was an illusion, but for him, time seemed to slow. Tom's gaze immediately locked on his. Henry couldn't look away. He couldn't find his voice.

Tom's gray eyes widened. Henry heard him suck in a surprised breath. His gaze dropped to Henry's big belly and then back up to Henry again. The surprise there faded, replaced with... Replaced with what? Henry found he couldn't tell. It looked as if a thousand thoughts were racing through the lone wolf's head, and the jumble was reflected in his eyes.

Before Henry could say anything, even the greeting he'd planned and practiced in front of the mirror, Tom switched seats to sit beside him. That was a good sign, right? Then Tom took Henry's shoulders in both his hands as he leaned in close.

Tom kissed him. Henry felt the pressure of tears behind his eyes as he surrendered to the kiss, barely holding back a sob.

The kiss was everything he'd been missing. He dared to hope that it meant Tom would forgive him for keeping this child of theirs a secret.

Tom drew back slowly, still looking into his eyes. He moved his hands to gently cup Henry's cheeks. "I missed you."

Henry could only close his tear-blurred eyes and lean into Tom's hands, desperate to touch him. Oh, how he'd missed this too. So very much.

Jacob Kross got into the limo, and the door shut. "I know you two have a lot to talk about, but we should get somewhere safe and quiet."

Tom nodded. His gaze lingered on Henry, his

eyes searching. "I agree. We have a lot to talk about."

Henry put his hands on his belly defensively. He kept thinking about the kiss. The kiss meant something. But did it mean forgiveness? No, he shouldn't reach that far.

But could it mean understanding? That was what he was praying for.

Tom and Henry were sitting together on the long leather seat on the right side of the limo. Jacob Kross and Gavin were sitting next to each other in the leather couch seat. The alpha was holding Gavin's hand in his, but the two of them were looking at Henry and Tom.

Tom glanced at them. "Where are we going?"

"To my place outside of town," Jake said. "Near the water. It's safest." He paused. "If that is all right with you. Like I told you, Henry has been staying with us for this last half a year. I have extensive security."

Half a year... It felt like half a decade since he'd been able to see Tom, to breathe in his scent again. And just like when they'd been together in Old Detroit, he immediately felt safe with the other wolf.

Tom's expression was hard to read as he nodded at the alpha. "Sounds good. For now."

Henry's heart was still pounding fast. His heartbeat hadn't slowed one bit. He couldn't believe that Tom was finally here with him. At the same time, he was terrified that this would somehow go wrong.

That something would steal his happiness.

Tom looked at him again...and then did something that won Henry's heart forever. He reached out and put his hand on Henry's belly. He didn't smile. His expression was intense, almost fascinated.

The baby turned and kicked as if he could sense his father's touch.

Tom's eyes widened. He tilted his head, still staring at Henry's big belly stretching the fabric of his shirt.

Henry didn't know what to say. He feared saying anything at all during such a fraught moment.

Tom didn't seem in any hurry to speak in front of Kross or Gavin. Henry couldn't blame him. He understood that Tom barely knew them. He knew Tom's feelings about alpha wolves.

The ride back to the mansion was strange for Henry. It seemed so long...and yet he barely remembered it. Gavin filled the air with light chatter, keeping the atmosphere from growing too intense. Tom and Jacob seemed wary but respectful of each other. And Henry kept having to bite his tongue to keep from talking to Tom about their baby. He wanted to let Tom take the lead there. After all, Tom was the one who'd finally learned the truth only minutes ago. That kiss gave Henry hope, yet he knew full well that he wasn't out of the woods yet.

Even though he appreciated Gavin for his light

chit-chat and helping tamp down the tension, being trapped in his own head with all his thoughts and worries was still a torment. His stomach was unsettled. He felt like he might throw up, a throwback to the bouts of morning sickness he'd suffered early on.

Finally, the limo pulled off the main road and drove up the long driveway to Kross's mansion. Danny parked in front of the mansion's front steps. He got out and hurried around to the back to let them out.

Jacob and Gavin climbed out first. Then Tom, who lingered at the door to give his hand to Henry and help him out too. The help was appreciated. He wasn't very nimble with all this baby inside him. And their son wasn't going to be a tiny baby either.

"I can show you around inside, Mr. Reinhart," Jacob Kross said formally. "If you're hungry, I'll have the cook make you a meal. I'm sure it will be far better than jail food."

"That sounds good," Tom replied. "But for now, I'd like to walk with Henry." He glanced at Henry and held his gaze. "If you're up for it."

Henry nodded, his heart lodged in his throat. This was it. They would finally be alone and could talk about the elephant in the room. "I can walk. It isn't pretty. But I can do it."

Tom's lips quirked in a smile. He gave Henry his arm, and Henry took it. He had forgotten how tall

Tom was. And how good-looking. And his wonderful scent…

Henry had to tear his gaze away from Tom. He smiled at Jacob and Gavin. "I'll walk him around the grounds."

"Don't tire yourself out," Jacob Kross said.

Tom frowned and slipped an arm around Henry's shoulders. "I'll watch him."

His tone held a note of warning…and a bit of challenge. As if Tom was telling the alpha that Henry belonged to him, and that was that.

The alpha nodded, not seeming angry or provoked by the possessive vibes Tom was giving off like heat from a bonfire. "We'll be inside if you need us."

"Dinner will be great!" Gavin said. "That's a promise." He pulled the alpha along toward the house. "Come on, Jake. Let's go find our kid and rescue his babysitter. I'm sure he misses his daddies."

Henry and Tom began walking along the front and then the side of the mansion. He wanted to take Tom around to the backyard lawns that sprawled to the tree line. Beyond the trees, they would be able to see the lake. It was pretty, and being outside soothed his wolf.

They walked for a while in silence. Henry was holding Tom, their arms interlinked, as they moved at an easy pace.

"The baby's mine," Tom said all at once.

Henry nodded. His stomach felt full of butterflies. "I wanted to tell you. I wanted so badly."

"Why didn't you?"

"There were so many reasons." And right now, none of them sounded good. The explanations caught in his throat. He couldn't seem to speak.

"Tell me."

"I didn't…" He swallowed and forced the words out. "I didn't want you to worry. I didn't want to lose you. And…and I needed to see you when you found out the truth. I needed to look into your eyes. I needed to see if you were disappointed. Or if you would hate me. Or hate our son."

His last words came out as half a sob. He didn't even bother to fight the tears. He simply cried and tried to keep his crying as quiet as possible.

Tom scowled at him. His gray eyes were fierce. "Do you really think I would do that? Hate you or our son?"

"I was afraid. You weren't here. I was trapped with my own fears. I'm so sorry. I was…I was wrong. But…"

He shook his head, knowing his words sounded weak and unconvincing.

Tom turned to face him. He took both Henry's hands in his. He looked down into Henry's eyes. "I'm sorry I wasn't there for you."

Never once had Henry expected an apology. The words staggered him. "You're...you're not angry?"

"It *is* a lot to take in. It rocked me back on my heels. But I'm not angry with you. Don't ever think that. Hell, how could I be angry? We did this together."

"I didn't get pregnant on purpose." That was one of the things he feared. That Tom would believe he got pregnant to tie the two of them together. He didn't want to be an anchor around anyone's neck.

"I didn't think you did." He sighed. "We didn't use protection." A wry smile appeared on his lips. "Guess our luck ran out."

Henry didn't say anything. He didn't know how to respond to that last thing Tom had said. Henry was worried, yes. But he also felt...lucky. Just lucky. Lucky to have escaped Old Detroit. Lucky to have found Tom. Lucky to have a healthy child growing inside him. Lucky that Tom hadn't been sent to prison. Lucky to be part of a good pack of good people.

Lucky.

"My luck didn't run out," Henry said, his confidence suddenly swelling. "I might've made a mistake, but my luck changed for the better." *When I met you.*

Tom looked pleased, seeming to read the rest of Henry's thought. "Well, if it was a mistake, then it is *our* mistake. But I never want to call our child a mistake. So let's agree not to do that from now on."

"You're right." He took a deep breath, trying to get his emotions under control. He wiped at the tears on his cheeks. "I would understand if you were angry with me. I...kept something from you. Something huge. I don't expect to be forgiven."

He didn't know why he was pushing this, as if trying to provoke Tom into being furious with him. Was he so desperate for Tom to agree that Henry had done something terrible? Maybe he *wanted* Tom to be angry with him. He didn't know why. It was crazy, but...

Tom gave him a puzzled look. "Do you feel guilty?"

"Yes." He barely got the word out.

"Don't."

"But you're taking it so well. *Too* well. It's not...normal."

Tom chuckled. "Guess I can't win. If I blow up, I'm a bastard. If I stay calm, I'm not normal."

Henry looked away, shame burning inside him. It seemed like he couldn't say the right thing. He'd never been all that great at conversation. Then he'd been alone for years with no one sane to talk with. But the last six months, he'd really worked at overcoming that. He'd worked at coming out of his shell instead of retreating into it. The letters had helped. He was a better writer than he was a talker. Gavin and Jake and the rest of the pack had helped too, but clearly, he had a long way to go.

"You're right," he finally said. "I guess I want to beat myself up. Because I'm afraid that I've destroyed your life..."

"You didn't destroy my life." Tom held him by the shoulders and looked into his eyes with an intensity that demanded Henry's full attention. Slowly, Tom's lips curled into a half-smile. "Didn't you read any of those letters I sent to you? Did you forget everything I said in them?"

He hadn't forgotten them. Many of those words were burned into his heart. The compliments. The expressions of desire. The love. None of them were particularly fancy words, but that made perfect sense. Tom wasn't fancy. But those words were blunt and simple and impossible to misconstrue. The kind words kept Henry's spirits high. The romantic ones lifted his heart. The sexy ones got his blood racing and stirred his body.

How could he ever forget that?

"I didn't forget," he said, lifting his chin. His words had a hint of challenge to them. "They meant everything to me. But...they are making me fall..." He took a deep breath and then grimly pushed on. He was afraid to be vulnerable, but maybe Tom was the one person he could be completely vulnerable with. "They made me fall in love with you. That's why I'm pushing you away."

Tom's smile was kind. He lifted a hand from Henry's shoulder and traced the tip of his index finger along Henry's cheek as if memorizing it by touch.

"I don't understand that," Tom said. "But I'm going to deal with it. Because the only thing that matters is the first part of what you said. And I feel the same." His smile widened, his eyes were soft. "I never would've imagined falling for someone over a bunch of letters. But since I couldn't touch you, kiss you, it only made it more intense while we were apart. I feel like I know you. As if I know you better than anyone else in the world. I don't always understand you, but I *know* you. Does that make any sense?"

Slowly, Henry nodded. It made sense in a crazy sort of way. Most people wouldn't believe you could fall in love and truly get to know someone over letters or emails or online things like that. Henry knew differently—at least when it came to himself. They had formed a connection that seemed deep and strong. It was the strongest he'd ever had in his life. Even stronger than the one he'd had with Max.

So was that what Henry had been doing? Stress testing this connection by trying to provoke Tom into getting mad at him for getting pregnant? Was he so insecure and needy? Was he so determined to sabotage himself?

Maybe. But Tom hadn't flinched. He seemed too

good to be true. Nothing had been sabotaged.

And that was why Henry was so terrified to lose him.

He leaned in and stood on his tiptoes to kiss Tom. The kiss was hard, desperate. But Tom sensed his need. The other wolf's strong arms slipped around him, pulling Henry close, shielding him. Henry's big belly kept him from pressing up against Tom completely, but he did the best he could.

Tom kissed him back with passion. Henry melted into the kiss. God, it had been so long since he'd been touched. That one night he'd shared with Tom had brought back all his long-suppressed physical needs. This man turned him on like no other.

Their kiss grew more passionate. Finally, Tom drew back. Both of them were breathing hard. Henry's cock was a hard rod throbbing inside his pants. Just because he was pregnant didn't mean he was dead.

Tom grinned. "I heard somewhere once that it's safe to have sex while you're preggers. If we don't get too acrobatic."

Henry's cheeks heated even as he burst out laughing. "Did you just say 'preggers?'"

Tom pretended to be affronted. "What? Is something wrong with that? I hate to break it to you, but you're showing, with my kid in you, and I find that sexy as hell."

"I look like a blimp on two skinny legs. And I

want better dirty talk. Like the kind you used in all those letters."

Tom's grin got positively wolf-like. "Oh, you do, do you? I think I can handle that. Are we done with all this talking? Because I need to get you somewhere private. Now."

Henry couldn't help but laugh even though his blood was heating. Pregnant sex was never going to be the most graceful thing in the world...or win any beauty awards...but right now, pleasuring Tom was what he wanted most in the world. He somehow needed to show this incredible man his love any way he could.

Because Tom hadn't ditched him when Henry had shown up pregnant. He hadn't accused Henry of lying when Henry had hidden the truth until he couldn't anymore. He didn't blame Henry for what had happened. Not being jailed and put on trial because of Old Detroit. Not getting knocked up and upending both their lives forever. No, all Henry felt from him was love.

This was a man Henry loved with all his heart. A man he saw as a hero. A man who would be a good father to their child.

A man he desperately wanted to be worthy of.

CHAPTER TWELVE

Tom had one arm around his lover and the other behind his head as he stared up at the raised ceilings above the bed. The room was dim with twilight, but he could see easily enough.

The guest suite at Kross's mansion seemed too rich for his blood. Lofty ceilings. Art on the walls that was so ugly it had to be ridiculously expensive. Furniture that looked so pricey you didn't want to put your ass on it. Carpet so thick you practically had to swim your way across it. That kind of showy stuff.

His hand idly stroked Henry's smooth, bare back as his thoughts drifted. Henry was sleeping in his arms, his breathing slow and steady.

Sex had been a new challenge, dealing with

Henry's swollen belly, making sure to keep their child safe, but also because Henry wasn't comfortable lying on his back. But it had forced Tom to be inventive. He didn't like to brag, but he was pretty damn talented with his tongue. He had some mouth-work skills in his repertoire. Judging by how Henry's eyes had rolled up when Tom had gone down on him showed that yeah, Henry was a believer now too.

After that, it had been spoony sex. Slow and tender. His balls had been aching with the need to come, but he'd drawn their sex out as long as he could, driving into Henry's ass with slow, deep thrusts. He'd done a little reach around on his adorable little omega too. Henry had been quite surprised by a second orgasm after filling Tom's mouth with his seed earlier. His omega had trembled and cried out, going rigid with the waves of pleasure taking him.

After that, Henry had fallen into an exhausted and sated sleep as a result of Tom's efforts. It made his ego swell. But now that Henry was sleeping, Tom found himself feeling restless. It was strange. He usually liked to sleep after sex, but right now, he felt as if he'd just downed two coffees.

Or maybe it wasn't strange. Today had been one hell of a day.

His life would never be the same. That was a lot to think about.

He was going to be a father. Hell, he knew they'd taken a risk that first night when they'd made love. He wasn't a naïve fool. But at the time...what? At the time, he'd felt reckless. They'd had lagodire hunting them. They had a huge wall between them and freedom. They had almost died on that rooftop. He'd wanted sex. Right then, he'd been willing to take the risk to get what he'd wanted.

Now he needed to deal with the consequences.

Henry seemed shocked that Tom wasn't furious that he'd ended up pregnant. Or maybe that wasn't it exactly. Maybe he expected Tom to be angry that Henry had kept it a secret for so long. But he wasn't angry. Not really. He wasn't a particularly forgiving person, but he wasn't holding that lie by omission against Henry.

Why not? Was it simply because he loved the omega?

That word... Love. It was a powerful word, but not one that Tom feared. He knew the feelings inside him could only be love. And he knew Henry. Maybe better than anyone else these days. Henry had poured out his heart to him in letter after letter. The omega was thoughtful and sensitive. Maybe he spent too much time self-reflecting, but no one was perfect. Tom hadn't been much for self-reflection himself...until spending six months in jail. There was a lot of time to sit around on your ass and reflect in a jail cell.

He could forgive Henry for not telling him about their child. He knew he had the right to be angry, but he wasn't. He understood. Henry had been essentially feral, cut off from civilization, doing whatever he had to do in order to survive in a nightmare he could not escape. Henry feared that Tom would reject him for getting pregnant. Or that Tom would flip out about being forced to be a father. That he'd blame Henry for ruining his life.

But Tom had always wanted children. Not right away, but hey, time was moving on, wasn't it? He liked kids. Or most of them. Some were definitely a pain in the ass. He smirked. Actually, all of them were a pain in the ass from a certain point of view.

But he believed he had a lot to give to a child. He was determined to be a good father. It wasn't going to be easy. He knew it. He was…a little nervous about it. The more he thought about it, the more it really sank in. But that also only made him more determined.

He was going to do this right.

First, he'd get Henry the hell out of New Detroit. It was nice of Kross and Gavin to look after Henry while Tom had been locked up, but now it was time to go their own way. He had enough savings to pay the hospital bills without relying on Kross's money. It wasn't safe for either of them to linger in New Detroit because of the Metro Pack. That bastard Eddie Carson had already tried to murder Henry once. That fact filled Tom with cold, seething rage, but he knew there was a downside to being a lone wolf. Carson had an entire pack to back him up. Tom was on his own. That was the way he liked it, but there was definitely a cost.

Tom didn't intend to stick around and risk giving Carson a second chance at Henry. Besides, Tom might be the one to put a bullet in Carson for what he'd done to Henry. As good as that might feel, he wasn't eager to end up right back in jail after just getting out today.

On top of that, Tom wouldn't be on good standing with the Metro alpha anyway. He'd given up the run to retrieve that diamond necklace. Carson wouldn't be pleased about that. Although Tom would be happy to tell the alpha to go fuck himself.

He knew that once they were out of New Detroit, he and Henry would be safe. Hell, he could put his place up for rent and move south. He'd always liked Miami. Or there was California. Putting a hell of a lot of miles between him and the Metro Pack seemed like the best choice.

He looked at the vertical blinds across the room. Outside the window was a little balcony. This mansion had an incredible view and a small section of woods to run around as a wolf. The desire to shift and run was almost as powerful as his need to make love to Henry again, to claim him once more in that most intimate of ways. But he would need to put that off. At least until Henry could safely shift again. When females or omegas were pregnant, their bodies would not shift forms from human to wolf to avoid harming the life they carried inside.

Besides, he didn't want to run on St. Clair Pack land. He would go somewhere else. There would be no more charity accepted from Kross or his pack. Tom was done with that. And now, Henry had him to keep him safe.

There had always been a low-grade tension between him and the alpha. Kross knew he couldn't control Tom. That always pissed off alphas, ruffled their fur, got their balls in a knot. Yeah, Tom might owe the guy for looking after Henry—and maybe for the lawyers—but he was done with alphas and pack hierarchies for good. It was all bullshit. And his kid wasn't being raised in that kind of medieval-era bullshit either.

Still, owing Kross a favor worried him. It didn't sit easy with him. He couldn't puzzle out why Jacob Kross was so generous to two wolves who weren't part of his pack. To be fair, he probably wouldn't trust any answer that Kross gave him.

Damn it. His thoughts were spinning in his head. He wasn't going to be able to nap or even relax, it looked like. He might as well get up. Maybe find a gym and work off some steam. This place must have a gym, right? Or maybe he'd shift into his wolf and run the woods after all. He'd be sure to piss on a few trees and mark the territory, just to tweak the pack wolves off.

Henry was sleeping cuddled up beside him. That forced Tom to slowly and carefully slip free of the omega. He winced as the bedsprings groaned under his weight, but Henry didn't stir. Quickly, he went to gather his clothes but stopped before putting them on again.

More borrowed clothes. He was so tired of that.

Instead, he padded across the room to the double doors leading to the balcony. He opened them silently and stepped naked into the cool twilight. The guest suite was on the second floor. The grounds beyond the house glowed with decorative lights along the terrace.

He moved to the railing, inhaling deeply. It was good to have the scents of trees and grass back in his head after all the concrete, ashes, and rusting metal in the ruins. Or the jail, which stank of urine, sweat, and disinfectant.

He took another deep breath, letting the woods call to him. The purple sky had only thin wisps of clouds high overhead. A handful of stars shone in the gloaming.

Tom reached inside of himself, embracing his wolf side. The change in his physical form began as pain ripped through him at a cellular level. He gritted his teeth, used to the pain after all these years, but that didn't make it a joy ride.

Gradually, his new form emerged. Long muzzle. Powerful shoulders on his four-legged body, covered with thick gray fur. His wolf nature took front and center in his brain, and he completed his shift.

He looked out on the world with new eyes. The shadows weren't as dark. The night was alive with intriguing scents, all of them calling to him. He kept himself from letting out a joyful howl because it felt so good to be back in wolf form again and free. Holding back the howl was a very near thing. He didn't want to wake anyone, but suppressing the howl was like trying not to sneeze.

Enough time had been wasted. He leaped toward the balcony railing and used it to launch himself off. His jump carried him down to the terrace. He barely felt the impact and didn't even stumble in the least.

His wolf raced past the outdoor kitchen and bar, past the pool and in-ground hot tub. His claws clicked on the stonework. He leaped from the terrace down to the lawn and began to run as fast as he could toward the trees.

He wished that Henry could be here at his side. He'd wanted to wait for his omega, but he simply couldn't. His need was too great after being locked up in a jail cell for so long. After their child was born, he would take Henry somewhere far from cities and people, and they would run together as wolves.

But Henry needed his sleep and couldn't shift

anyway, so tonight's run was for Tom. Now that he was a free man, he needed his soul to touch nature again. That might sound like New Age bologna, but it was true. It was especially hard on shifters not to change into their animals and escape from the asphalt, smog, and concrete to recharge their batteries.

He sprinted through the trees, leaping rocks, dodging fallen trunks, and rushing through the undergrowth. When he finally reached the shores of Lake Erie, he lifted his head and let out the howl that had been building inside him since he'd shifted.

After the howl, he felt better. More centered. Calmer. He turned and ran back for the mansion, burning through the rest of the pent-up energy inside. It wasn't long before he shot out onto the lawn behind the mansion again. He slowed to a trot as he headed for the wide stairs to the terrace.

Jacob Kross was waiting for him. The alpha sat in a chair next to a patio table. He held a glass of wine in his hand. His form was backlit by the lights from the mansion. As Tom crossed the lawn, he noticed a second wineglass sitting on the table and a robe draped over the opposite chair.

It seemed as if Tom was expected. He shouldn't have been surprised. His howl hadn't exactly been quiet. He'd missed his chance to mark some territory, though. When the time had come, it had seemed too petty. Funny, but juvenile.

Tom walked up the steps in wolf form as Kross watched him with calm eyes.

"Welcome back," the alpha said.

Tom shifted back into human form. It always felt like taking a deep breath and pulling the wolf back inside like inhaling mist. Not caging him, but not letting him run rampant any longer. And all of that inside his head. Still, it felt just as painful shifting from a wolf back to a human.

Kross watched with a neutral expression as Tom stretched, now fully back in human form and working out the lingering kinks.

The alpha nodded at the robe. "I brought that for you. I didn't see any discarded clothing on the terrace, so I thought you might need it."

Tom nodded his thanks but didn't bother to explain that he'd jumped off the balcony.

"A beautiful night," Jacob Kross said, turning to stare out toward the trees. "I don't blame you for a midnight run."

Here it came. He knew it. Kross was here to call in his favor. This was Kross's property. Alphas were territorial, so letting them stay here was a big deal. Tom did owe the man for helping Henry. And maybe for the fancy lawyer team. And maybe for the fancy suit.

"Let's talk," Tom said gruffly, slipping on the robe. It actually fit his broad shoulders, even though he wasn't a robe kind of guy. He usually went naked without an ounce of shame. "I'm guessing that's why you're out here waiting."

"Would you like some wine?" Kross asked, glancing at the bottle and the other glass.

"Not much of a wine guy. Always thought the hubbub around wine was a status thing. And it gives me a headache."

"Fair enough. Would you like me to get you something else to drink?"

Tom tilted his head as he took the chair opposite Kross. He didn't really want the alpha waiting on him. Too much civility from alphas made him edgy.

"I'm fine, thank you."

While he was thanking people, he might as well get the gratitude portion of tonight's program out of the way. His mother had raised him right, even though he sure as hell hadn't made it easy on her. Maybe that was why she'd eventually found religion and now believed shifters were abominations in the eyes of God. "Thank you for the lawyers too. And the suit. But mostly, thank you for watching out for Henry when I couldn't."

"You're welcome," Kross said simply. "That's what pack means. Watching out for one another."

Tom had heard that line plenty of times before. It was mostly bullshit. Pack meant obeying the alpha. There was no democracy in a shifter pack. Not with wolves anyway.

"Maybe, but you don't owe Henry anything. He isn't part of your pack."

A puzzled frown darkened the alpha's features. "Henry is part of the St. Clair wolves."

Tom froze, his hands gripping the arms of the patio chair so hard the metal creaked. He had to have misheard the guy. "What was that?"

"You didn't know."

He felt cold inside. And furious. He leaned forward, his voice like ice. "You pressured him into joining your pack? That was your price for help?"

He didn't fear the alpha. He gave himself better than even odds in a knock-down, drag-out fight against a rich, pampered alpha. Even a powerful one like Kross. The only thing working against him was the fact that he'd been locked up for so long. Oh, and Kross's bodyguards here at the mansion. That would complicate things. Especially if they shot him.

Jacob Kross watched him with cool blue eyes. "I don't put conditions on my help."

"Then how the hell is Henry suddenly part of your pack? He already had a pack. They tried to kill him."

"It was his request. Henry asked Gavin for it, and Gavin came to me. It was a simple choice for me. Henry is a good person. He deserves safety."

"You're damn right he does. But I'll be the one to

give it to him." This news had gutted him and, at the same time, enraged him. Why hadn't Henry mentioned this? It was yet another huge thing the omega had not bothered to share. What other lies by omission were floating out there right now?

Was Tom the fool, being manipulated by Henry, suckered in by a sob story, some puppy dog eyes, and a cute ass? Did the omega believe Tom's patience and understanding had no limits? Or did he believe Tom would forgive him for anything and everything forever?

"You should speak to Henry about this," Kross said, still sounding irritatingly calm. Maybe the alpha was smart enough to realize that coming back hard against Tom would push things out of control.

"Thanks for the advice. I sure as hell will since this is the second surprise he's sprung on me today." He stood. It was difficult to look badass in a bathrobe, but he didn't give a damn. He leaned forward. "I blame you for this, *alpha*. And I'm not happy."

"I don't like threats. Especially not in my home."

"I don't care. In my mind, you just stole the man I love from me. I don't give a damn if you paid for a thousand lawyers for me. You took advantage of a lonely and needy omega, you son of a bitch. *My* omega."

"It wasn't like that. Go talk to the man you love. Learn the truth."

"Learn the truth? That would be a nice change."

He stalked away, fists clenched. His head was throbbing. He'd felt rejuvenated after his wolf run, but all that peace had vanished, burned away to nothing. It had been replaced with fury, dread, and turmoil.

He shoved through the back doors, striding through the mansion toward the stairs. He needed to get dressed and get out.

His emotions had been ripped up and torn apart today. From the highs of being set free, seeing Henry again and making love with him, to the lows of right now. Learning that he would be a father was both a high and…not a low, but a complicated mess of hope and worries and change. He was exhausted by these whip-sawing emotions.

He was just tired, period.

He'd need money for a ride. He sure as hell wasn't going to beg Kross for any more help. The alpha had done enough.

He only had the cash he'd had on hand before jumping into Old Detroit so many months ago. His truck was parked in Cleveland at a private airfield near the shores of Lake Erie. If it hadn't been towed already. The battery was probably dead by now. It was going to cost a fortune to use a rideshare to get his ass back to Cleveland, so he should head to the New Detroit airport and rent a car to make the trip.

He focused on his plan of action, on solving the

problem in front of him. It was easier than thinking about what had happened to him today. He was beginning to believe he'd been the biggest damned idiot on the planet. He'd fallen in love with a man who kept huge secrets from him. He'd thought Henry had opened his heart and poured it out on the pages of the letters he'd sent. Clearly not. Nothing had been mentioned about their child...and nothing had been said about Henry joining a pack.

In fact, he didn't even care about the reasons anymore. It was the deception that destroyed everything. Not a whisper, not a peep from Henry about such a monumental decision. It didn't matter if it was a lack of trust or fear or whatever. Tom had tried to fool himself into believing a person could fall in love from long distance, over letters and words. But clearly, that had a very real downside, didn't it? You were completely vulnerable to lies. Especially lies by omission.

He reached the guestroom and quietly entered. He would be keeping the suit. The gear he'd worn into Old Detroit was ruined. He didn't have anything else right now. So he dressed, not looking at Henry as he slept on the bed, still curled up.

He waited until he was fully dressed and ready to leave before waking Henry up. Because he was going, but he wasn't going to leave without talking with Henry first. He wasn't a coward.

Besides, he wanted to give Henry one last chance to leave this pack and come with him. He should just write the whole thing off. That might be healthiest after being lied to so much. But he needed to hear Henry out. He needed to give him a final chance.

He sat down on the bed, listening to Henry sleep-breathe. The omega did look so peaceful and happy right now. Tom felt a flash of guilt for ruining it.

But this couldn't stand. It couldn't even wait until morning. He needed to be free of Kross. He wasn't going to owe the damned alpha anything else. He wasn't going to stay here under the bastard's leash for a minute more.

Gently, he put a hand on Henry's shoulder and shook him awake. Henry stirred and blinked. He sat up, rubbing his eyes. His short hair stood up in patches, and he immediately yawned.

"What time is it?" Henry asked.

"Late. We need to talk."

The tone of his voice cut through Henry's sleepy disorientation. He blinked and stared at Tom with wide eyes. "What's wrong?"

Where did he begin? So damned much was wrong. Everything was wrong.

"You joined this pack."

Henry frowned. "Of course I did. They were protecting me."

He was staggered at how Henry didn't seem to

have any concept of why Tom was pissed, why he felt betrayed. Maybe it was because Henry had just been woken up. He was still blinking owlishly.

"Did they force you to join?"

"No. Never."

"Listen to me. It didn't need to be an overt threat. Did they pressure you by saying they'd remove their support? Kick you out on the street? Anything like that?" Because if they had, he was going to have some more words with Jacob Kross. And they wouldn't be nice words.

"No. Gavin would never do that. He's my friend. And Jake wouldn't do that either."

"Jake? You should call him *Alpha* Kross. He's your alpha, isn't he?"

"Why are you being like this?"

"Because there are only so many lies a guy can take."

"I was alone. I didn't have anything." Henry sat up and began pulling on his clothes angrily. "My old alpha tried to kill me. And you weren't here—"

"Because I was in jail. Because of you."

Henry froze. The look he gave Tom was deeply hurt. He stood there in the dark room for a moment that seemed to last forever. Then he slowly began to pull on the rest of his clothes. There were tears on his cheeks, but he was crying quietly.

The tears only made Tom angrier. They made him

feel like he'd been punched in the gut, and he was tired of being manipulated. "Say something, damn it!"

"I can't say anything. You're right. You were in jail because of me." His tone was quiet, defeated. But his voice was steady, despite the tears.

"You should've told me. First, you didn't tell me you were pregnant. In all this time, not one word. Now this. You joined this pack. Without even asking what I thought or how I felt about it."

"I did. I couldn't see you. I was afraid. I needed people to help me. But you're right. It was wrong of me to hide our son from you. I knew I wasn't worthy of you when you forgave me for it. In some ways, that made me so happy, but it also hurt me because I knew I didn't deserve to have someone like you." He turned to look at Tom, tears glittering on his cheeks. "But this is the one you can't forgive me for, is that it? Joining a wolf pack again."

Tom shoved aside thoughts of forgiveness or whether it made sense to be so pissed about this but instantly forgive Henry for the other deception. Right now, logic could go straight to Hell.

"What else is there that I don't know?" he demanded. "Did you murder someone? Is that why your other pack dumped you in Old Detroit? Is your real name even Henry Wright?"

"I didn't murder anyone. I would never," Henry replied quietly, staring at him with those big, hurt amber eyes. "I told you the truth about the Metro Pack. My name really is Henry Wright."

"You hide so much that I don't know what to believe."

Henry nodded, looking down again and shrugging into his shirt. "You're right. And I should've thought more about the...repercussions of joining the St. Clair Pack. But I was so alone. I didn't want to be alone anymore."

It was crazy. He was still furious, but his heart was breaking too. Not only because this was going to cost him Henry, but because he understood why Henry would do it. The omega had been alone for so long. Like it or not, Tom hadn't been there for him because of the fucking government and maybe a few stupid laws that he'd broken. So Tom might've beaten the rap—at least for now—but he'd certainly paid a huge price to walk out of jail.

"Leave the pack." He took a few steps toward Henry but stopped short of touching him. "Go to Kross and tell him your decision. Or I can do it. I don't fear him."

"But they've become like family to me. Gavin is my friend—"

"You don't need to be pack property for him to stay your friend. You're mine. Not theirs."

Henry froze. He stared at Tom, uncertainty in his body language, his eyes more vulnerable than Tom had ever seen. He took a deep, shuddering breath.

"I will…" he said in an uneven voice. "I will do that if you make me. But…you need to do something for me."

"Do you really believe you have the leverage to make demands right now?"

"I don't. You're right. But I need to anyway."

The fucking brass balls it took to say something like that when it had just come out you'd been hiding so much bullshit was so staggering that Tom actually admired it.

"Fine. What do you want?"

"Stop going into Old Detroit. Never go back inside the walls."

"That's how I make my damned living," he snarled. He swept a hand around at the elegant room. "I'm not some filthy rich bastard who can sit on his ass and live off of stock dividends." He leaned in closer, showing teeth. "And I won't take pack charity."

Henry didn't draw back and had no scent of fear. He knew Tom would never hurt him. But the pain and sorrow in his scent did not lessen. If anything, it grew even more intense.

"I don't want to lose you again," Henry said. "I would be terrified every time you went behind those walls. Terrified that one day, you simply wouldn't come home. I wouldn't even have a body to bury." He began crying again. And this time, his voice broke a little. "I can't, Tom. I don't care if we're poor. I want to be with you. I want to raise our son with you. And I don't want our child to lose a father."

"He won't lose a father because I'm the best at what I do." He softened his tone, seeing how much this was upsetting Henry. He even gave the omega a half-smile. "I got you out of there, didn't I?"

"You did. You saved my life. I will always love you for that. But you want me to leave this pack, the people who have been there for me these past few months, who like me as a person. My friends. I'll do that...for you. The father of my child." His hand moved to his belly and rested there. "But you need to do something for us too. You need to be there for us. We can't lose you."

The word love should've sent his heart soaring, but there was so much pain and strife in the air that it simply didn't.

"No," he said bluntly. "I'm not going to work some nine-to-five job, punching a clock. That's not me. No one would hire me. This is what I do. It's who I am. Either you have faith in me coming home to the both of you, or you don't. I never wanted our son to grow up chained to a pack." He stared at Henry coldly. "But I guess I don't have any choice in the matter, do I?"

Henry took a step toward him, holding out a hand. Tom ignored that hand and turned his back.

He felt betrayed. Inside, he felt filled with rusting pieces of metal, sharp and jagged. All the deceptions behind the words of love. All the love letters from Henry that he'd kept, all meant nothing. They were only words.

Henry should've known. There was one thing Tom could never accept, and that was being leashed to a pack, under the thumb of another alpha. And yet that had been exactly the thing Henry had done—joining a new pack—and then kept silent about until the truth had spilled tonight. When the alpha "let it slip." No doubt, it had been to show Tom where he stood.

It had been a terrible mistake to ever accept help from Kross. He had made a deal with the devil. He'd known it...and he'd done it anyway. For Henry.

But it had bitten him in the ass. So he was done. He might make a fool of himself once, but he wouldn't hesitate to change directions and change his ways if necessary.

He stopped and looked at Henry. "What are you going to name our son?"

Henry appeared thrown off-balance, jarred by the sudden change in conversation. "I don't know... I wanted to talk with you about it."

"You pick the name. Don't let anyone else in the pack tell you what to name him. *You* do it."

"No one here would do that, Tom. If you only had

the chance to know them—"

"I need some time," he said, cutting Henry off. "To get my head right. I spent months in jail thinking. And those thoughts were all wasted because I didn't know the situation." He took a deep breath. The pain in Henry's eyes—those damn tears—were cutting right through him like a scalpel. "I'm not going to run out on our son. But I won't be part of raising him in a pack either. I'm going. I can't stand this place any longer."

He turned on his heel and headed for the door. He felt like a hole had opened up inside him. Something that could never be filled again.

"Tom, wait! Please!"

He didn't wait. He didn't turn around. What else needed to be said? There were lines in the sand. They had been crossed. It was unfair to expect him to be a part of any pack. He might be a wolf, but he would never be someone's bitch. He'd had enough of people ordering him around in the military. He'd had enough of bad packs with tyrannical leaders to last three lifetimes.

He was done. Now he needed to focus on picking up the pieces. This was going to cost him. There was no doubt about that. And not just the cost of replacing his lost and damaged equipment. No, this cost would be far higher.

Tom left the room, closing the door behind him.

Henry didn't run after him. Maybe that was because he was pregnant. Maybe that was because he knew it was over.

The mansion had a landline. He used it to call a taxi. He'd get a ride to a hotel near the airport, rent a car tomorrow, pick up his truck or have it towed from Cleveland, and head back home. It was a plan, such as it was.

He was keeping the damned suit, though. It was far from a fair exchange, but Kross was getting the omega that Tom loved, so yeah, he'd be keeping the designer suit.

Outside, the night air was cool and dry. He could smell the trees and the distant water. Katydids and crickets filled the air with sounds. He shoved his hands in his pockets and started up the long driveway toward the main gates. It would be a long walk. He'd given instructions to the taxi to meet him outside the gates. It was better than asking the "alpha" for the gate code. Kross could go to hell.

Before he even crossed the courtyard in front of the house, a voice called out to him.

"Tom, wait!"

It wasn't Henry. That would've been better. If it had been Henry changing his mind and leaving the pack without demanding that Tom give up the only thing he could do to put bread on the table, Tom would've been willing to put it all behind him.

No, the voice belonged to Gavin Harris.

He turned and frowned at the omega. Had his fight with Henry been overheard? Or had Henry gone crying to the alpha and they'd sent out Gavin to patch things up?

Either way, it wasn't going to work.

He stopped anyway and waited as Gavin hurried down the mansion's front steps and crossed the courtyard to him.

"I hope our fight didn't wake your baby," he said, suddenly remembering that he'd been a guest in a house with a small child. He felt a little guilty. He'd been so wrapped up in his own shit that he hadn't even considered the noise might wake the child. He was going to have to learn to be a lot more damned considerate if he was going to make a good father.

"No, you didn't wake him, don't worry. Ryan sleeps through the night most of the time. He actually sleeps like his father." Gavin smiled. "Like a hibernating bear. I guess that makes me lucky. I've always been a lighter sleeper."

Tom nodded, trying to fight back his impatience. He was tired of talking. His throat felt raw. He was exhausted. He couldn't leave soon enough. He glanced down the driveway, wondering how long it would take for the taxi to arrive.

"You're angry," Gavin said, watching him. "And you're leaving."

He looked at the omega again. The other man was lean, short, with dirty-blond hair so short it stood up in spikes. He had almost feminine features, but they were attractive enough. His wide, dark eyes always seemed filled with emotion. Or maybe it was his body language. There was something about him that shouted "caring" and "nurturing" and all of that. An omega thing—must be. Henry had the same aura. Maybe it was one of the reasons he'd fallen so hard for Henry.

"It's best that I go," he finally replied. "I don't belong with your pack." He gave Gavin a hard stare. He couldn't help it. Merely saying the word "pack" brought back all his anger.

"He made a mistake, Tom," Gavin said softly. "You're right to feel hurt. But Henry knows he screwed up."

"Is that what he said to you? I didn't realize he had enough time to spill his guts about our business to the *pack*. But I guess you're his family now."

Gavin winced. "Henry was crying. He was going after you. I was awake and heard people moving around. I asked him what was wrong, and he told me. I'm his friend, Tom. I would like to be your friend as well."

"I don't need more friends. Especially not friends who take advantage of a vulnerable and scared wolf."

"Is that what you think we did?" Gavin's eyes

were piercing. "Because I'm an omega too. I know all about what it feels like to be alone. To struggle. To have no one on your side."

"It doesn't matter now. I'll never call another wolf alpha again. I'll never bare my throat in submission. And I won't bargain away my life just to get what I deserve."

"What do you deserve?"

"Henry," he growled.

Gavin nodded, not intimidated by the growl. For an omega, the other wolf had his own set of steel balls. Maybe having a kid turned you into some kind of badass.

"Maybe Henry deserves a father for his child that he knows will always be there."

"No one will always be there. Hell, I saved his life—from the lagodire, from an alpha who tried to kill him—and I ended up in jail. Life doesn't let you always be there. He needs to acknowledge that."

"Okay. Maybe you're right. But he loves you. You can see it. All he ever talks about is you, Tom. I can see it shining in his eyes every time he mentions your name."

"Who said love was enough for anything?" Now he was just being venomous, but he was tired of being lectured. He needed time to stitch up a few wounds. "Love. Trust. Truth? Doesn't seem to mean much to the people around me."

Gavin reached out and put a hand on his arm. He tipped his head to the side and gave Tom a look of understanding. "I'd like you to stay. At least until morning. Don't let this drive you both apart."

"No." He drew away. He didn't like all the compassion coming from this omega. It was undermining his anger. He had a right to be angry.

"Okay. I don't know all the details about the fight. It's not my business—"

"You're right."

Gavin smiled and continued. "But he desperately loves you. He keeps one of your letters on him at all times. In his pocket, in his wallet, all folded up. You didn't know that, did you?"

"No."

"Remember that. Later on, after some time has passed, remember it. People screw up all the time. But sometimes love requires understanding and forgiveness. We all need some of that, don't we?"

"I don't need a sermon, thanks."

Gavin sighed. "You're right. It breaks my heart to see this happen. I just want to fix everything if I can. But I've taken enough of your time." His brown eyes lifted and locked with Tom's. "Good luck, Tom. I mean it."

"I don't need luck." His eyes narrowed. "But I want you to tell your big bad alpha one last thing since he's not around for me to say this to his face.

You lured Henry into your pack, so I expect you to keep him safe. Eddie Carson tried to kill Henry and murdered his lover. So keep Henry safe, and keep my son safe, or your pack will find out I'm not nearly as nice and cuddly as an alpha is."

The threat was overkill. He felt bad about it as soon as it left his lips. Especially about making it to someone like Gavin, who seemed as if he wouldn't hurt a fly. The other omega's heart seemed to be on his sleeve but also in the right place, if that made any damn sense at all. But Tom was leaving, Jacob Kross wasn't here to tell it to his face, and the point needed to be made.

He walked away, putting the mansion in his rearview mirror. It was a long walk to the gates of the property.

The gates swung open when he crossed the sensor line. He went through and stood near the side of the road, just past the gates and a fancy, black-and-gold plaque with the street numbers on it.

He couldn't see the mansion from here. The drive was too long, and there were too many trees. But he didn't care. He wasn't looking back.

The taxi finally showed up. Tom left.

CHAPTER THIRTEEN

It was evening when the cab finally dropped Tom off at his ranch house in Braxton, suburbs of New Detroit. He paid the cabbie and headed for his front door.

A full day had passed since he'd walked out on Henry. It felt like a month. He kept playing his memories of the scene over and over in his brain, judging himself, getting angry again, feeling the stab of betrayal, the sting of those lies.

Forgiving others had never been his strong suit. It had been easy to forgive Henry for not telling him about being pregnant until he could do it in person. It had been easy because he understood—and Tom had been responsible for getting the omega pregnant. So he took responsibility. He wouldn't have wanted to learn about it in a letter. As surprised as he'd been to actually love writing back and forth with Henry, the moment he learned he would be having a son was one he would've wanted to share with Henry in person. He wanted to be able to hold his mate and kiss him.

And he had.

But then the bullshit about the pack had ruined everything.

Bah. He was thinking too much again. Brains were the most frustrating things in the universe. It was easier when you did all your thinking with your cock and your fists. Fucking and punching things.

He snorted. That was such a stupid and juvenile thing to think. It was dumb, even for him. A new low. Clearly, it was time to hang up his spurs for the day. He was going to grab a beer and then go to bed. He felt exhausted. Worn down. Empty.

Tomorrow would be another pain in the ass. He'd need to spend the day getting out to Cleveland, getting his truck, and then resupplying what he could. That last run in Old Detroit had cost him a lot of pricey gear. He needed to get it all replaced before his next run into the ruins.

And next time? The damned military wasn't going to catch him.

He was unlocking his front door when he heard a car coming up the street. That was nothing noteworthy, but the sound of this engine—buttery smooth, almost a purr—set off some intuition alarm. He tensed, his senses sharpening. A glance up the street showed him a silver Rolls Royce with heavily tinted windows gliding along the otherwise empty neighborhood road.

He recognized the vehicle instantly. They weren't that common in Ohio. The Rolls belonged to Eddie Carson. The son of a bitch alpha of the Metro Pack. The bastard who had tried to murder Henry, the omega that Tom loved. A wolf with innocent blood on his muzzle, costing Henry his lover, a human named Max, who hadn't deserved to die because of shifter bullshit politics.

The elegant car pulled to the curb in front of Tom's dandelion-infested front lawn. For a moment, Tom hesitated. He could go inside his house and grab a handgun or even the shotgun for protection. Although he doubted his neighbors would appreciate him walking around armed to the teeth. There were kids in this neighborhood and a lot of friendly working families and retirees.

He kept his hand on the doorknob, watching, ready to move. The driver got out of the Rolls and hurried around to the back. The wolf shifter was clearly a bodyguard doubling as a driver, but he didn't even glance Tom's way. He swept open the car's rear door and stood there, almost at attention.

That made him relax a little. That meant Carson had come to talk, not to try something rougher. Fine. Tom would talk. This was going to be ugly either way. He wasn't in a good mood.

Eddie Carson climbed out of the Rolls and buttoned the second-to-the-bottom button of his suit jacket. He smiled at Tom and walked up the front path. Tom decided to meet him halfway, not pleased the man was on his territory. Not pleased at all.

The alpha looked as if he belonged working on a dock somewhere, if not for the pricey Italian threads he wore. He had big hands with thick fingers and hairy knuckles. He was burly, muscled, with a shaved head and a goatee. The bastard looked like he'd watched too many mafia movies, trying too hard to look like a crime boss. Alpha intensity came off Carson in waves—that force of power and dominance they gave off, a product of their position at the head of a pack.

Tom had never been impressed by that bullshit, even as a punk, know-nothing kid.

"Tom," the alpha said as they met halfway. He didn't bother to hold out a hand to shake, which was fine because Tom wouldn't have shaken it. "It's been a while. I heard you had some problems with the law."

Tom figured he had a few options right now, and he wasn't sure which one he'd pick. He could stroll right back into his house, grab the shotgun from his gun safe, waltz right back out, and shoot Eddie Carson in his lying, scheming alpha face.

That would land him back in jail and eventually in prison for murder. His son would grow up without a father. Tom's life would essentially be over.

His other option was to stand here and find out what the hell this bastard wanted and how much of a threat he still was to Henry. Even though Henry had chosen the safety of a pack over Tom, he still felt extremely protective of his omega. He always would. It was that simple.

He chose option two. He looked Carson in the eyes, but he didn't pretend to hide his anger or his barely leashed aggression.

"My problems just ended." Tom lifted his arms, palms up. "I'm a free man, ready to get back into trouble."

"*Have* your problems ended? I guess we'll see, won't we?"

"Is there a reason you're on my lawn, Carson? Because five minutes ago, it was free of dog shit, but now that's changed, and it's kinda pissing me off."

Carson's eyes flashed with anger, but his smile stayed jovial and very wide. "Now, now. Is that how you talk to a client?"

"Ex-client. I didn't get your diamond necklace. Sorry. Send your complaint to customer service. They'll round file it for you."

Even Carson's jovial smile slipped a little, but Tom didn't care. He wasn't in the mood for alphas, and he sure as hell wasn't in the mood for Carson. He glanced over at Carson's driver. The bodyguard was standing by the driver's side door, trying to look menacing. But Carson had only brought one bodyguard.

Two on one? Tom would take those odds. Who needed a pack to back you up when running alone kept things so dangerously interesting?

Carson sighed. "That doesn't make me happy, Tom."

"Welcome to the club, Eddie."

"All right, all right. Clearly, we got off on the wrong foot. Probably because I didn't send you a fruit basket in prison."

"That must be it. But thanks for stopping by. I'm going to get a beer."

"I wouldn't want to keep a hardworking fella from his beer," Carson said. "But before you go, we have something to discuss."

Tom waited, keeping himself loose and ready to act. He knew Carson was baiting him into talking about Henry. He was certain the alpha knew that an omega from his pack—the one he'd tried to feed to the lagodire—was back in New Detroit. And he knew Carson would want to correct that oversight because Henry was a danger to him. The things Henry knew were a danger to Eddie Carson and his standing as alpha and a member of the Council.

When it was clear Tom wouldn't speak, Carson pressed on.

"My necklace. The Lumiere Soleil."

"The run was a bust. I never found your necklace. And you can find someone else to track it down."

"We had a contract."

Tom gave a derisive snort. "You didn't pay any money upfront. So you aren't owed anything. And I don't know if you realize it, but trespassing in a restricted zone is illegal. I'm a changed man. An upstanding citizen."

"I think you *did* get my necklace," Carson said, his words dangerously friendly. "I think you're going to sell it to someone else. Am I right?"

"No."

"How about I up my offer? I'll give you a hundred grand. Free and clear. That's double our first agreement."

"That's good money, but you're still out of luck. I don't have your necklace. I was busy doing something else."

"That something else wouldn't be an omega named Henry Wright, would it?"

There it was. What Tom had been waiting for. "If I did meet someone inside the walls, he probably had an interesting story for why he was there."

Alpha Carson's eyes were cold, intense, and he smelled of danger and anger.

Tom stared back at him, waiting to see what would happen.

Alphas were so used to dominating and being the toughest hombre in the room that sometimes they didn't know what to do if you stood up to them and refused to submit. Tom hadn't been in the mood to submit since he'd gotten his ass tossed from the only pack he'd been a part of all those years ago.

He sure as hell wasn't going to start now.

Because right now, he was simply happy to be pissing this alpha off. After the past few days, he needed a way to blow off some steam. Especially if he wasn't going to get the chance to rearrange this guy's goatee with his fist. Or watch him go to jail for what he did to Henry and Max and who knew how many other wolves.

Although he preferred the punching option, and Tom's wolf preferred the throat-ripping option. That furry bastard didn't mess around.

"Cute. But Tom, my friend, there's no need for us to be at each other's throats like this. I'm going to believe you when you say you didn't get my necklace."

"I have an honest face, huh? Can't say the same for you."

"Such an angry young man. Luckily, I like some

hot sauce in my employees." Carson shrugged. "Besides, the feds would've confiscated it from you when you were so sloppy and got arrested. My sources would've told me you had it."

"So that was all a test? Posturing? What a boring waste of time."

"Maybe. But it lets me get to my point. I want my necklace. I want you to go and get it like we agreed. I'll ignore everything else you've done, every little slight and problem you've caused me. I'll even pay you the hundred grand. People would say that was very generous. Very generous."

"No."

"Let me be clear." Carson's fake-friendly smile vanished. "If you don't want to do it for the money, do it for the omega. The one you knocked up."

"You know I'll kill you if you try to hurt him again." He said it as casually as announcing it was a beautiful day out. No trace of growl. No glares or scowls. A simple fact.

But inside, his wolf was pacing in his head, snarling, so eager to go after this smug bastard that he could barely keep it contained.

The only thing keeping him in check was that he knew Henry was safe with the St. Clair Pack at Kross's mansion. Kross had bodyguards, security. The pack itself was the strongest in New Detroit. So as much as he hated to admit it, right now, he was glad Henry was there, surrounded by friends, instead of here. Clearly, Tom's house wasn't safe.

Carson didn't seem unnerved by Tom's threat. Maybe he was used to getting them.

"I'm sure you might try. I admire your joie de vivre. I think I'm being very fair. Especially since you...understand a little more about me these days, don't you?"

"I understand plenty. But the answer's still no."

Carson fixed him with a flat stare. "A hundred and fifty grand. That's my final offer."

"Do you not understand English? No."

"You're the one who tracked down that diamond. I'm not willing to start over from scratch." He leaned forward, and Tom shifted his weight, ready to get in a fighting stance and tangle. But Carson abruptly settled back on his heels. He stroked a finger along his goatee. "Fine. We're at an impasse. At least until something changes."

"Nothing's going to change." He chose to ignore the implied threat. Henry was safe at the Kross mansion. He had security. Carson couldn't touch him. And Tom didn't fear Carson. He didn't fear any alpha.

"I guess we'll see," Eddie Carson said with a shrug. He walked back to his Rolls Royce as Tom watched him go.

He didn't relax until the car pulled away from the curb and cruised up the street, the fading afternoon light making the silver paint job look dull.

Only then did Tom head inside again. He punched in the alarm code and then walked through his entire stale-air house. All his services were on autopay from his account, so even though he'd been in jail, his bills had been paid. His place was still secure, even after all this time. No one had broken in. He'd wondered if Carson would send some thugs to break in and look for the necklace, but the alpha had been right about one thing. If Tom had the necklace when escaping Old Detroit, the government would've impounded it when they took him and Henry into custody.

He immediately went to his gun safe and opened it. He took out another pistol, a Glock, and another holster. He would be going around armed from now on. Luckily, he hadn't been convicted, so his concealed carry permit was still good.

He found his cell phone and plugged it in to charge. The batteries were long dead. He didn't take the phone with him on retriever runs. He didn't want to be tracked…and a spam call at the wrong moment? Yeah, that could bring the monsters down on you fast.

He desperately wanted to call Henry and warn him to keep his head down, even though he knew Henry was doing exactly that. He wanted to hear Henry's voice. But his omega was safe at the mansion with all its security. Besides, he had a big problem. He didn't have Henry's smartphone number. They had never exchanged that kind of information before Tom took off that night.

He didn't have a number for Kross's mansion either, or any other way to call his pack. But tomorrow, he would get his truck from the airfield in Cleveland where it had been sitting all this time. At some point tomorrow, he would drive to see Kross. Probably at that big skyscraper downtown. Tom didn't know if he could handle seeing Henry right now. It felt...too soon. Tom's head was still a mess about everything that had gone down. But he damn well was going to make sure his omega was safe.

That was the least he could do.

He knew he wasn't going to be getting much sleep tonight. He knew he'd be lying there awake, thinking about Henry, worrying about him and worrying about the son who was growing inside his womb.

CHAPTER FOURTEEN

The next day…

Henry needed to think of his baby. The life inside him needed to be his focus. He couldn't afford to wallow in his own grief. He couldn't let sorrow drag him down. He couldn't allow his loss to drown him.

That was far easier said than done, wasn't it? Especially when your heart was broken.

He sat on the covered glider swing and stared at the swimming pool. Gavin was wading around the shallow end with a baby in his arms. Ryan wasn't quite a year old, but the kid loved the water. He would splash and clap and kick his legs. Gavin was an attentive parent. His attention never strayed. He always made sure the boy had plenty of sunblock and didn't let him turn into a waterlogged prune, things like that. Little things that showed his care and love.

Henry put his hand on his big belly. That was one thing his belly was good for—a hand rest. Or a book rest. He smiled. His little one had been quiet for the last hour without the usual somersaults and kicking. Maybe the rocking motion of the swing had put him to sleep.

What was he going to name their son? Tom wanted him to pick the name. That was one of the last things Tom said to him before he...before he left. Henry blinked back the tears that blurred his eyes. Right now, he wished Tom was here to help him.

Guilt threatened to drown him. This was his fault. He'd known Tom distrusted alphas. Tom hadn't kept any secrets. It was Henry who had the secrets. He'd believed the one about being pregnant had been the volatile secret, but he'd been blindsided by the other. He hadn't talked about the St. Clair Pack to Tom. He'd written pages and pages about his thoughts and other tiny details about his day...but he'd kept that back. He had no right to feel surprised at Tom's reaction. Henry had brought this on himself.

He closed his eyes, taking slow, deep breaths. It was almost like Lamaze breathing. He tried not to think of anything, not to feel the pain aching inside him. He tried to simply breathe.

It only helped a little. He still felt Tom's loss keenly. It was far worse than when Tom had been in a jail cell. At least then, Henry could look forward to his letters. But now he had nothing.

Earlier, Gavin told Henry about how he'd tried to talk with Tom that night. Henry appreciated it, but he could've told his friend it was doomed to fail. Tom was headstrong, independent, and self-reliant in ways that Henry deeply admired. But the downside was that Tom wasn't going to turn back once he set his course. It wasn't in his nature.

And why should he turn back? I lied to him. Over and over again. I lied to him because I was afraid.

He was always afraid. Fear had been the driving force for most of his life. When he ignored that fear, as he had when he'd fallen in love with Max, it always came back to hurt him. But even when he didn't ignore the fear, like when he'd become a part of the St. Clair Pack, it had also come back to bite him in the ass.

He tried to push those thoughts away and took a sip from his sparkling water. He was trying to avoid soda. He was probably overreacting, being too cautious. He would talk to Dr. Arlington about whether he was going off the deep end and being too paranoid protective over things that didn't matter.

He shifted on the swing chair and couldn't help but look at the folded piece of paper on the little table next to the swing. The paper was heavily creased from being opened and folded over and over again.

It was a letter from Tom. One of his favorites. Having it out here with him by the pool was silly. It was downright sappy and sentimental, actually, but he liked to keep one of Tom's letters with him...or at least somewhere close. It was his silly way of keeping Tom close to his son.

Like he'd said, foolishly sentimental.

He practically knew the letter by heart. He knew quite a few of them by heart. In this letter, Tom talked a little about his time in the military, an airborne division where he'd learned to jump out of planes. His stories were nothing too intense—some details, some pranks they'd pulled on each other, and some of the dumb things they'd done as young men. Later in the letter, Tom talked a little about his childhood. His father, a man he deeply admired, had been lost in the fall of Detroit. Tom joked around about how bad the jail food was. He joked around about how bad his own cooking was and how Henry would prefer jail food if he ever had the chance to taste Tom's cooking. He talked about moving to somewhere close to the Rocky Mountains. Having a place in the mountains or the foothills...but not too far from civilization. Somewhere quiet. Somewhere they could run as wolves in peace. Somewhere *theirs*.

He talked about how beautiful Henry was. How

he wanted to kiss his way down Henry's neck, to nip and nibble at his ear, to murmur all the naughty things he was going to do to his "sexy little omega." He talked about the color of Henry's eyes. The way he loved coaxing out a smile. Other stuff like that. Words that made Henry feel important, cherished, loved, special. And that wasn't even counting the sexier parts...

Now that was gone.

Sometimes Henry wondered if things would've been better if the two of them had simply stayed in Old Detroit. It was ridiculous, of course. The city had been a nightmare full of danger...but he couldn't help but wonder if they could've found a safe place somewhere hidden from the lagodire and simply lived together. Relying on each other. Being happy.

He missed Tom. Missed him so much. And the missing him had only just begun...

He still wanted Tom with him when he gave birth. The thought of not having Tom with him filled him with a low-grade panic. He needed his lone wolf at his side.

Gavin wandered over from the pool, holding little Ryan in his arms. They were both still damp. Ryan was swinging around Gavin's bright yellow swimming goggles and making excited baby sounds.

"Mind if we join you?" Gavin asked.

"Be my guest," he said, smiling. "It's your swing."

Gavin sat down, balancing Ryan on his thigh. He held the child around the waist and began to bounce his leg as the swing rocked slightly. Ryan turned to stare at Henry with huge blue eyes. He had Gavin's eye shape, but the color was all Jake. It was also clear to everyone that the kid was going to grow up to be as handsome as sin because he was an adorable baby. He had a face made for baby food commercials.

"Thinking about him, aren't you?" Gavin asked softly.

"That's all I do. Be pregnant, eat, pee all the time, and think about Tom and how I messed everything up."

Gavin had warned him about keeping his pregnancy secret from Tom. But Henry had believed he'd known what was best. No, that wasn't it. He'd been too afraid that the truth would cost him Tom.

There it was again. Fear. It seemed to influence every part of his life.

Gavin nudged him with his shoulder. "I'm a firm believer that everything can be fixed. Once, I believed Jake was going to kick me out of his life after our child was born. I was afraid that Jake would choose his father's dream instead of following his heart and forging his own path. He surprised me. He changed me. But I changed him too." His eyes were kind. "Tom's going to need some time. But I know with all my heart that he'll be back."

"How do you know that?"

"Because I saw how he reacted when he climbed into the limo and saw you again—and learned that you were pregnant. He's not an idiot. He knew it was his kid. But he was so tender with you. So understanding. That means something."

"More understanding than I deserved."

"He loves you." Gavin leaned forward and planted a kiss on the back of little Ryan's head. Ryan ignored him, still staring at Henry with those big baby blues, the goggle strap still clutched in one fat baby fist. "Sometimes it's that simple."

"But he left. Because I didn't tell him that I joined a pack. But…I was so afraid he'd go to prison. I was alone and afraid. I didn't have a job or any money. I didn't have any health care. I'm pregnant. And…my old alpha…"

He didn't know why he was saying all of this again. Was he trying to justify his actions to Gavin…or to himself?

Either way, it was hard to even say the words aloud. His previous alpha had left him to die, abandoning him in Old Detroit so the lagodire could do his dirty work for him. And it had cost Max his life.

Gavin's eyes flashed. "Eddie Carson. He tried to have you killed because of someone you loved. I'm very aware of Eddie Carson's feelings about omegas." He sighed and tickled Ryan. The child squeaked like a doggie toy and started to giggle. The sound brought a smile to both their faces.

"I'm not here to beat you up over what happened, Henry," Gavin continued. "I've made my share of mistakes."

"But you and Jake are still together. And you're thinking about having another kid soon. The St. Clair Pack accepted you. Just like it accepted me. I was sure they would accept Tom too…"

Gavin's eyes were sympathetic. "Tom's a lone wolf. It happens."

"You make it sound like a debilitating condition."

Gavin grinned. "No, I didn't mean it that way. I was on my own for a very long time. So I understand him. And I understand you. I am a fountain of understanding. But he might not ever want to join our pack. Even if it costs him you. Or he could change. *I* changed. I'm not the omega I was, and I like myself just fine. But change or not, I think he loves you far too much to stay away."

"He asked me to leave the pack."

"What did you say?" Gavin asked warily, suddenly still.

"I said I would. For him. But I wanted him to do something for me."

"You are killing me here. *What* did you want?"

"For him to stop going into Old Detroit. I think…I think he might be a little crazy. I think part of him loves the danger, the thrill. But I don't want our son to lose his father. I...I don't want to lose Tom either."

Henry knew the risks in Old Detroit better than anyone. Tom was tough and smart and fearless, but it was easy to die in the violent, chaotic ruins. And there was no easy escape. They had proved that themselves.

"What did he say?" Although from Gavin's tone, he already knew the answer.

"He wouldn't stop. Not even for his kid."

Gavin sighed. He looked at Ryan for a while. The kiddo was playing with the goggles but was getting squirmier. "I know that sounds strange...but we need to see his point of view too. His life is in freefall. He was in jail. He has a kid coming. He lost you—"

"But he can *have* me. He just has to choose. Or...he just has to forgive me... Or let me stay with the pack..." He shook his head. "I sound really selfish, don't I?"

"Not too bad. You want it all. For you and for your baby. It's hard to blame you after all you've been through." He shook his head. "I could ask Jake to give Tom a job. Tom has a good 'don't mess with me' face. I got a full dose of it the night he left. He told me we needed to protect you and protect his son. It was pretty intense."

"I'm sorry. He was really worked up because of me."

"You don't have to apologize. I didn't take it

personally." He flashed a charming smile. "I'm in love with an alpha, so I know all about the flexing. Tom might not be an alpha, but he's a wolf who shares a lot of the characteristics. Or that's the impression I get."

"Yeah. You're right." He sighed. It felt good to talk, but it made him focus on what he'd done wrong. "I shouldn't have put any conditions on him. I knew he didn't like packs. He thought I believed the same way...and I did...until I met you and Jake and the people of St. Clair. I know that if he could just get to know everyone like I know them, he would come to see them as family."

"He might. I did. But he might not. You have to prepare yourself for that."

"If that's the case...I'm going to leave the pack. I need to. I love you all, but he's my mate."

Gavin sighed. He seemed sad. "You can't have too much family, Henry. So...is leaving really what you want?"

"No. Yes... It doesn't matter. I need to do something to make it up to Tom—make up for all the things I've done. The problems I've caused him."

"Are you sure that's the way to think about it? We're both omegas. We tend to put our own needs last. We have a submissive streak. It's how we're made. You joined us for a few reasons, and they were good ones. I'm not saying it would be easy, but you could stay with our pack and still be a lover and partner to Tom."

He was so very tempted to try that. It was what he'd hoped would happen, even though he'd known it wasn't realistic. Tom had made his scorn for alphas clear. He had his own deep issues with packs. Henry understood that better than anyone, and he accepted it.

But bad experiences didn't mean every pack and every alpha was bad. Tom was too independent and downright stubborn to ever accept an alpha. Fine. Tom had no interest in ordering other people around, so he would never make a good alpha for a pack. He was a lone wolf to his core. That was fine, too. So was there a way for both their needs to be met? Was there a way for Henry to keep enjoying the security, the sense of family, and the friends he'd found here and still give Tom the freedom he needed to be happy?

Unfortunately, he didn't think there was a way to have both. Those things were at opposite ends of the spectrum. No matter how much he might want to have the best of both worlds, he couldn't.

"I'm torn between two things I want so much," he finally said. "I'm afraid to make a choice. I feel paralyzed."

Ryan had grown restless over the past few minutes. He was squirming, apparently trying to throw himself out of Gavin's lap and off the swing entirely. Gavin kept a firm hold on him and stood, resting the boy on his hip. "I need to go feed him. I was supposed to meet Jake for lunch today. Let me call him and tell him I'm going to miss it. I want to keep talking this through with you."

Henry shook his head. "Absolutely not. Ryan has already missed his snack because of me. You keep your plans and go see your man. I'm not going to get in the way of that." How selfish would that be? He always seemed to be making problems for people. "Besides, I need some time to think through this myself. I need to get my head straight."

"Are you sure?" Gavin was looking at him with compassionate but knowing eyes. "I want to be here for you if you need me. That's what friends are for."

"Thank you. But we can talk later. I've been enough of a burden." He held up a hand when Gavin started to protest. "You don't have to say anything. I owe you and Jake so much. But this is something I need to resolve myself."

"I understand. But if you need me, you have my cell number. Don't hesitate to call." Ryan was whining now, and Gavin rolled his eyes. "The young prince has lost all patience. I'd better tend to him. I'll see you later this afternoon after we get back."

Henry watched Gavin carry Ryan back inside the big house. The other omega was a great parent. Henry watched everything Gavin did with keen interest. He was memorizing it all. All the little details, the trials and tribulations of being a parent. He intended to be the best parent to his son that he could be. Since Henry had no parents to help him, it was a lucky break to be staying with Gavin and helping with Ryan. It was like on-the-job training.

It seemed so quiet without Ryan or Gavin out here. The breeze whispered in the trees. The water in the pool splashed and sloshed. It wasn't as nice as waves on the beach, but it was strangely comforting. He knew he needed to enjoy these peaceful moments while he could.

But the peace and beauty around him were at odds with the turmoil inside him. Because he had already taken too long to decide. His choices were stark. Leave the pack for Tom. Or let Tom leave him so Henry could stay within the security and comfort of the pack. All the talk with Gavin had only shown Henry that not only did he need to make a choice, but that he needed to do it himself. No one else, no matter how much their heart might be in the right place, could make the right choice for him and for his baby.

Gavin was his friend. It had been a very long time since he'd had a good friend. The wolves of the St. Clair Pack had become like family to him. They had been so accepting and supportive.

But he loved Tom. He missed Tom so much. His heart had broken when Tom left...and every hour since then felt as if he had a hole inside himself.

Something that couldn't be filled until Tom returned. He missed the kisses. The smiles. The confidence. The intimacy. The little compliments that made him feel wanted. He missed the feeling of safety when he was with Tom. Sure, he felt safe with the pack, but that feeling of safety shot into the stratosphere when he was in Tom's arms.

He still wanted Tom to stop his scavenging missions into Old Detroit. He didn't care if they had to struggle to make ends meet. He didn't care if they needed to eat cheap spaghetti dinners six nights of the week or get second-hand clothes and toys for the baby. He didn't care about money. He didn't want Tom to go missing someday. Because it *would* happen. Someday, Tom's luck would run out. That would leave Henry a widower and their son without a father.

He knew it. He'd lived in the ruins. The sand in his own hourglass had nearly run out. If it hadn't been for Tom's rescue, he wouldn't be here today.

But maybe Tom wasn't there yet in his headspace to see things the same way. As much as it terrified him, maybe Henry needed to stay patient. Their son would be coming soon. That changed men. Becoming a father put things in an entirely different framework.

It was time for a big choice. It would change his life. But then again, when hadn't his life been changing? His life had been a mess of twists and turns. That wasn't new.

So did he stay with the pack and lose Tom? Or did he go to Tom—the man he loved, the father of the baby inside him—and maybe someday lose Tom to the lagodire if Tom never changed?

Neither option was perfect. But he couldn't live like he was right now. In limbo, aching for Tom but too afraid to take a chance…

That was it, wasn't it? Fear. It always came down to fear. He was afraid to leave this pack because he was afraid to be alone and vulnerable. He was afraid to be on his own with enemies out there who wanted him dead for reasons that didn't make a bit of sense to him. But Tom had promised to care for him. So, did he trust the man to keep his word?

Was that ever in doubt? Tom had put everything, including his life, at risk to save Henry. He knew he could trust the other wolf. With his life…and with his heart.

He loved Tom. It was that simple. He needed him. As badly as he wanted Tom to stop living such a dangerous life, Henry still wanted to spend every moment he could with him. He wanted to cherish those moments because, like the love letters they'd sent each other when they'd been forced apart, they meant so very much to him.

Henry would need to leave the St. Clair Pack. He needed to put his fears behind him and go after what he wanted most. He was caring, determined, and loving. Those were some of his greatest strengths. He didn't want to lose his friends, but he needed Tom. He wanted Tom.

He would miss his life here. He would have to tell Gavin about his choice. He wasn't looking forward to that, even though he knew Gavin would understand. But he was far less sure about Jake. Telling an alpha you were leaving the pack after accepting their invitation to join...that was scary. Even if you liked the alpha.

So he would do that later. Maybe with Tom at his side for moral support. Because first he needed to talk to Tom. He needed to fix things between them.

Henry carefully pushed himself to his feet. With this belly, he felt like a camel with a misplaced hump. He liked to believe he'd had a little bit of grace in his movements before getting pregnant, but he'd definitely lost it all carrying around this child.

He smiled and gently rubbed his belly. His boy was quiet, but he'd probably be up and active again soon. And Henry wanted him to hear Tom's voice again. That was yet another horrible thing about Tom being locked up. Their baby didn't get to hear his voice.

By the time he got inside, the mansion felt empty. It was clear that Gavin had left with Ryan. Now that he thought about it, he had heard one of the cars driving off. He'd been too lost in his thoughts to really pay attention to it.

It was fifteen minutes or so until noon. The cook would be in the kitchen, prepping for dinner tonight, but Henry wasn't hungry. Danny had left to take Gavin downtown to Jake for their lunch, so Henry would need to get a cab or use ride sharing to get to Tom.

The mansion had plenty of computers. One of them that he liked to use was in the library. He used a search engine to look up Tom Reinhart. He knew Tom lived in New Detroit, in the Braxton suburb, but he didn't know the street address. Lots of names came up with his search, but it didn't take him long to find the correct address for the correct Tom Reinhart. It was a little scary how easy it was to find information on people on the internet.

With Tom's address on a piece of notepad paper, Henry found a local cab company and placed an order for a cab ride. He gave the pickup and drop-off addresses and got a calculated fare and a time to expect arrival. He marked that he would be paying cash since that was all he had. He wrote Gavin a note telling him where he was going. He didn't want anyone to panic. Besides, he'd be back later this afternoon for sure.

After that, he simply walked out the front door. He waved to Duncan. Duncan waved back. Henry went for exercise walks all the time. The bodyguard had no reason to suspect that Henry would be leaving for a while. But Henry didn't want Duncan calling Jacob Kross. Besides, Tom could give him a ride back here. Then Henry could break the news that he would be leaving the pack.

The entire property was closed in by walls and a high fence, including a massive gate. But the gate opened automatically from inside if you walked through the sensors. When he finally reached the gate, sweating more than a little, the cab was waiting for him by the mailboxes.

As Henry climbed into the back of the cab, a thought suddenly hit him out of the blue. He knew what he wanted to name his son.

He wanted to name him Max.

CHAPTER FIFTEEN

Henry's cab pulled to the curb in front of a ranch-style house. The house was painted light gray with dark gray shutters. The neighborhood was cute and well-maintained but so different from Kross's estate that it was staggering. The garage door was down, so he couldn't tell if Tom was home or not. Tom owned a truck, but Henry had never seen it. Like so much else about Tom, he knew about it from their letters.

His cab driver, a human woman wearing big round sunglasses, a floppy hat, and a blouse with huge flowers on it, turned and looked at him. "Here we are, hon."

"Thanks." He reached for the door handle. He'd

already paid for the ride in cash because he didn't have a credit or debit card. He would pay back the cash as soon as he returned to the mansion. Well, he was hoping that Tom could spot him the money, of course. It was embarrassing not to have any money and to need it.

"It's none of my business, hon, and I don't mean to be rude," the human driver said, smiling at him. Henry froze, a bit uneasy. People usually said that right before saying something rude. "But you're one of those shifters, aren't you? The pregger ones."

He raised his eyebrows, biting his tongue on a sarcastic reply. *What tipped you off? The fact that I'm smuggling a watermelon beneath my stretch pants?* Instead, he smiled. "An omega wolf. Yeah."

"Wow. It's so exciting to meet you! I have two children myself. It's so good to meet a man who understands what us girls go through." She paused, chewing on her lower lip. "Do you consider yourself a man? Oh, forgive me. That sounds downright horrible to ask. Never could stop myself from saying something stupid."

"No, it's okay. I'm a man. I have all the equipment plus bonus stuff."

She laughed. "Well, all right then. And look at me. I'm so curious I could pester you with questions all day long. I was biting my tongue this entire ride, you don't even know. Sorry, sorry. One more question.

Promise. Are you having a girl or a boy?"

"A boy. Omegas always have boys."

"Well, now, I hope that boy is as healthy as can be." She winked. "I wish you and your baby boy all the best. We mothers have to stick together."

He laughed a little because it was both strange and sort of fitting in a weird way to be called a mother. It probably should've made him remember how different he was, as a shifter, as an omega, from every other creature on the planet. Or how his kind were a strange genetic manipulation created by scientists tinkering with things probably best left alone. But the human woman seemed friendly, if a bit forward. He didn't catch any sense of condemnation or hostility from her. His life had made him very attuned to that. So he decided to take her best wishes and camaraderie in good faith.

He tipped her the absolute last of his money, and she drove off with a wave.

Henry turned his attention back to Tom's house. He'd been hoping Tom would see him and come rushing out to greet him. But that didn't happen. In fact, looking at the house, he had the growing sense that it was empty. The driveway was empty. He couldn't see into the garage, so maybe that was empty too.

If Tom wasn't home, Henry was going to have to wait for him. He hoped he didn't have to sit on the concrete steps in front of the door for long. His butt would pay a high price. If he took too long before getting back, Gavin would return from lunch and panic if Henry was gone and he didn't find the note. He didn't want to worry anyone.

Henry crossed the cement path and walked up the three stairs to the front door. He rang the doorbell, hearing it chime inside the house. But the door stayed shut. He knocked on the storm door. Again, there was no answer.

Great. It looked like he was going to wait after all. He lowered himself onto the front steps with a groan. He wished he owned a cell phone. He could amuse himself by playing a game or surfing the internet or something. Now he got to be bored as he waited.

Well, what did he expect with this ad hoc plan? He'd made his decision and was so eager to see Tom again that he'd charged ahead fearlessly...

He had to grin and shake his head at himself. His first fearless action...and he ended up sitting on his butt, waiting around like a lost puppy.

The baby inside him kicked and shifted positions, evidently excited about something. Or maybe he'd woken up after the long cab ride.

"You're eager for your daddy, aren't you?" he murmured. He'd long ago gotten over any self-consciousness about talking to his belly. "Me too."

The neighborhood street was quiet, but on the

opposite side of the street, a dark sedan with heavily tinted windows suddenly started up. Henry glanced that way. It looked like a government car. Or some kind of unmarked cop car.

Something twitched in his mind—some instinct, some sense of danger. He drew in a sharp breath and stood. He didn't know why, but he didn't like the look of that car.

The dark sedan pulled into the street and drove past the house. He couldn't see the driver or anyone in the back because of the tinted windows. But the hair on the back of his arms and neck was standing up. He had the feeling he was being watched.

Fear seeped through him. Maybe he was being paranoid, but he'd survived Old Detroit by being paranoid. He had *reasons* to be paranoid. Suddenly, it seemed a whole lot less romantic to come after Tom and a whole lot more reckless and stupid.

He gripped the black metal railing on the steps and managed to get himself back on his feet and moving. He was praying that the gate in the high fence around the house's backyard wasn't locked. It might be great to be fearless and bold and everything…but he was pregnant, alone, and an omega. For him, being brave didn't mean being stupid. So he was going to hide in the backyard until Tom got home. Maybe there would even be patio furniture to sit on. But he would stand if he needed to.

After barricading the gate and staying out of sight until Tom came home.

He reached the gate. There was a string hanging over the wood planks to pull and release the latch on the inside. He pulled on the string, but the latch mechanism clanked, and the gate didn't open. There had to be a padlock or something on the other side. Crap.

He could hear a car coming up the street. He glanced behind him, his heart pounding.

The black sedan was coming up the road again. His blood froze in his veins. His heart was pounding fast. The car pulled into the driveway, a couple dozen feet from him.

This wasn't good. Not good at all.

Henry began to cross the lawn to the neighbor's house. He needed witnesses. He needed someone to call the police. He was in danger.

The car kept its engine running, but the passenger-side front door opened, and someone got out. He was a wolf shifter, but Henry didn't recognize him. He had a thin mustache and a hatchet-like face with cold, dark eyes. The stranger was wearing jeans and a sports jacket from a basketball team.

Fear tried to paralyze him. He fought back against it desperately. His only thoughts were on getting away and protecting his baby.

He lurched into motion, breaking into an

awkward, lumbering run toward the neighbor's house.

The other shifter broke into a run, easily cutting him off long before Henry got close to the neighbor's front door. Henry didn't even know if the neighbors were home, but he yelled for help anyway.

The man's hand clamped down over Henry's mouth. His hand smelled like cheese, and Henry's stomach turned. The stranger's brown eyes flashed dangerously. "Quiet, freak. Or I'll give you some real motivation to squeal."

Henry tried to pull away, shoving at the man holding him. He tried to turn his head. But the stranger effortlessly swung Henry around to face him. He opened his jacket to show a holstered pistol. His lips drew back in a snarl.

"I told you to be quiet and mind yourself, you little bitch. Now come along. Your alpha wants to see you."

He lifted his chin defiantly, even though he was absolutely terrified and increasingly certain he was going to die. He had one last card to play. He didn't know if these were new wolves of the Metro Pack— ones he'd never seen before—or if they were hired thugs or what. But he was praying his old pack wouldn't want a war with the St. Clair Pack. "Jacob Kross is my alpha now."

"I don't see him around to stick up for you, freak

boy." The other wolf's voice was abrasive as a saw blade cutting metal. "And I'm not paid to give a damn about that anyway. So if you value that little abomination growing in your fat belly, you'll get in the back of the car all nice nice. Or I'll punch you in the gut and shoot you later."

All defiance drained out of Henry immediately. The thug grabbed him by the arm and dragged him toward the waiting car. Henry was praying that Tom's truck would come racing down the street and his lover would save him. But there was no sign of Tom as Henry was shoved into the back of the sedan. The thug got in the back next to him and slammed the door. The automatic locks *thunked*. The stranger pulled his pistol now that he was concealed by the tinted windows. He kept it low but pointed at Henry.

Not that the pistol was necessary or Henry could do anything. His fear for his child kept him paralyzed, unable to do anything but keep quiet and obey their demands. Another shifter—this one a bear shifter— was sitting behind the wheel. He was huge, with arms like tree trunks. He backed the car up and casually drove away without a word.

Mercenaries then. They were working for Carson. He must not want to risk using wolves from the Metro Pack to clean up this "problem." Or he didn't want to leave proof that the St. Clair Wolves could find and start a war.

Henry knew he was so screwed.

They didn't drive him downtown or to Carson's mansion or condo like he half expected. They didn't bother to blindfold him or even to bind his hands. It showed how little they feared him.

They drove him to a private airport in New Detroit, swinging wide to an entrance in the back fence, far from the runway. The car rolled up to a large helicopter sitting near a hangar. Two more dangerous-looking men were standing by the helicopter, and there was already a pilot inside, even though the blades weren't turning.

His stomach felt as if it dropped into his feet. He knew what they meant to do. He closed his eyes, not wanting to cry in front of them. He didn't want to give them the satisfaction.

The thug in the back dragged him out of the car. His big hand was clamped around Henry's arm so tightly it sent pulses of pain through him. "Move."

Henry moved. What other choice did he have?

One of the shifters by the helicopter—a cat shifter, by his scent, a leopard—watched him with cruel, arrogant eyes. He had a cell phone to his ear, but as Henry approached, he handed the cell phone to him.

"Someone wants to say hi," the cat shifter said in a mockingly friendly voice.

Henry took the phone in shaking hands. He lifted it to his ear. "Who is this?" he tried to demand, but his voice came out more like a mouse squeak.

"Henry, my little omega," Eddie Carson said. "I hear you've betrayed me and joined another pack."

"Betrayed you?" Raw outrage gave his voice strength. "You tried to fucking kill me! You killed Max! You kicked me out of your pack!"

Carson chuckled. "Wild accusations and unfounded allegations. But don't worry. You'll be taking a helicopter ride back to your home. That's right. Back to Old Detroit."

Henry didn't say anything because he couldn't. The crashing wave of fear had stolen every word from his mind. The helpless despair he felt seemed to hollow him out.

All he'd wanted to do was find Tom and tell him that he loved him, that he needed him. And now this...

"Don't worry," Carson continued in a jolly tone of voice. "I've hired some capable *friends* to look after you. I wouldn't piss them off, though. They might feed you to the lagodire even though I've made it clear that would make me quite cross."

"What do you want? I don't have anything for you. Why can't you leave me alone?"

"First, I don't want anything from you. I want something from the wolf who knocked you up. And no, you don't get to be left alone. No one walks away from my pack. I'm still your alpha."

"No, you're not. You'll never be my alpha again."

"Not for long, anyway, so I suppose that in a way, you're right. Goodbye."

The call disconnected. Henry lowered the cell phone, staring at it lying in his shaking hand.

The cat shifter snatched the phone back and signaled the pilot. The pilot began flipping switches in the helicopter cockpit. The rotor blades began to turn.

They dragged him to the helicopter. He couldn't fight them. He couldn't run. He was terrified and, at the same time, completely numb, as if he wasn't really in control of his body right now. Over and over again, he kept thinking of how this was like last time. The last time they'd thrown him into Old Detroit to die.

Only this time, he had a child inside him.

CHAPTER SIXTEEN

Tom had never known what people meant when they said something like "he left his heart" somewhere. Left his heart in his hometown. Left his heart in the South. Left his heart with his family. Stuff like that.

He'd never been a person to look backward. He always looked forward. He didn't go all tormented and broody about what his old wolf pack and alpha had done to him. He didn't complain about the risks his life choices forced him to make. He looked forward. His heart was always in the future. Maybe you could even say he was chasing the future. Or he had been chasing it, because now he *knew* where his heart was.

He'd left his heart with Henry Wright.

He was in his truck, on his way back from Cleveland. The radio was blasting, but it didn't help keep his thoughts off Henry. He felt hollow inside as he cruised down I90, headed back home. His truck had needed a new battery, so that had delayed him. The battery had been DOA when he'd finally got his ass out to the private airfield in Cleveland near the lake.

His mind kept returning to his little omega. The wolf who owned his heart. It couldn't be denied, so he didn't waste his breath trying. There wasn't an hour that he was awake that he didn't think about Henry. Having him and losing him again only sharpened that even more. And having Carson sniffing around yesterday...that made Tom want to go to war to protect his mate and his child.

Tom had always been something of a loner. He wasn't afraid to keep his own company. Sure, he'd had lovers. They came and went. He was still friends with a few of them. But no one had stolen his heart like Henry had.

It was love. Why waste time denying it? Every moment since he'd walked out on Henry had been one of heartache. And it wasn't only the heat of desire. No, it was the intimacy, both emotional and physical. It was the friendship. The caring. The connection. Simply, it was love.

Could he ever walk away from that? Even if he felt betrayed when Henry signed on the dotted line with another damned pack, could Tom walk away from the omega?

No. But maybe there was a better question to ask. Could he love a wolf who belonged to a pack? How could he trust that Henry's loyalties wouldn't be divided between Tom and his alpha? How could he make sure his son grew up believing in free will and equality?

His hands clenched on the steering wheel. It wasn't that simple, though, was it? Because Henry had said he would leave the pack for Tom, and that was no small thing. But he wanted something in return. He wanted Tom to stop his runs into Old Detroit.

How could he do that? It was the only way Tom was able to make enough money to keep food on the table and a roof overhead. He didn't know how to do anything else. His runs were dangerous, but he was good.

Damn it. How could he feel guilty about not giving Henry the one thing he'd ever asked for? Hell, Henry's life had been upended so many times already. Was it wrong for the omega to want some stability, some protection, some reassurance that he wouldn't suffer anymore? That's what had driven him into the arms of the St. Clair Pack. Tom had been in jail, and Henry needed protection. As much as he might want to, he couldn't blame the omega for doing what he needed to do.

But that was in the past. Tom wanted to make a family with Henry and their son. He wasn't afraid of that challenge. But he feared not being able to provide for them and keep them safe.

Of course, he couldn't do that dead, could he? And parachuting into Old Detroit to scavenge jewelry and valuables wasn't exactly safe, was it? Hell, he couldn't even get life insurance.

Maybe it was time to hang up his spurs. Retire from this dangerous life. Henry had a point. Tom didn't want their son to grow up without him—either dead or in prison. The more he thought about it, the more the possibility stirred a deep fear inside him.

At first, he'd accepted that he'd gotten Henry pregnant, accepted the dramatic change in his life because he'd come to love the omega. Not only from the night they'd shared together—the night that had given them their son—but from all their conversations through countless letters. Old-fashioned, yeah, but surprisingly effective.

Yet the pack loyalty had been the issue to destroy their relationship. Or maybe that was making it too simple. Because Henry had certainly kept plenty of things secret. It made sense in a way. The omega had been betrayed and hurt in the past by people he trusted. He'd lost the human he'd once loved. Tom could forgive the lies as long as Henry would work with him to find a real, honest trust together. No more lies. No more fear.

To give Henry that, Tom would need to stop his Old Detroit runs. No matter how much he might fear a future without that cash flow, or how much a crazy part of him would miss the adrenaline and danger, he needed to do it. If he wanted a family, if he wanted love, he needed to make a sacrifice.

That was it then. He had reached a decision, and he wasn't even home yet. He would grab a shower, scarf down a frozen dinner, and make the trip out to that alpha bastard's mansion and tell Henry he was done with Old Detroit for good. He was done with his old life. He wanted a new life with Henry. With their son.

Soon, he exited the freeway and made his way through the side streets to his quiet neighborhood. He slowed and scanned the street for Carson's Rolls Royce or any other strange car. But there was nothing out of the ordinary. No street-parked cars at all.

Still...he didn't feel secure. He probably wouldn't for a long time. That bastard Carson had gotten under his skin, showing up here.

He parked the truck in his driveway, scanning his house for anything out of the ordinary. But there was nothing.

Tom got out and headed for the front door. He

was glad to be carrying a weapon. Just in case there was—

He froze. A cheap, generic cell phone sat on the top step in front of his door. He stared at it, feeling ice water rushing through his veins. There was a sticky note on the back of the phone.

He glanced around his neighborhood again. Again, he saw nothing out of the ordinary, and he wasn't picking up any scents that raised the hair on his neck.

But clearly, someone had been here, and clearly, they had left this for him.

He picked up the phone and looked at the note. The message was simple. A phone number and the word *"call."*

He picked the phone up and dialed the number with fingers that felt stiff and unwieldy. His heartbeat was a dull, thudding rhythm. Someone answered on the second ring.

"Tom," Eddie Carson said. "I assume you recognize my voice. It hasn't been long since we chatted."

"What do you want, Carson?"

"Now, now. No names. I like being careful."

"Don't waste my time more than you already have."

"I have something that belongs to you."

Dread rushed through him. His first instinct was

that Carson meant Henry. But Henry was safe at Kross's mansion. So it had to be something else.

"Don't play around with me. What do you have, and what do you want?"

"I want my…package. The one I hired you to find."

The Lumiere Soleil diamond necklace. He should've known Carson would never let that go.

"I told you. I don't have it."

"And I told you, I want you to get it. To inspire you, I took your sweet, pregnant omega. So that means I also have your son."

His blood went colder than any stream of snowmelt. He almost crushed the small plastic cell phone in his hand as fear for Henry and his son surged inside him within a storm cloud of pure rage.

"I should kill you."

"I might actually believe you could…if you had a pack behind you. Since you don't, let's talk about our deal. You get the diamond. I give you back the omega and your son. Easy."

"I want to speak to Henry."

"That's a bit tough. Right now, Henry's in Old Detroit. Cell reception there is iffy. Don't worry. I have him somewhere safe. Way up high, where he can't be someone's snack. So he will be fine…probably. The mercenaries I hired aren't very nice, but I don't think they're into pregnant men. Then again, maybe they are kinky that way. Guess you'd better hurry and find my diamond necklace."

"You fucking bastard." He could barely speak. He could feel his inner wolf surging to the forefront, demanding he shift and find the alpha to rip out his throat. "You're gonna pay for that."

"That's unlikely. You can't even look after your own. They tell me they snatched him right from your doorstep. Imagine that. You left him all alone and vulnerable. Sadly, you weren't there to save him."

What the hell had Henry been doing here? He didn't think Henry had ever been here. Hell, he didn't think the omega had the remotest idea of what his address was. Yeah, Tom had mentioned the house in a few letters. Had that been enough for Henry to track it down? But why in God's name would he come here alone?

Unless he had left the St. Clair Pack. Unless he'd left them because Tom wanted him to…

He felt like someone had kicked him in the balls with a steel-toed boot. The guilt stole his breath away completely. It was like being buried by an avalanche, crushing him. Freezing him.

"If I get that damned diamond, you'll let Henry go?"

"Of course. You have my word."

"How do I know you won't just throw him off the building? Or feed him to the lagodire again?"

"You don't. But you don't have much choice either. Trust is such an exciting thing, isn't it?"

Tom didn't say anything. He couldn't. He hated feeling helpless. He hated having the omega he loved and his child in danger. It was nearly driving him into a mindless rage, but he knew he needed to keep his wits about him if he was going to have any hope of bringing Henry home safely.

"I'll take your silence as consent," the alpha said. "Keep this phone and use it to contact me after you have what I want. I recommend you work fast."

The cell phone went dead. It took all of Tom's self-control not to crush it into broken plastic.

He closed his eyes, breathing deeply, isolating the fear and the rage and cutting them loose. Strong emotions would only get in the way right now.

He unlocked his front door and pushed his way inside. He needed gear, weapons, and supplies. He needed a plane that could fly over Old Detroit so he could parachute into the city. He needed it all ASAP.

Jacob Kross was his first choice. The wealthy alpha had to own a private jet or something. Or he could hire a private plane on a second's notice.

Besides, the alpha had some explaining to do. Like why the fuck he had let Henry out alone. Henry was supposed to be part of Kross's pack. All other controlling bullshit aside, packs were supposed to keep their wolves safe. Kross knew that Henry had once been part of the Metro Wolves...and that Eddie Carson had tried to kill him. So why had this happened?

In no time, he'd packed up everything he needed for another run into Old Detroit. His spare parachutes and skydiving gear. Energy bars. Canteens. A new pistol with another illegal sound suppressor to replace the one he'd lost. Ammo. A first aid kid. He would need it all if he was going to pull this off.

After that, he set out for Jacob Kross's mansion— the last place he had seen Henry. He drove on autopilot, barely seeing the traffic around him, barely paying attention to it because his thoughts were centered on Henry and their unborn child like a spotlight. He was so twisted up with worry and rage that he could barely think. He could barely breathe. His heart felt like a motor running too fast but at the same time getting him nowhere.

When he arrived at the mansion, he didn't bother pushing the button at the gate to call the house. He simply shut off the truck's engine, put it in park, got out, and climbed over the huge gate. Nothing was going to keep him out.

He ran up the long driveway. He was barely breathing hard by the time he reached the house. The bodyguards had been closing in on him, but they stopped when they recognized him. One of them spoke into a headset earpiece.

He ignored them and ran up the front steps to the big double doors. He didn't bother ringing the doorbell. He wasn't feeling particularly civilized. Instead, he pounded on the door so hard it shook in its frame.

"Kross! Get out here! *Now!*"

He stepped back and began to pace, waiting for the alpha to respond. The bodyguards eyed him warily but didn't come close. They stayed a dozen meters away. That was good. For them.

He was about to pound on the door again—or maybe kick it in—when the right-side door swung inward. Jacob Kross stood there, still wearing one of those damned designer suits he liked so much. If Tom never had to wear another suit in his life, it would be too soon. He was nothing like this other wolf.

Nothing like him.

Kross watched him with cold blue eyes. The intensity of that alpha stare would've been enough to make other wolves back off. But not Tom. He didn't give a damn. He wasn't afraid of any alpha. And he wanted answers.

He let his teeth show in a snarl. Kross's eyes narrowed. He didn't invite Tom inside, but his scent was...concerned.

"Tom," the alpha finally said. "I was about to call—"

"Were you now? I find that convenient. Because

I'm here to ask why the fuck you let Henry leave. He was one of your fucking pack. Or doesn't that count for anything?"

Gavin appeared at the alpha's side. His big eyes were full of deepening concern. He was rubbing a hand across his mouth and jaw while his other arm hugged tight to his body. The worry from the other omega dampened some of Tom's fury. It wasn't worry because of Tom. It had to be worry over Henry.

"Henry left a note…" Gavin said, his voice not quite steady. "He went to see you. I came home with Ryan, and Henry was gone. Duncan saw him leave the house. But he thought Henry was going for a walk like he does all the time. No one thought… Tom, tell me he's with you."

Tom felt like a jagged piece of metal had lodged in his throat, making it nearly impossible to get the words out. "He's not with me. That bastard Eddie Carson has him." He shoved his hand in his pocket and pulled out the cheap cell phone left for him on his front step. "Carson talked to me on this. I found it on my doorstep. He told me he has Henry and our child somewhere in Old Detroit."

Gavin closed his eyes, his face going pale. All hope seemed to drain out of him as he sagged against Kross. The alpha kept a protective arm around Gavin, but his eyes flashed, and his jaw muscles bulged because he was gritting his teeth so hard. "Come inside. We need to talk."

Kross turned and headed deeper into the mansion, moving with furious strides. Gavin had to nearly jog to keep up with him.

Tom followed inside and shut the door, glancing around as more bodyguards from the St. Clair Pack made themselves visible. Big wolves that he knew were armed. He wasn't intimidated. Right now, he felt like he could tear his way through an entire pack if it meant getting to Henry and their unborn child.

He followed Jacob Kross and Gavin into a private study. Kross held the door for him, gesturing him to a seat.

"I'll stand," Tom snarled.

Kross only nodded. He moved behind a huge desk and sat on the edge. Gavin moved to the window, staring out the glass toward the lake. Every line of him told his anguish.

That anguish soothed Tom a little—or at least told him he didn't need to see these two as enemies. He hated everything about packs and distrusted them completely, but it was clear Gavin cared deeply for Henry. Kross must care at least a little as well, especially if he took his duty as alpha seriously. So Tom needed to be calmer. These two could be powerful allies. Right now, he would do anything he needed to do to get Henry and his son back safely.

Anything.

"There have been rumors about Eddie Carson and the Metro Wolves for years," Kross said, his expression grim. "It was nothing I could act on as head of the council. Each pack is responsible for itself and its own justice—within reason. We must obey the Accords, but there is plenty of maneuvering room even in the shifter laws."

"I don't give a damn about pack politics bullshit," Tom said savagely. "Henry wasn't with me because of you. He chose your pack over me." That wasn't exactly true, but he didn't want to waste a lot of time and breath over a lot of blurry details. He wanted *action*, damn it. "So that means you were responsible for protecting him and my son. You failed. Now, you're going to help me get him back."

Gavin surprised him by answering. "Of course we will, Tom. Anything you need. He's part of our family too."

The alpha gave a rueful smile. "My omega beat me to the punch again." He locked eyes with Tom. "But you're right. I failed Henry. From what we can piece together from security cameras and browsing history, he hired a cab to pick him up past the gate. His note was for Gavin. Henry left to talk to you, and clearly, it was very important. We were trying to find a way to touch base with you and make sure he arrived safely, the situation being what it is."

"He showed up at my house. That's where

Carson's hired thugs kidnapped him."

"What is Carson after?" Kross asked. "Not Henry. Not directly. Or he wouldn't have called you on some throwaway phone."

"He wants me to go back into Old Detroit. He wants me to get him the damned diamond necklace he has such a hard-on for. If I do, he says he'll let Henry go."

Kross's eyes narrowed. "Do you trust him?"

"No. Not even close. He already tried to kill Henry once. He dangled Henry in front of the lagodire like a chew toy. Carson has blood on his hands already. He killed a human—someone Henry loved before I was on the scene. Hell, Henry is a witness and a victim. Even if I give Carson what he wants, he won't let Henry go." Tom gave a bitter smile. "He can't risk it. Henry might mess up his business empire. Or make him look bad in front of the precious council."

"I was thinking the same thing," Kross said. "Carson would deny that he has Henry. That's part of the reason he's keeping Henry in Old Detroit and using hired thugs this time around. But make no mistake, this is an act of war against the St. Clair Pack."

"I'm not part of your damned pack," Tom said. "I'm going to get Henry and my son back. That's all I care about. But you're going to help me do it. I need a plane to fly me over Old Detroit. I'll take things from there."

Gavin's eyes went wide. "You're going alone?"

"I always go alone. That's how I run."

"You can't land a plane in Old Detroit anymore. Carson must have used a helicopter to get over the walls and inside the city—"

"I don't need a helicopter to get in. I need a plane to fly as close to the ruins as possible. I'll jump out of the plane and parachute down. I do it all the time. So get me a plane."

"So you're going to give Carson his diamond? He'll betray you once you have it. Just like you said."

"I'm not giving him any diamond," Tom said coldly. "I'm going to rescue Henry and kill anyone who tries to stop me."

"How are you going to get out?" Gavin asked.

"I've been thinking about that. It's where you come in again. You hire a helicopter and fly us off the roof. I'm not swimming out under the walls. Once was enough. And he's too pregnant."

Kross was frowning, but it looked as if he was carefully considering the idea. "I have some contacts in the military. I can pull some strings, call in a lot of favors, and arrange to get a helicopter through restricted airspace. The plane flight would be relatively easy. But I don't want you going alone."

"Too bad. That's how I work. Relying on other

people will only get me killed. Besides, if a wolf relies on a pack, there's always a debt to pay. I owe you enough already."

"No debts," Gavin said. "We care about Henry. He's our friend. Part of our family."

"He's part of the pack," Kross added with a fierce nod. "I failed to protect him. I failed you. And I failed your unborn son. I need to make this right. If Carson and the Metro Pack want a war, then we will give him what he wants. Carson will pay for this."

Tom wasn't going to admit it, but what Kross said touched him. It almost made him feel the way he'd felt back in the 82nd Airborne when you could count on the soldier at your back, and everyone worked together for the mission.

"Going in with a bunch of wolves at once is too dangerous in Old Detroit," Tom said slowly, mulling it over. "It will draw too much attention on the ground, meaning we'll have to deal with hordes of lagodire. If you try a helicopter assault on the roof, they could kill Henry and fight you off before you could land or drop people on the building. No. It's too dangerous."

"You have another plan?" There was no challenge in the alpha's voice, just a willingness to hear him out as if Tom was an equal.

He liked that too.

"Yeah. I parachute in at night. It's quiet. I land,

take out the mercs guarding Henry, and once the rooftop is secure, I call for extraction."

"Do you know what building roof they're holding him on?" Gavin asked quietly.

"Carson didn't say specifically. But it has to be a high rooftop. There aren't that many skyscrapers. And they'll probably have lights where they camp. Even if they don't. I can use infrared to find them."

"You need to know before you jump," Kross said. "You won't have time to locate them on the way down. I'll handle this. Like I said, I have some friends in the military. I can get some real-time drone camera footage if I call in the right favors. That will tell us what building they're hiding on."

Tom nodded, his hope rising inside him. That intelligence could make all the difference in the world. He was actually grateful. But out of pure principle, he wasn't about to let this alpha know he was grateful.

"So we're going to work together. Fine. I'll take your help because it helps Henry." He glanced at Gavin. "And because I believe you really do care about him. But when I get him out, I'm not joining your pack…and I'm not going to owe you a damned thing for this. You're not my alpha and never will be. Make no mistake. I'll never serve another."

A smirk appeared on Kross's face. "I think you've made that abundantly clear. I respect that." He took a deep breath and looked Tom in the eyes. "Thank you for letting my pack help in the rescue."

That surprised him so much that he groped for a reply. "You're thanking me?"

"Of course. I know your feelings about packs. Gavin told me it has complicated your relationship between you and Henry. We care about Henry, and we care about your child. You can choose whether to believe my words or not, but I intend to show you through our actions. So, yes, I'm thanking you. If Henry stays a member of the St. Clair Pack or whether he leaves us for a different future with you, it doesn't matter. Because he will always be family."

Tom felt a surge of relief and gratitude swelling inside him that he suddenly had to choke back down. He didn't want to give this alpha any leverage over him...although it seemed like he had misjudged the wolf. Jacob Kross wasn't like any alpha Tom had ever met.

But it didn't matter. Because right now, all he cared about was saving Henry and their son.

"All right," Tom said. "That's settled." He jerked his thumb over his shoulder in a vague direction behind him. "My truck's at the gate. It has my gear and guns. Let's get this ball rolling. I intend to make my move tonight." His eyes narrowed. "Can you pull that off on your end?"

"We'll make it happen," Kross said. He pulled out his smartphone. "If you'll excuse me, I need to alert the pack and call in a lot of favors. Get yourself ready to go. It's going to be a long night."

Tom nodded. He and the alpha shared a moment, staring at each other. Respect maybe. Understanding. Or even just a truce. Whatever it was, Tom felt relieved that Kross was using his power to help. That raised the odds in their favor. But Tom would've done this whether the St. Clair Pack decided to help or not.

Henry needed him. His child needed him. He would never fail them.

Tonight, Tom was going back to Old Detroit with a plan. A crazy one, but it technically qualified as a plan.

He would be leaving the ruins with Henry and their child safe in his arms…or he wouldn't be leaving at all.

CHAPTER SEVENTEEN

The moon was fat and beautiful. Henry had been watching as it curved its way across the sky. There were clouds to the west but none overhead. The stars were pinpricks of light in the dark sky. Around him was the constant rush of wind. This high up, you couldn't escape the wind. It roared and moaned and buffeted you constantly.

He was handcuffed, but that was all. No gags, no blindfold, and no leg irons. His captors had cuffed him to the camp chair at first...but then they kept having to free him so he could pee. That got old for them. Besides...it was a camp chair. Not exactly very solid and heavy.

So they made a lot of threats about throwing him

off the skyscraper if he pissed them off and cuffed his hands together instead of cuffing him to a folding canvas chair frame. All so he could pee and leave them in peace.

Henry was on top of the tallest building in Old Detroit. He'd never been up here, even in all his days trapped in the ruins. All of downtown to the riverfront was infested with lagodire and warring clans and packs. This building—he didn't know its name—was in the center of four shorter skyscraper buildings arranged symmetrically around it. One of those buildings had partially collapsed during the fires. It had fallen and smashed into the side of another building. Now it leaned against the other like a drunken man being helped along by a friend. Henry could hear the metal ominously creaking and groaning in the wind.

He'd been here on this rooftop where the wind never stopped for what seemed like forever. Johnny and Mikey B., the two mercenaries who had driven him to the helicopter, were sitting on camp chairs with two other shifters. Another wolf called Reed and a cat shifter named Brad. Johnny the Wolf, Brad the Kitty, Reed the Other Wolf, and finally Mikey B. the Bear. Did B stand for bear? He didn't know.

Johnny walked over from the makeshift camp. He was smoking a cigarette. The tip glowed red as he drew on it. The wind tore away the smoke and shredded it into nothing. He loomed over Henry, leaning in close, staring at him.

"Can you *not* smoke around me?" Henry said. "I'm pregnant if you hadn't noticed."

Johnny leaned in even closer, took a long drag, and blew smoke right in his face. Except it didn't really work. The wind instantly blew it all away. That seemed to piss Johnny off.

"I hope you fucking choke, freak." He reached out and flicked Henry's nose hard.

His nose stung, and his eyes watered. It was such a stupid assault. Something a little kid would do. He couldn't even be mad. Well...not *that* mad.

Johnny laughed and paced off. The other mercs were sitting in camp chairs together, drinking beers from a big cooler they'd brought off the helicopter. There was no fire, but there were a few camp lanterns and some supply crates they were using as a windbreak. They had put Henry off in his own chair a dozen or so meters away from theirs. Close enough to watch, but not close enough to annoy them. Or to remind them why they were here tonight.

But Johnny kept getting up and pacing the rooftop. Or the inner part of the rooftop. It was a strange roof. The center circle was raised up at least ten feet and surrounded by tons of antennas around the edge but no barrier or railing. That was down a level. Henry had no idea why they were up here where the wind was the worst. Maybe because this was where the helicopter dumped them?

Johnny would stand at the edge, the tips of his boots hanging over as he stared at the huge wall that surrounded the city, cutting the ruins off from the world. Then he would walk back for another beer, exchange a few words with the other mercs, and set off pacing again. He was clearly agitated, and that made Henry uneasy.

From listening in, Henry thought Johnny the Wolf was nothing more than a greedy and cruel thug. You could smell it on him.

There was a seventy, maybe seventy-five percent chance that Brad the Kitty was psychotic. He was cold and arrogant and smelled ruthless beyond compare. His scent was always the same—very little change in emotion. No real anger. No joy. He was the scariest of the mercs who guarded him.

Henry couldn't get a good sense of Reed the Other Wolf. He mostly kept to himself. Drank beer like a thirsty fish. Mikey B. the Bear was the biggest of them all, with huge shoulders and slabs of muscle, but he was easily ordered around by the others. Still, Mikey seemed like the kindest of these four mercenaries. Mikey at least brought him water and asked if he needed a blanket against the wind.

Nothing much had happened since the helicopter departed. The helicopter had touched its three wheels down on the roof of the center skyscraper. They were maybe seventy or so stories above the streets and away from the lagodire. But it wasn't a helicopter pad, so the pilot had ordered them off with the helicopter blades still spinning while cursing the crosswinds the entire time. The four mercs had dragged him off along with their supplies. The helicopter had immediately zoomed off again, veering a little in the crosswinds, and flew back over the water toward New Detroit.

Since then, it had been nothing but waiting. They weren't the first ones up here either. There was an exterior elevator, but it was barricaded and didn't have any power anyway. There were already camp chairs up here. On the level ledge below, there were tents that had blown over at some point. There was even a little portable grill with propane. He could smell that it had been used before.

How many times had Alpha Eddie Carson used this crude rooftop camp? How many "problems" had he dumped here? Henry knew Carson paid bribes to people in the military to let the helicopter violate the restricted airspace. He knew because he overheard the nervous pilot's radio chatter on the way out here. That corruption made him feel even worse in some ways. He knew the Metro Pack was bad—not everyone there, of course, but a fish rotted from the head, right? How many of his former packmates had ever wondered where their pack's omega had vanished to?

How many turned a blind eye to their alpha's corruption and violence?

They are afraid. Like you were afraid.

He understood that better than anyone. That was one of the reasons he admired Tom so much. Tom wasn't afraid. He was the bravest person Henry had ever met. He wished with all his heart that he could be more like the lone wolf. Right now, he was trying his best. He was trying to be brave for their child.

Because even his captors were afraid. He could smell their fear whenever they were close. They were afraid of the lagodire. They were afraid of being abandoned and trapped in the ruins with no hope of escape.

Henry had no pity for them. They had made their decisions. He'd made his own. And if some of Henry's decisions had been mistakes, he knew Tom would forgive him for it. Henry's heart was simply bigger than his brain. He'd chosen the wrong time in life to get brave and make changes. But his heart had been in the right place. They could write that on his tombstone.

No. Hold on to your hope. You have friends now. You have someone who loves you. Someone strong and brave, who already proved himself a hundred times over.

He had Tom, the father of the precious life growing inside him.

He put his handcuffed hands on his belly and

hummed a soft song to their son. He looked up at the moon. He thought about a children's book about saying goodnight to the moon that he wanted to read to his son for bed. He looked forward to that—bedtime stories. He looked forward to so much with his son...

He needed to stay strong. He couldn't fight these shifters. He wasn't strong enough even when he hadn't been pregnant and super-sized. But he would do everything he could to keep his child safe. He owed it to his baby, and he owed it to Tom.

Johnny wandered back over. He couldn't seem to stay away. Henry could smell the anger smoldering inside him. It stank like an electrical fire.

"I hope you're happy, you little freak," Johnny snarled. "Your kind never learns your lesson."

"What lesson is that?" He didn't want to know. But he didn't want Johnny to hit him until he replied either.

"That abominations like you need to die."

Abominations. It was such an ugly term but so absurdly over the top. "All shifters were created in a government lab. So I guess we all have a bit of the freak inside. And I guess we all need to die, according to you."

He usually wasn't so bold. Pissing off a wolf like Johnny was insane. But he was so tired of being called a freak and an abomination. He only wanted what everyone else wanted. To be happy. To find some love and some friends. To have healthy children and the joy, tears, and challenge of raising them, of making a family. He couldn't help what he was. He didn't know why people hated him for something he couldn't change, but he was so very tired of it.

"That mealy-mouthed talk is so typical of the weak. We aren't even close to the same, you little shit. Everything about you disgusts me." Johnny squatted down and pulled a folding knife from his pocket. With one hand, he opened it. The blade gleamed in the moonlight. "You're weak. You're a freak. You don't even like pussy. I want to get your stink out of my nose. All that fear turns my stomach even more than looking at you."

He moved the knife closer, resting the tip on the cloth of Henry's shirt, right near his belly button. Henry froze, not daring to breathe. Afraid? Yes, he was terrified again. He should've kept his mouth shut. Provoking Johnny was a very bad idea.

"Oh, nothing to say now? I thought so. You're a little cowardly shit, aren't you?" Johnny leaned even closer, smiling sweetly. "I'll let you in on a secret. You'd better grow yourself some wings real quick. Because the rest of us, we're flying out on the helicopter. You? You're flying out a different way."

Henry's blood froze in his veins. He could only stare at the other wolf in dread. It wasn't a surprise.

Deep down, he'd guessed as much. After all, Henry was a threat to Carson and his position with the New Detroit Wolf Council. Jake Kross was head of that council. Kross knew everything, and Carson had to know that, but without Henry there to give testimony, there would never be any consequences for an alpha. Especially if they left his body in Old Detroit. No one would ever know Henry's bones were any different from the thousands who had died when the city fell to the lagodire.

"Hey, Johnny," Mikey B. called, walking over to them. "Go sit down and have a beer. Stop messing with that omega."

"Why the hell should I? It's fun."

Mikey B. snorted, pulling up short and putting his big fists on his hips as he stared at Henry. Then he threw a sidelong glance at Johnny. "People are gonna think you like omega tail if you keep going over to him."

"Fuck you, Mikey." Johnny turned and backhanded Henry so hard the world spun wildly. Mikey B. was far bigger and heavier than Johnny, so apparently, Johnny was going to take out his rage over having his sexuality questioned on Henry. Wonderful. "I'm gonna gut this freak. That's what I'm gonna *like*."

Henry's heart was pounding. He could taste blood. His head was still spinning from the blow, and his cheek felt like it was on fire. He didn't say anything. He didn't dare look at Johnny for fear of provoking him. He'd wanted to believe he'd become braver after Tom, braver for his child. But that wasn't the case, was it? He still felt all the fear—maybe even more—but now it was fear for the safety of his baby.

"Stop being a psycho and come play some poker. Texas hold 'em. Nothing else to do, so why don't you let me take all your money?"

Johnny made a sound of contempt in his throat. "The fucking wind blows the cards everywhere."

"So try holding on to 'em for once. Now, you coming, or what?"

Johnny stood and started back toward the chairs and small camp table the other shifters were sitting around. "I'm going to kick your ass this time."

"Yeah. Yeah," Mikey said. He turned his gaze on Henry. Those eyes glittered in the moonlight. They weren't kind, but they weren't nearly as hateful as Johnny's. "You need anything?"

"I'd like…some paper and a pen. To write a letter. And maybe a lantern?"

"Who the fuck writes letters?" Despite the harsh language, Mikey's words were more baffled than angry or confrontational.

"I do. I like it."

"Whatever." The bear shifter shook his large head. "We didn't bring paper. I don't think we have pens. So you're out of luck."

"Seems to be a lot of that going around lately."

"Yeah. I hear you." Mikey B. turned and began to walk away. He glanced back over his shoulder. "Let me know if you need to take another piss."

Henry watched him go, letting out a long, shuddering breath, glad to be left alone. Especially glad that Johnny wasn't close anymore. Henry was going to be safe. For now, at least.

His unborn child turned and kicked inside him, stirred up by all the adrenaline and stress in Henry's body. Henry put his handcuffed hands on his belly again, trying to give what comfort he could. He took another risk and began to hum softly to his child, songs he'd known all his life.

The mercenaries left him alone, playing their game of poker, their harsh faces lit by the glow of the electric lanterns. Henry watched the moon and thought of Tom. He thought of his child, of their family, and their future.

Tears quietly ran down his cheeks, but he kept humming his soothing tunes, his hands on his belly as he watched the moon, wondering if Tom saw it too.

CHAPTER EIGHTEEN

Tom Reinhart stared down at the dark swath of Old Detroit ruins. There were plenty of lights on the Canadian side of the border. A huge sea of lights south of Lake Erie. New Detroit stretching from Toledo to Cleveland was a carpet of jewels.

He was standing in the back of a plane, heavy with gear. He had his parachute. His weapons. Some food, some water. Handheld metal cutters in case they'd handcuffed or chained Henry to something. A knife in case he had to cut through duct tape or rope. And the most important thing aside from his pistol: a high-powered radio receiver that would let him call in the helicopter for a rescue.

He had never been so on edge in his life, so

frustrated, so desperate to go. To do something. To save his omega and their child. No pain compared to the torture of waiting helplessly while someone you loved was in danger.

He'd needed to rely on others for the first time in forever to pull this off. At least since leaving the military. No, that wasn't exactly true. Because he had relied on Kross once already, hadn't he? For the lawyers that had won him that hung jury and kept his ass out of prison.

This was getting to be a disturbing habit.

Whatever. It didn't matter. He needed to do what he needed to do. And there was nothing he wouldn't do for Henry and for their son.

The door in the back of the plane was open. Wind beat at him as he stood there gripping a handle on the fuselage and looking out at the darkness of Old Detroit. The moon was full. The roar of the wind and the plane engines drowned out all other sounds.

He was waiting for his cue to jump. More waiting, but this was better than the earlier frustration of relying on Kross to arrange all the parts of this plan that Tom couldn't. Kross had called in his "soldiers," the strongest, most loyal wolves of the St. Clair Pack. He'd arranged for a plane Tom could parachute out of, securing clearance through restricted airspace. Tom had no idea how the alpha had pulled it off—either with money or influence—but it was amazing. Every other time Tom had parachuted into Old Detroit, the planes he'd hired had been forced to stay out of restricted airspace, which meant he needed to "fly" himself into the city and over the walls while skydiving.

On top of that, Kross had scrambled to get his company helicopter standing by for the last phase of the rescue. The exfiltration. The trip home again. Assuming Tom could find Henry, deal with his captors, and send the signal.

It wouldn't be easy, but he did have a few advantages. Again, thanks to Kross. He was going to owe that bastard so much after this. But he didn't care. He'd sell his soul to any alpha that would help him rescue Henry.

One advantage was that Tom knew exactly where they were keeping Henry, all because of Kross's contacts with the human military. It was extremely valuable intelligence. A military drone patrolling the skies, making sure the lagodire didn't try escaping the walls, had spotted a helicopter violating restricted airspace. The helicopter had dropped off five people onto a cluster of buildings in Old Detroit—the Renaissance Center central skyscraper—and flew off again like a bat out of hell. Other high-resolution camera shots, including infrared, showed a small camp set up on the roof.

Now Tom had a target location, and he knew how

many enemies he faced. Four mercenary shifters. He was outnumbered, but surprise would be the key. Kross had offered to send a helicopter in with the pack's strongest wolf shifters to back Tom up, but that was too dangerous. The mercenaries would hear the helicopter approaching. They might kill Henry before there was a chance to rescue him. Tom didn't want vengeance. He wanted Henry and his son, safe in his arms again. That was his only goal. Nothing must endanger that.

So his plan was simple, as the best ones needed to be. Simple, but it did have a downside. It was highly dangerous.

Tom would parachute into the city, landing on the top of the seventy story skyscraper. That wouldn't be easy with the cross-currents of air rushing up the sides of the buildings. At least the wind would help cover the sound of the parachute flapping or snagging on something. Tom would pull his pistol and remove the mercenary threat. Once the area was secure, he'd free Henry and call in Kross's rescue chopper. Simple but not easy. So much could go wrong. But he was determined to make everything go right. By sheer force of will, if necessary.

They were across the water and over the city now. He glanced down the plane's interior, waiting on his signal. It came moments later. A St. Clair Pack wolf named Chris pointed at him and gave him the thumbs up.

Tom nodded and turned back to the door. He positioned himself and pushed off, falling forward and away from the plane so the tail wouldn't hit him.

The rush of freefall was like nothing else in the world. The rush of the wind. The ground racing up to meet you. The incredible, breathtaking speed. It wasn't like flying, but it was definitely falling with style.

He spread his arms and legs out, keeping himself horizontal. He could see the cluster of buildings with the tall skyscraper in the center, not far from the water and the wall. The pilot had gotten him far closer to the city than he'd ever been before.

His deploy shoot altitude alarm went off, and he pulled the ripcord. There was always that sudden jerk of deceleration as the chute filled with air, slowing him dramatically. He took hold of the steering toggles and began to guide himself toward the rooftop seventy-three stories above the dark and dangerous ruins. He used every technique he had—swooping to increase his speed, taking measured turns to keep on target.

He angled in with slow turns, controlling his descent, getting a feel for the crosswinds. They would get worse the closer he got to the buildings. He could feel the adrenaline burning in his veins, but at the same time, he felt utterly cold and focused. He'd managed to put all his fears and worries about Henry and their child into a lockbox inside his mind and push it out of his thoughts. For now, at least. He was focused on the challenge of landing a parachute on a skyscraper rooftop without immediately alerting everyone there and getting shot.

The moon being out tonight wasn't to his advantage, but as he looped around the skyscraper in ever-tightening circles, he spotted the tiny forms of four men sitting in the dim glow of electric lanterns on the raised circular section of the rooftop.

Then he spotted another form in a chair a little ways away from the others, positioned near a spiderweb tangle of lines and cords on the white rooftop.

Henry. It had to be.

Good. Perfect. The mercenaries' night vision would be hurt by the lights. Tom was coming in almost soundlessly. He needed to watch out for other sentries on the level he meant to land on. But the drone pictures had only shown four enemies, and he had a visual on all of them.

He circled in closer yet, turning hard. His heart was beating fast as the moment of truth quickly approached. There had been no going back after he'd jumped from the plane, but there was *really* no going back now. He was angling in for his landing. He was aiming for a narrow section of roof on a circular skyscraper, trying to land as far away from the men sitting around a table with electric lanterns as possible.

He pulled hard on one of the steering toggles, sweeping in fast. His brain kept judging the distance, his approach speed and angle, as he made small adjustments. The crosswinds buffeted him hard. They actually sent him off at the wrong angle for a second or so before he wrenched the parachute back on course. His heart was pounding so hard that he felt like he'd just sprinted five miles.

The round rooftop of the center skyscraper was rushing at him fast. He flared at the perfect moment to slow himself for the touchdown. Undershooting would have him veering wildly to avoid smashing into the side of the building. Overshooting would be almost as bad. He'd have to break into the building and climb a million steps. The exterior elevator wouldn't work. And the place had to be burned out, damaged, and barricaded beyond belief. And possibly infested with lagodire.

Not ideal.

He came in faster than he wanted, but he hit his target area, running as his boots touched down on the rooftop. In an instant, he pulled his knife and was slicing through the harness straps as the parachute caught wind from behind and began to haul him toward the curving ledge. If the parachute pulled him over before he could cut the lines, he was dead.

Because he'd already cut too many lines to use the chute again.

The knife blade sliced through the last chute line as the ledge came rushing toward him. The parachute, now cut free, went sailing and flapping over the ledge and into the darkness.

Tom fetched up against the building ledge itself. His blood was rushing in his ears. He felt half crazy after that. Almost drunk with adrenaline. As if he was untouchable for pulling it off.

He rolled back into a crouch, forcing his thoughts back to his mission. Landing was only step one. Things were going to get more dangerous from here.

He was now at the farthest diagonal angle from the mercenaries. The rooftop had two levels, both circular, and he was down on the second. All the equipment and vents, antennas, cable trays, and mechanical floor inflow and outflow exhausts were scattered around the circular rooftop in the center or at its base.

The wind was a constant low roar. He shrugged out of his harness and drew his pistol. He already had a round chambered. He moved forward in a crouch. The constant motion of the air and crosswinds made catching scents almost impossible. That worked for him, and it worked against him. Luckily, he knew where they were all clustered. And if his luck had held, they had no idea he'd joined them.

He stalked forward, scanning for a ladder to the upper part of the roof. The lower roof was littered with twisted, broken antennas and oddly shaped communications equipment and cables. It made the going slower than he wanted. Someone had ripped them off or bent them down so a helicopter could get close. He passed the exterior elevator, the top of the narrow elevator tube running up the side of the building. There was no power, so it was useless, but then again, that was why the mercenaries were being so careless. They were bored, and they believed they were safe from the lagodire up here, seven hundred feet above the streets.

He saw the metal ladder leading up to the topmost roof section—the windowless inner circle within the circle, a story above the top public floor. It had no railing along the edge and was at least ten, maybe twelve feet up.

Once he was up there, things would happen fast. He needed to deal with these bastards ruthlessly. He was outnumbered, and they had already endangered the life of his lover and child. He needed to end this quickly. He couldn't hold back and have Henry end up dead because Tom couldn't do what he needed to do.

He reached the ladder. Adrenaline rushed through his veins. That would give him strength but also affect the steadiness of his aim. He took a second to focus. His child was in danger. Henry was in danger. He needed to check his targets and save his family.

This was it. The reason for his existence. He felt that deep down in his bones. All his training, all the danger and experience, all his living life on the edge. His existence came down to something simple but true to its heart. Protecting the weak, guarding those who needed it, using his strength to save lives. Saving those he loved.

He slipped the pistol back in his shoulder holster and began to climb. The metal rungs were cold beneath his hands, even through his gloves. The roar of the wind never seemed to stop, but sometimes it came and went in surges, like waves. Now it pushed at him hard from the side. He compensated for it and ignored it. Wind already had its chance to stop him and failed.

He reached the top of the ladder and could now see over the topmost ledge. The four mercenary shifters were still in the center of the circular upper rooftop. They were still sitting next to a broken radio antenna—a huge gridwork of metal that had been toppled over—sheltered against the wind by some equipment, electrical boxes or HVAC equipment. They were playing cards in the light of battery-powered lamps. Even over the wind, he could hear their voices as they played and cursed each other.

Henry was huddled in a camp chair midway between the center of the circular rooftop and the outer edge. Thank God he was out of the line of fire. Tom had to resist the overpowering urge to run to him. To make sure he was okay.

He had business to handle first.

Tom slipped the rest of the way onto the roof, keeping low and drawing his pistol again. He raised it, taking aim at the enemy shifters.

Old Detroit was dark and silent around them. But Tom's shape and outline might still be noticed, even though the unceasing wind blew his scent away from the other shifters and covered the sound of any footstep. He closed in with smooth, even steps. He would be getting as close as possible. He wanted zero chance that any stray fire or ricochets would come anywhere near Henry.

He wasn't going to take any chances with Henry's life or the life of his unborn child.

The wind on the very top of the tallest building in Old Detroit was the worst yet, pushing hard against him as if it hated him. Tom lined up the pistol's sights on the closest mercenary—a skinny guy—as he moved in even closer.

He didn't know if they finally heard him or if he'd moved close enough for the light to illuminate him, but one of the mercs suddenly cursed and tossed his cards. He scrambled out of the camp chair, pointing at

Tom and shouting. He reached for the pistol shoved in his waistband.

Tom shot him. The sound of the shot with the suppressor was barely audible over the wind. The enemy shifter crumpled. Two of the other mercenaries began to stand, reaching for weapons. The third one, for some reason, shoved backward and tipped over his chair, crashing to the rooftop with a scream.

Tom opened fire in rapid succession, putting two bullets into each of the enemy mercenaries grabbing for their guns. As they fell, Tom swung his pistol around to the last merc. This shifter was a wolf. He was nimble, Tom had to give him that. The merc had rolled back to his feet from his fall and was running hard.

But he was running straight toward Henry. If Tom hesitated, the enemy wolf would soon be too close to shoot. Henry would be in the line of fire. He knew what the bastard intended. He wanted to use Henry as a shield. To try and bargain for his life.

Tom shot the enemy wolf down. He didn't even flinch from shooting the man in the back. He wasn't going to stand on any principle if it meant endangering Henry and their child.

The last mercenary fell dead without a sound and lay still on the rooftop, his blood pooling beneath him.

Tom scanned for any other enemies, but there were none. He holstered his pistol and ran to Henry.

Henry was staring at him with wide, unbelieving eyes. His face appeared very pale in the faint glow of the electric lanterns. Tom slid to a stop and crouched in front of him, his heart pounding even harder than it had when the parachute dragged him toward the ledge.

"Henry, I'm here. Are you okay? Did they hurt you?"

Henry leaned forward in the chair, moving into Tom's arms. His wrists were cuffed, so he hooked them over Tom's head to hug him the only way he could.

"Tom. Oh, God, Tom. Are you real? You can't be real…"

Tom was grinning and laughing. Relief was going to drown him. "I'm real. I'm here. Don't worry. I'm here for you."

He hugged Henry tight against him—as tight as he could with the awkward positions they were in. He drew back enough to cup Henry's face in both his hands, looking into his eyes for a moment before kissing him. He poured every bit of his love and joy into that kiss.

He believed Henry got the message.

But they couldn't kiss forever. He wanted Henry out of here. Yesterday. So he ended the kiss and got back to business.

"Let me cut those cuffs off," he said, raising his

voice to be heard over the wind. He pulled the metal cutters free of his belt.

Henry dutifully held out his wrists. Tom cut the chain between the handcuffs. The metal bracelets remained, but at least Henry could freely use his arms again.

Tom pulled him in for another hug. Honestly, he loved that Henry's big belly got between them. It made it a three-way hug.

"Are you okay? They didn't hurt our baby, did they?"

Henry was smiling and shaking. He stroked a soft hand down Tom's cheek. "No. They didn't hurt the baby. They had me scared to death, though. They...they weren't going to let me go. Even if you gave them what they wanted. They were going to kill me."

"Then I don't regret killing them first," he said coldly. Then he gave Henry a grin, putting the wolves he'd shot out of his mind. "Listen. I have a ride. It's not a limo like you're used to, but it should work."

Henry laughed and shook his head. He still sounded a little dazed, as if he couldn't believe this was really happening. "I'm so glad to see you that I'm choosing to ignore that cheap shot."

"Good. I'll make it up to you later." He pulled the radio handset from his military harness. Tom had come through on his end, despite the odds against him. Kross had better come through on his end.

He double-checked the radio frequency. He didn't bother with a bunch of military radio protocols. He kept it simple and to the point. "This is Tom. I've got him. Get us out."

"This is Echo One," a voice he didn't recognize replied. "Copy that. On our way. ETA ten minutes."

Tom put the radio away. He pulled Henry into his arms again. That was where the omega belonged. In his arms. Forever.

He looked down into Henry's beautiful amber eyes. "I thought I'd lost you. Both of you. I couldn't allow that."

Henry closed his eyes. There were tears on his cheeks. "I thought the same. I was so scared. I'm sorry. I was so reckless, but I had to see you. I had to tell you that I love you. That I will—"

Tom cut him off by leaning forward and claiming the omega's lips in a fierce kiss. He didn't need to know any more than that. Henry loved him. He loved Henry. Once they were free of this nightmare city, he would never come here again. This was the last time, no matter what.

He had what he wanted right here in his arms. Henry and his unborn son. And kissing the man he loved? That was the sweetest thing.

*

Henry was terrified about only one thing — that this was all a dream.

But the kiss was too good. This close, Tom's scent filled him, and Tom's arms around him felt incredible. He hadn't experienced anywhere near enough time in this man's arms. The universe owed him.

He didn't look at the bodies of the mercenaries who'd kidnapped him and taken him here. He didn't need those memories, those images in his head. He had enough already. He had seen Tom shoot them. Johnny had come running for Henry at the end. His eyes had been full of hate. Henry had no illusions. Johnny intended to hurt or kill him or use him as a hostage against Tom. So even though Henry was crying right now, they were tears of relief and joy, but not tears for anyone else. They'd meant to kill him and his child. Maybe someday he could forgive that, but he would never forget it.

He stayed safe in Tom's arms as the wind rushed and roared and blew against them. A short time later, how long he couldn't tell, the *thump thump* of helicopter rotors filled the air. Tom turned to look as a sleek helicopter approached from the west.

The radio squawked. "This is Echo One. We're on our approach. Is the rooftop secure, over?"

Tom pulled the radio to reply. "We see you, Echo One. The rooftop is secure. Only friendlies, over."

"Copy that."

They moved closer to the edge of the rooftop to give the helicopter enough room to touch down. It was a dangerous approach, not just because of the crosswinds, but because of all the junk, the bent and destroyed antennas and equipment and cables all around.

But the pilot was skilled. This helicopter had wheels like the one the mercenaries used to take him here. The copter hovered overhead as the pilot corrected for the gusts of wind and slowly descended. The doors opened. St. Clair Wolves with assault rifles jumped out.

Tom had his arm around Henry's shoulders. Henry clutched him tightly as they walked toward the helicopter. The downwash from the spinning blades was forceful. The noise was even worse. But Tom stayed with him the whole way. He helped boost Henry into the helicopter, then climbed in beside him, hovering over him like a mother and making sure he was strapped in properly.

Henry didn't mind. It felt good to be taken care of right now. He was still reeling—in a good way—from suddenly seeing Tom appear as if by magic and save him. He hadn't dared to hope, but Tom had come for him. The man never had to say another word to him in his life and Henry would still be absolutely certain of Tom's love. Because the sacrifices his lone wolf had made were superhuman. So yes, Tom had won his heart. He would make the best father, caring and brave and ready to do anything and everything for the people he loved. The people he considered family.

Henry was simply glad with all his heart that he fit into that category. That he was part of Tom's family, and that Tom was part of his.

He'd expected to take off again right away. The helicopter's engines were still going, the blades still turning. But the St. Clair wolves were busy on the rooftop. It took him a moment to realize what they were doing. They were dragging the bodies of the dead mercenaries to the lower ledges of the tower and throwing them off.

"Why are they doing that?" he asked Tom, leaning close and nearly yelling in the other man's ear to be heard.

It seemed harsh somehow. They had already lost their lives, and now their bodies were being thrown off a skyscraper.

Tom looked at him with grave eyes. "So there won't be as much evidence of what happened when Carson's helicopter comes back." He frowned, staring out the helicopter's open door. "It probably won't fool them. There is blood. And my shell casings. And the elevator doesn't work, so it couldn't have been the lagodire. But the questions might be enough to hold off a war between the two packs. For now, anyway."

A war. Over him. He closed his eyes and tried not to think about it. But then again, he had never done anything to anyone. It finally felt good to have some friends on his side. And more than that, it felt wonderful to have someone like Tom to love him.

It felt like forever, but finally, the other wolves climbed back onto the upper roof and ran back to the helicopter. They put their weapons away as they strapped in and greeted him with warm smiles and kind words. He could tell they were glad to have him back. It really made him feel like he belonged. It was a feeling that he cherished.

Meanwhile, Tom sat next to him, holding his hand as the helicopter door was shut and the helicopter lifted off.

He didn't remember much about the flight across the water, back to New Detroit, Ohio. He couldn't seem to form any focused thoughts. His emotions were too strong. He was exhausted, but he was also filled with joy and relief and a kind of dazed wonder that this had all happened. Because he'd already been dumped in Old Detroit once and had barely survived, with no one caring that he'd vanished and no one to help him. But now, so many people had come to his aid. Tom most of all.

They didn't land at an airport like he'd expected.

No, they flew straight to Redstone Meredith Hospital. When Tom noticed his surprise, the lone wolf gave him a tight smile.

"We're getting you and our kid checked out by the best physicians in the city," he said.

Henry put one hand on his belly and could only nod. He hadn't been hurt, but he wasn't going to argue. As long as Tom would stay with him for as long as he could...

"How did you arrange this?" he finally asked in wonder as they landed on the helipad.

Tom smirked. "Kross donates a ton of money and knows a bunch of people on the board. Guess it's good to be king. Or king of New Detroit."

"Don't be angry with him," Henry chided gently. "He is a good person."

"Yeah. He is. But don't tell him I said that. That bastard doesn't need his ego inflated."

Henry laughed. His heart filled with simple and powerful love for his lone wolf.

There were orderlies and nurses waiting for them with a gurney and a wheelchair when they landed. Henry chose the wheelchair since he wasn't seriously hurt and lying on his back was very uncomfortable. They rushed him inside the hospital. The whole time, Tom stayed at his side, eating up the distance with his long strides.

After that, Henry was examined by two

physicians who poked and prodded him and asked all kinds of questions. They declared him dehydrated and put him on an IV. At least the angle of the hospital bed was more comfortable than lying flat on his back. The hospital staff was very attentive, though. He couldn't thank them enough.

Henry even had his own hospital room to himself. He could certainly get used to being rich.

Eventually, he was alone with Tom again after all the noise and hubbub. Tom sat next to his bed, holding Henry's hand. Suddenly, Tom leaned in close and kissed him. It was a sweet kiss, tender and loving. The kind of kiss between a married couple whose trust was as deep as their passion.

"I love you," Tom said after he drew back enough to look into Henry's eyes. "I love the life growing inside you, and I love *you*. That will never change. I swear it."

Henry had to close his eyes, which were suddenly prickling with tears. "I love you so much, Tom. You mean everything to me. You'll make the best father. I know that in my heart."

Tom was grinning, his eyes shining with pleasure. He stole another quick kiss. "I think that's the best thing anyone has ever said to me. I don't think I'll ever forget it."

"You'd better not. Because you're making me tear up, and you got the baby all excited. See?" He took

Tom's hand and placed it on his belly, letting him feel their child kicking up the dickens.

"He's an adrenaline junkie. Like one of his two fathers." The look in his eyes was tender as he smiled and kept his big hand on Henry's belly.

"I know what I want to name him. But...I want to know what you think."

Tom's eyebrows shot up. He stared at Henry curiously. "Tell me."

"Max. I want to name him Max."

"A good name," Tom said at once. His mouth curved into a smile. "I think the Max you lost would like that."

"Would that...bother you? Knowing who he's named after? Someone I loved before you. Because you have a vote in this too."

"I'm not a jealous man. Never have been. I never had the chance to meet Max, but from what you've shared of him, I think we'd get along." His grin widened. "We both have great taste in men."

Henry laughed, closing his eyes as tears squeezed out. He didn't want to turn into a blubbering tear factory, but these days, he couldn't help it. At least he could blame it on being pregnant. "Thank you."

Tom was holding his hand. Now he lifted Henry's hand to his and kissed the back of it. "Nah, love. Thank *you*. You've given me everything. You're my happiness. And our son is part of that. I'm so glad I got you both back where you belong. With me." His expression grew serious. "But from now on, I'm not letting you out of my sight."

Henry took a deep, shaky breath. "I shouldn't have gone to you alone. That was a mistake. I tried to believe they wouldn't do anything to me because I was with Gavin and Jake, with the pack. But...I also realized how much I needed you. I decided I'm leaving the St. Clair Pack. For you. No conditions. I don't want you going back into Old Detroit because I don't want to lose you, but I'll take any time with you that I can get, for as long as I can get."

Tom closed his eyes and sighed. But that smile still lingered on his handsome face. "You're not leaving the pack."

"But, I thought...?"

"They care for you. Deeply. Gavin's your friend. I would never come between that. You need family, and they're one big, extended family. Besides, Kross came through for me tonight. I couldn't have rescued you without his help. I certainly couldn't have gotten you out of the city again without his helicopter."

Henry was shocked to his core. He gaped at Tom, his thoughts spinning inside his head. "I...I don't know what to say right now."

Tom's smirk deepened. "Well, don't think I'm going soft on alphas. *I'm* not joining any pack. Ever. I'm a free wolf, born and bred." His smile vanished, and his eyes flashed. "But all bets are off if your alpha won't let me marry you. So I guess we'll have to wait and see what Kross says. If he says no, you're quitting the pack, and we're running off to Las Vegas."

At the door to the hospital room, Kross and Gavin—with a sleeping Ryan in his arms—appeared in the doorway.

"What's this about me saying no to something?" Kross asked. He was impeccably dressed as usual. Designer suit. Pocket square that matched his silk tie. Not a hair out of place.

Tom turned to face him. He was still wearing his gear from the mission in Old Detroit—black fatigues and boots—although he'd left his weapons and tools and the rest on the helicopter to be flown back to the private airport. Both wolves were strikingly handsome, although Jacob Kross had an aristocratic air of leadership...or maybe nobility...that in part came from his alpha-ness. Meanwhile, Tom was all brazen strength and headstrong resilience. More laid-back but just as proud. The lone wolf should have some tattoo that said Don't Tread on Me or something—a phrase that went back to the American Revolution.

And of course, there was Gavin, who was beaming from ear to ear and giddily waved at Henry with his free hand, since his other arm was full of sleeping baby. And Henry, grinning hugely, waved back and motioned Gavin over to his bedside. Gavin came eagerly, still cradling their son in his arms.

"I'm so glad you're safe," Gavin said, his big eyes very sincere. "I was so sick with worry. I think I ate four boxes of cheese crackers, one after another. I almost made myself puke." He closed his eyes and shook his head. "Listen to me. I'm such an idiot. You almost lost your life, and I'm complaining about eating all the crackers."

Henry laughed and patted his hand. "You're not an idiot. It's so sweet of you to be worried. And thank you. For helping Tom. I'll never forget it."

"Well, of course we would help him," Gavin said, seeming honestly perplexed. "You're both family."

Tom cocked his head to the side. "Last time I checked, I wasn't part of your pack."

Gavin snorted. "You're part of the pack whether you want it or not. Because I said so."

Jacob Kross was laughing. "They say I'm the alpha, but I simply let my beloved little omega have anything he wants."

"And your beloved little son, too," Gavin added, looking fondly at the baby sleeping in his arms.

Henry put his hand on his belly again, feeling the little one doing somersaults. He was going to have to get the kid into gymnastics or karate or something. Seeing Gavin's love for his son only made Henry feel the same excitement and love for the life growing inside him.

Tom was looking at Jake Kross. There was challenge in his eyes. "I'm marrying Henry. I'm not asking your permission."

Henry's heart began to pound fast. He opened his mouth, not sure what would come out. He ended up saying, "That's if I say yes."

Frowning, Tom turned to him. "Will you say yes?"

"I will *if* you give me a romantic proposal. Hospitals aren't romantic."

Tom snorted and looked back at Kross. "I'm marrying Henry after I figure out something romantic to do that doesn't involve medical care. And I'm not asking your permission, and I'm not joining your pack."

A slight smile appeared on the alpha's face. "I see. It looks like I have no other choice than to make a special exception for you, Tom Reinhart."

"What exception? Don't tell me it's that easy."

"Why not? I'm alpha. I want things to be easy. You already know how much Henry means to us. But I've seen that you're a good man, too. You're fearless. You protect the weak, and you protect your own. You're a hero in my book, whether you join us officially or not."

Tom didn't seem to know what to say to that. He seemed ready for a fight, not agreement. "So...what happens?"

"You can be an honorary member of the St. Clair Pack. And I won't be your alpha. You'll essentially be a brother to the pack wolves, with some of the benefits because of Henry, but you can still be your…independent self."

"His *ornery* self, you mean," Henry corrected, giving Tom a loving look. "His grumpy, get-off-my-lawn, nobody-tells-me-what-to-do self."

"Hey, hey, hey," Tom said, smirking. "You made your point." He looked back at the alpha and then at Gavin. "Thank you. I'm no fool. I know I owe you. I'll help you and your pack however I can. You can count on me when you need it."

Gavin spoke up. "Will you be going back into Old Detroit again?"

Henry tensed. He had been afraid to bring that up.

But Tom slowly shook his head. "Tonight was the last time. I've risked my life in there enough. Besides," he said, glancing at Henry, "I have a family to look after now."

"Do you have a job lined up?" Gavin asked, pressing on boldly. For an omega, Gavin was apparently fearless. Henry hoped someday he could be that bold.

"I just retired from my career. I guess you could say I'm between prospects."

Gavin looked at Jake Kross, who nodded. "I don't

want to overstep, but maybe we can help you out with that. Maybe something with the council. Or security, given your training and skills. We'll work something out."

"The council," Tom said, his voice taking on a razor edge. His lip curled. "What are we going to do about Eddie Carson?"

"We bloodied his nose tonight," Kross said. "But I intend to take him and his pack down. Through the council, using the Accords. He flaunts the laws, both human and shifter. I intend to use the law to bring him to justice." He held Tom's gaze. "But from here on out, Henry, your son, and even you are under the protection of the St. Clair wolves."

"Well, then," Tom replied in almost a drawl. "Guess I owe you another one. I want to take Carson down. For what he did to Henry. So whatever jobs you have for me, any way you think I can help you out, I'm there."

Tom turned back to Henry and leaned in for a kiss. A tender smile was on his face as he drew back and spoke softly. "As for you, my omega... I'll never leave you. I'll always love you, always protect you and our family. And I promise, I *will* think up some romantic way to propose to you." A teasing smile appeared on his face. "Maybe through a letter?"

"Tom Reinhart! If you propose to me over a letter, I'm going to skin you alive!"

Tom was laughing. Gavin and Jake were laughing. And Henry joined them. For the first time, he let himself embrace the thought that things would turn out all right. He had a man who loved him. He had a beautiful child coming that he would love with all his heart and do his best to raise right. And he had a pack—an extended family, something he'd never had before, not truly. He had friends who loved him and cared for him and cherished him.

His joy was simple. His love was deep. And he was not ashamed to feel deeply and truly happy. His little pack—Tom and Max and Henry—would give the love he'd always needed. And he knew that his heart was easily big enough to give Tom, Max, and any other child they wanted to have all the love in the world.

EPILOGUE

Nothing in the world made Tom prouder than holding his newborn son in his arms.

It was an incredible feeling. It made him feel both humble and powerful. He had helped create this beautiful life. Maybe Henry had done all the heavy lifting, especially during the birth less than an hour ago…but Tom had helped.

More than that, holding his child only reinforced how much his life had changed. It made his duty to those he loved all the more clear. His duty not only to protect his son but to raise him to be a good man. His duty to cherish Henry, to love him, and to keep him safe and secure. To work as a team to raise a child in a world that was not always kind or forgiving.

"He's beautiful," Tom murmured to Henry. He didn't look up from his son's sleeping face, with that cute little baby hat on, all swaddled tightly in his arms. But his smile felt like it was going to stretch his mouth permanently out of proportion. "You do good work."

Henry gave a tired chuckle. "I do. I really do. It was worth feeling like I've been backed over by a dump truck. Twice."

His omega's voice was strained and raspy. There were dark circles under his eyes. His short hair was sweaty and sticking up in erratic spikes. He looked like he was ready to sleep for at least fifteen hours.

It had been a long labor. Tom had been there for all of it. Hell, they couldn't have thrown him out, even if they'd wanted to. He'd felt helpless in a way, hating to see his mate in the pain of childbirth. He wanted to take that pain and endure it for Henry, but he couldn't. He could only be there to hold his hand and join him in the breathing exercises, giving him chips of ice and wiping his forehead from time to time. He could only be there to look into his eyes and tell him how strong he was. How proud Tom was of his mate.

But it was over now, and all that stress and pain was behind them. Their son had arrived in the world. And he was one of the most beautiful things Tom had ever seen.

Henry was watching him hold little Max through

half-lidded eyes. Max was healthy, weighing in at eight point two pounds. His cries were even adorable. Little "wah" sounds. He knew babies got louder, but right now, he thought that sound was as precious as it came.

He'd been practicing changing diapers. He trained with the same determination and focus that he put into his time on the gun range or with skydiving. His child deserved a clean diaper and reliable diaper rotation, and he was damn well going to make sure it happened.

Max was snoozing. Being born had to be as exhausting as giving birth...although he was no expert. He couldn't get over how tiny a newborn was. Sure, he'd seen plenty of Gavin and Jake's kid. Hell, he even liked the brat and played a mean game of peek-a-boo with him. But there was nothing like holding someone you considered "your child." Your child, with all the weight and responsibilities and love it came with.

He was ready to be a father. He knew he had plenty to learn. He knew he would make mistakes. But he was dedicated. No matter what, he would always strive to do the best by Max. He would do the same for Henry...and for any other child they had together. Because right now, he was imagining having at least three. Maybe more.

But...he was going to keep that suggestion to

himself. Henry didn't seem like he'd be in the mood to consider two more kiddos at the moment. It might be a wise move to give Henry some time.

"I love you, little guy," he said softly to Max. He looked up and met Henry's gaze. "And I love you too, big guy."

Henry closed his eyes and gave a tired laugh. "I love seeing you hold him." He gave a contented sigh. "I'm the luckiest wolf in the world."

"Yeah, you're wrong about that. Because I own that title right now."

"I'm too tired to argue about how wrong you are."

"Good," Tom said, grinning. "That means I win the argument by default."

"Do you hear your father, Max? He likes being difficult. Don't take after him."

"No, he's going to take after you. He's perfect."

Henry's eyes went soft, happy. "You say the most wonderful things to me. I kept all your letters, did you know that? Every single one you sent me."

He knew that. He knew that Henry kept them in a fancy keepsake box under his side of the bed.

"I kept yours too. You're a much better writer, so I made out like a bandit."

Henry snorted. "You just keep on believing that. I know what's in those letters. They have the words of a sweet man with a good soul."

Tom began to rock gently from side to side as he

cradled Max in his arms. So delicate. So perfect. Just looking at his child's face brought every one of his protective instincts surging forward.

Much had changed since the night he'd rescued Henry. He'd married Henry for starters. He'd flown Henry out to Kauai, Hawaii, and proposed on the beach, in the moonlight, as the ocean waves rolled in. He'd pretended to find the ring in a piece of driftwood and then slipped the ring on Henry's hand. It was stupid and cheesy, maybe, but it was the best he could do. Henry had said yes, so he counted it as a win.

Big things were happening in the New Detroit political world. Or the shifter part of it, anyway. Jake had initiated an investigation into the actions of the Metro Pack, using his position as head of the council to push forward. Eddie Carson was not pleased. The council had split into two factions and might even be disbanded. The human population of New Detroit, by far the largest population, was even paying attention to the intricate shifter politics, which threatened to drag in other shifters, like big cats and even bear shifters. It was a mess. No wonder Tom had always loathed politics.

As for Eddie Carson, no mention had ever been made of the mercenaries Tom had killed to save Henry's life. Killing was not something Tom took pleasure in, but at least open war hadn't broken out...yet. Right now, it was all political maneuvering.

It wasn't easy to touch an alpha like Carson. In a way, packs acted like mafias. Secrecy and sometimes violence.

But the St. Clair Pack was different. True, Tom had stuck by his guns and hadn't joined, but Henry was still a part of them, and the wolf pack treated the omega like family. They were warier around Tom, but he understood that. Still, they treated Tom like family too, even though he wasn't officially part of the pack—maybe like third-cousin family, but still, family.

Despite all that, and despite Carson not being sent to prison—*yet*—Tom still had hope. He knew happiness was in their future. That was one of the reasons why he felt so much hope right now.

That hope was why he'd stayed in New Detroit, even though there was still a threat to his family. Enough of a threat that he was living in Kross's mansion and renting out his own place for now. He still didn't like having to rely on the alpha—it went against the grain with him, rubbed his fur the wrong way, all of that. But this wasn't about him or his pride. It was about Henry's safety...and little Max's safety. Kross had plenty of security on the grounds. He'd even put in a bunch more security around the property lines—cameras and high-tech sensors. He always had at least two armed pack wolves on duty.

The oddest thing was that, over these final months of Henry's pregnancy, Tom had come to like Jake

Kross. Despite all his intentions to the contrary. The guy wasn't bad. Actually, he was in danger of becoming a friend. Kross wasn't the raised pinkie, tea and wine sipping, smug, rich, domineering jerk that Tom expected. Yeah, the guy did wear ridiculously pricey suits too often, but no one was perfect. Kross really cared about Gavin, loved the omega deeply, and that was something the two of them shared—loving omega wolves. Also, Gavin and Henry were inseparable friends. It brought the four of them together, especially since Tom and Henry were living in the east wing guestroom.

Tom began to pace around the hospital room, humming softly to Max as he bounced and swayed, keeping the newborn asleep. He felt like he could hold his child in his arms forever. He'd built a bassinet and tons of baby equipment back at the manor, even though it would be a while before most of it would be used. He even liked putting together baby equipment. How insane was that?

As for Tom, he'd kept his word to Henry. He hadn't gone back behind the walls of Old Detroit, and he never would. That dangerous part of his life was behind him. He had a family that needed him. And he needed to protect them because the threats were real. These days, he was an unaffiliated part of the St. Clair Pack security force. His experience and military training were the only things he had to rely on, but right now, they were necessary. It was a strange situation. He wasn't part of the pack, and Kross wasn't his boss, but Tom was still dedicated to protecting their territory from very real threats.

Hell, it gave him something important to do while he figured out his next career. Besides, he got plenty of time to look after Henry. And after spending so many months in jail, he felt the universe owed him that.

"I'm going to take a nap," Henry said with a tired smile. "I think I've earned it."

Tom chuckled. "You've more than earned it, love. Do you need anything?"

"Promise me you'll be here when I wake up?"

"I'll be here," he said, meeting Henry's gaze. "You can count on me."

"I know," Henry replied, closing his eyes, his face weary but peaceful.

Tom stayed with his omega, holding his newborn child, and he too was at peace.

Omega Rescue
Max Rose

He saved an omega's life...only to lose his heart.

Firefighter and alpha wolf Darren Drake charges into a burning building only to discover the man he's rescuing is an omega shifter...and his mate. Alex Carson is a photographer and an omega wolf with the most stunning blue eyes and gentle spirit that Darren has ever encountered. Since Darren is an alpha, bringing the now-homeless omega into his house is the only honorable thing to do. Besides, he isn't letting his mate out of his sight, because he intends to win Alex's love and loyalty, no matter what. But after a single, blazing-hot night of passion, Darren wakes to discover that his mate has vanished, leaving only a note behind...

Alex lives a footloose existence, traveling the world, taking stunning photos, and never staying in one place for long. But when the fire that nearly takes his life also destroys his laptop and his cameras, he's left in a desperate situation. That's when Darren, the sexy, alpha firefighter built like a demigod, comes through for him again, letting him stay in his home until Alex can get back on his feet. Alex knows how badly he aches for Darren, but the big firefighter doesn't understand Alex's rootless existence. Even though the alpha seems to command Alex's heart, he isn't ready to be tied down forever. But after Alex shows up pregnant on Darren's doorstep, is there any hope for rekindling their thwarted love when an alpha and an omega want very different things?

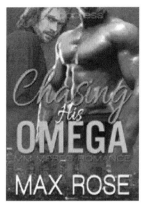

Chasing His Omega
Max Rose

An omega who lives life on the run, and an alpha who will never give up...

Mike Sloan is U.S. Army Airborne and as tough as they come. He's just retired after a distinguished career and is enjoying a drink in a Detroit bar when Colin Parker walks through the door. The attraction is instant and staggering. Colin is everything Mike wants in a man—lean, gorgeous, and with soulful, unforgettable eyes. Perfect for a night of hot fun. There's also something about Colin that Mike can't deny, something that draws him irresistibly toward the other man. But the bar is a rough one, and not friendly to men who love men. Mike isn't worried. No one dares mess with him. But Colin is ambushed in the back of the bar when he's alone. Mike rushes to his rescue, saving him from a brutal attack. Blaming himself for not stopping it sooner, Mike's only choice now is to take Colin home and make him feel so incredible he will forget every bruise. But when Mike wakes after an incredible night together, Colin is gone...

Not only is Colin gay, but he also has the rare omega gene, which means he can get pregnant. He's been on his own for years, roaming the country, never putting down roots. He distrusts strangers, but after Mike comes to his rescue, he loses all sense and gives in to his heart. But a scorching-hot night with Mike isn't enough to make him settle down anywhere for long. He's been on the road ever since his family disowned him for what he was. It's only a matter of time until Mike rejects him too, so it is best to leave. Only his luck has run out. He's pregnant with Mike's child. How can he ever face the man again? Little does he know that Mike is not a man to give up—ever—on having the thing he wants. And what he wants is Colin.

Printed in Poland
by Amazon Fulfillment
Poland Sp. z o.o., Wrocław

63932113R00211